COMPLICATIONS

What Reviewers Say About MJ Williamz's Work

Shots Fired

"MJ Williamz, in her first romantic thriller has done an impressive job of building up the tension and suspense. Williamz has a firm grasp of keeping the reader guessing and quickly turning the pages to get to the bottom of the mystery. *Shots Fired* clearly shows the author's ability to spin an engaging tale and is sure to be just the beginning of great things to follow as the author matures."—*Lambda Literary*

"Williamz tells her story in the voices of Kyla, Echo, and Detective Pat Silverton. She does a great job with the twists and turns of the story, along with the secondary plot. The police procedure is first rate, as are the scenes between Kyla and Echo, as they try to keep their relationship alive through the stress and mistrust."—*Just About Write*

Forbidden Passions

"*Forbidden Passions* is 192 pages of bodice ripping antebellum erotica not so gently wrapped in the moistest, muskiest pantalets of lesbian horn dog high jinks ever written. While the book is joyfully and un-abashedly smut, the love story is well written and the characters are multi-dimensional. ...*Forbidden Passions* is the very model of modern major erotica, but hidden within the sweet swells and trembling clefts of that erotica is a beautiful May–September romance between two wonderful and memorable characters."—*The Rainbow Reader*

Visit us at www.boldstrokesbooks.com

By the Author

Shots Fired

Forbidden Passions

Initiation by Desire

Speakeasy

Escapades

Sheltered Love

Summer Passion

Heartscapes

Love on Liberty

Love Down Under

Complications

COMPLICATIONS

by

MJ Williamz

2017

COMPLICATIONS

ISBN 13: 978-1-62639-769-9

This Trade Paperback Original Is Published By
Bold Strokes Books, Inc.
P.O. Box 249
Valley Falls, NY 12185

First Edition: June 2017

CREDITS
EDITOR: Cindy Cresap
PRODUCTION DESIGN: Susan Ramundo
COVER DESIGN By Sheri (GRAPHICARTIST2020@HOTMAIL.COM)

Acknowledgments

First of all, I'd like to thank Laydin for always being there for me. I couldn't do this without her. I'd also like to thank Rad, Sandy, and Cindy from Bold Strokes for all their support and help to make me a better author.

I'd also like to thank Sarah and Inger for their input as the tale unfolded.

And last, but certainly not least, a huge thank you to you, the readers who make my job as enjoyable as it is.

Dedication

For Laydin—For Life

CHAPTER ONE

Mel O'Brien rolled over in bed to find Mandy, the luscious redhead from the previous night, still sleeping soundly. She watched her pert breasts heave slightly with each breath she took. Mel had known Mandy for a few months but had only gotten up the nerve to ask her out a week ago. She really liked her and had high hopes she might be the one.

Mel couldn't look at Mandy's naked body without touching it. She skimmed her hand over the length of it, stopping where her legs met. She slipped her hand between her legs and found her still moist from the night before. She rubbed her clit, and Mandy got wetter. Mel slipped her fingers inside.

Mandy stirred, but barely. Mel kept her fingers moving in and out until Mandy woke completely.

"Oh, my," she said. "What a way to wake up."

"Mm," Mel said.

"Holy shit, Mel. Oh, my God. I'm going to come."

"That's the idea," Mel said.

"Oh, God. Oh, dear God," Mandy cried as she rode the orgasm.

Mel waited until the shudders ceased, then pulled Mandy into her arms.

"You're so much fun," she said.

"So are you."

"So, can I see you again?"

"Oh, Mel, I don't know…"

Mel propped herself up on an elbow and looked down at Mandy.

"Why not? We had a good time, right?"

"Yeah, we did. But I'm not looking for anything serious right now."

"So, another date would mean we're serious?" Mel asked.

"It could lead to it, and I mean it. I really don't want a relationship."

Mandy got out of bed and quickly dressed.

"Hey, what's the hurry?" Mel said. "You can hang out for a little while. I'll make breakfast."

"No, I need to go. But thanks." She kissed Mel on the cheek and left.

"Damn it," Mel said to herself. She was sick and tired of one-night stands. Sure, they'd been fun when it was her and Joey on the prowl, but now that she was solo and a little older, she really wanted to settle down. But she couldn't find a woman who was interested.

She was bummed and thought about the rest of her day. It was Saturday and she had no plans. She called Joey to see if she wanted to catch some waves.

"Hey, Joey, what are you doing?"

"Getting ready to take DJ to the park. What are you up to?"

"Nothin'."

"How'd things go last night?" Joey said.

"The usual. It went great. We came back to my place, had a rockin' night, and she left this morning."

"Good for you, my friend."

"Not good for me. She doesn't want to see me again. I swear, Joey, I'm so tired of one-night stands."

Joey laughed.

"There was a time we lived for them."

"Those days are over."

"Man, you sound miserable," Joey said. "Come to the park with us. That should cheer you up."

"Okay. What time?"

"Meet us at noon."

"Will do."

Mel hung up feeling a little better. The promise of some time on the beach with Joey and her son cheered her somewhat. She opened her refrigerator and found some two-day-old cold pizza. That would serve as breakfast. Mel loved to cook, but cooking for herself was too depressing. She wanted to make breakfast for a woman. Her woman. She sighed, ate the pizza, and wandered down the hall to take a shower.

She showed up at the park at five after twelve and, not surprisingly, there was no sign of Joey. She was notoriously late when she had to be somewhere with DJ and Samantha wasn't involved. Samantha had no trouble getting DJ ready to go, but Joey was still figuring that out. Mel didn't worry. She just sat on a swing and enjoyed the beautiful day.

The sun was shining, the sky was cloudless, and the temperature was in the mid seventies. It was a perfect summer day. She saw Joey's pickup pull up and sauntered over to help her get DJ out.

"Meow!" DJ yelled, still unable to pronounce Mel's name.

"Hey, buddy. How you doin'?"

"Good."

"Hey, Joey," Mel said.

"Hey, Mel. Sorry we're late."

"That's okay. I expected it."

"Fuck you."

"Language," Mel said.

"Oh, yeah."

"You're the parent."

"I know. I just sometimes forget that he's a sponge."

"Yep. The last thing you want is for that language to come out of his mouth around his other mom or at daycare."

Mel got DJ out of the car and took him over to the little kid play area. He toddled over to the play structure. Mel and Joey followed him. They lifted him up so he could go down the slide over and over.

"You know, I don't get you," Joey said. "I mean, heck yeah, I'm happy as hell with Samantha, but you're free. You should be loving life. Just keep getting laid. Life is good."

"Yeah, but I want what you and Samantha have. I'm tired of a different woman every week or so. I want one woman."

"Well, quit trying so hard then. Just enjoy what you've got, and sooner or later the right woman will come along. Go with the flow. Relax."

"I wish I could."

"I wish I could help you out."

"The only thing that's going to help me is finding someone who wants me for more than one night."

"Man, you're bummed hard-core today. Who were you with last night?"

"Mandy Hawkins. You know. She's the redheaded professor who works in Somerset and lives here."

"Yeah. I know her. She's a hot piece."

"Meow?"

Mel looked down and saw DJ looking up at her.

"Pway wif me?"

"Sure thing, little bud."

She spent the next half hour watching DJ on the play structure, playing with the pirate's steering wheel, turning over tic-tac-toe pieces and crawling through tubes. She was having as much fun as he was. She wondered where Joey was. She looked over and saw her on the phone.

Joey wandered over to DJ and Mel.

"You having fun?" she asked.

DJ nodded and smiled brightly.

"What about you?" she said to Mel.

"Yeah. I love this little guy."

"He loves you, too. So, I just got off the phone with Samantha. She wants you to come over for dinner. What do you say?"

Mel was used to eating with the Scarpetti family a couple of times a month. Samantha and Joey were both wonderful cooks. Sometimes they'd even let Mel cook.

"Sure. That'd be great."

"Most excellent. She also said we can bring DJ home and hit the waves, if you're up for it."

"Yeah. I could use some surf time."

Mel drove home to change her clothes while Joey took DJ home. She drove back to the beach and parked in the lot of The Shack, a burger joint where Joey and Mel had shared many meals and beers over the years. She waited until Joey showed up, then crossed the street with her and made her way to the shore.

The waves were breaking nicely, and it lifted her spirits to be there. They paddled out. The cool water on her legs refreshed her. She was ready to catch some waves. She caught one and rode it all the way in.

She popped up from underwater to see Joey near her.

"That was awesome!" Joey called to her.

"Yeah, it was!"

They climbed back on their boards and paddled out again. They surfed for two hours and had many great rides. Mel was revitalized and had almost forgotten her troubles when they finally paddled back to shore and called it a day.

They crossed the street, stored their boards, and went into The Shack to grab a couple of beers before heading back to Joey's house.

"You remember the time we came here and it was Tiffany's eighteenth birthday?" Joey said.

"Of course. She was a lot of fun. I wonder how she's doing in college."

"She must be loving it. I haven't seen her around town since she left for school."

"Neither have I."

"She'd be good for you," Joey said.

"She's too young."

"Yeah, but you could just fuck her and not worry about a future. You know she'd be up for that, too."

"That's true. I suppose it wouldn't be bad to have a playmate until I found the one. Still, that playmate can't be Tiffany because she's not around."

"Well, we'll find you someone. Now finish your beer. Samantha will be waiting for us."

Mel knew she'd be okay making a comment about Joey being whipped, but she wasn't in the mood. She wanted to be whipped, too. She wanted to have someone to be accountable to, so she didn't make fun of Joey.

She followed Joey to her house.

"Oh, man. I didn't bring anything with me," she said when she and Joey got to the front door.

"Dude, you're family. You don't need to bring anything."

"Samantha's gonna think I have no social skills."

"She already knows that." Joey patted her back. "Come on in. And would you relax? You've been in a funk all day. Get over it and relax, okay?"

"I'm trying. And surfing helped."

"Good."

"Mel!" Samantha called from the kitchen. She rushed into the front room and gave Mel a big hug and a kiss on the cheek.

"Sorry. I came empty-handed."

"Don't be silly. That's no big deal. Now have a seat at the bar while Joey opens the wine."

Mel did as she was told. She watched Joey and Samantha, her favorite couple, work around each other in the kitchen. Joey gave her a glass of wine. Mel brushed her bangs out of her eyes, only to have them fall back down.

"You've got the most adorable habit of doing that," Samantha said. "I can't believe any woman who's single and has seen you do that didn't fall for you."

"No such luck," Mel said.

"So Joey tells me you're getting tired of the chase?"

"I am. I'm ready to settle down, but no one seems interested."

"I have a hard time buying that," Samantha said. "Just give it time. You'll find someone. And it'll be right. In the meantime, enjoy being single."

"Being single has its perks," Mel said. "And I can't believe I'm saying this, but I'm tired of a new woman every week or so. I was telling Joey that this afternoon. I want someone to come home to, like she has."

"What you need to remember is that neither of us was looking when it happened for us. You need to not try so hard. Trust me."

❖

Susan Maloney unpacked most of her boxes and sat down to rest. Moving was hard work. But she was very excited to be in her new home. The community of Maybon Tir seemed like just the place to start over. Living as a waitress in Los Angeles was difficult at best, and she was hoping it would be easier in the small women's community. She was looking for a new start. She was happy to be away from Dorinda, her girlfriend of seven years who was verbally, emotionally, and mentally abusive to her. Susan had finally had enough. She'd packed up and left. Fortunately, the cute little bungalow on Seventh Street had been available and she'd snatched it right up. She hoped to rent for only a short period and to be able to buy her own place soon. She'd checked the local listings. House prices were very reasonable. She was sure she was going to like it there.

Susan stood and looked around the room at the mess. She didn't feel like dealing with it any more at that moment. Instead, she put on a swimsuit under her shorts and T-shirt and headed down to the beach. There weren't a lot of people since it was late afternoon. The two surfers out in the ocean caught her attention, and she watched them for a while before spreading out her towel and catching some rays.

She fell asleep and woke to an empty beach. Even the surfers had gone in. She put her clothes on over her suit again, grabbed her towel, and made her way back home. She took a shower and dressed, then looked into her empty refrigerator. Her cupboards, too, were bare. She was hungry and tired and not really in the mood to cook.

Susan Googled nearby restaurants and found a place called Suzette's, a crepe house. That sounded good. She thought it was probably a bit pricey for her, but she was willing to splurge on her first night in town. She deserved to celebrate her new life.

She drove to the center of town and found Suzette's. There was a wait, but she didn't mind. She sat in the foyer and watched all the couples enjoying their dinner. At first, it was like a punch in the gut, seeing everyone so happy with their partners and spouses, but then she reminded herself that she was single by choice and single she would stay. She was happy without a significant other. She didn't need another person to complete her.

The hostess finally came over to take her to a table.

"You don't look familiar," the hostess said.

"No. I just moved to town. Today, actually."

"Oh, well, welcome. What will you be doing here?"

"I'll be waitressing at Kindred Spirits. Do you know it?"

"Honey, I've lived here for ten years. I don't think there's much about this town I don't know."

"Oh, then you do know it. I haven't been by there to check it out. I thought I'd go over after dinner."

"That's a good idea. Things there won't pick up until a little later anyway."

Susan ordered her dinner and relaxed while she enjoyed crepes made to perfection. She stopped occasionally to take in the sheer joy of being surrounded by nothing but women. Sure, the community was small, but it was a little slice of heaven as far as Susan was concerned. She hadn't seen anything yet to make her question her decision to move. But she still hadn't seen Kindred Spirits. She was anxious to finish her dinner and head over.

The waitress brought the bill and Susan paid. She walked down the street to her car. She breathed in the cool coastal air and felt a sense of comfort flow over her. She knew she had made the right decision. She was home.

Susan entered the address for Kindred Spirits into her phone and drove over. She had surprised herself that she took the job sight unseen, but the owner had been so nice to her on the phone and via emails. She was sure she would love working there.

She easily found the place, but it wasn't so easy to find a parking place. The lot was almost full. She finally found one and got out of her car. She smoothed her skirt, put her keys in her purse, and started toward the front door.

She could hear the music loud and clear before she even opened the door. When she did open it, the sounds from the bar rushed over her. She heard the music, as well as laughter and clinking glasses. She stood just inside the door and took everything in. Everyone seemed to be having a good time. She was happy she'd taken the job there.

Susan fought her way through the crowd until she came to the bar. She waited patiently for the bartender to come over and take her order. She felt herself being jostled and turned to her right to see who had bumped into her.

"Excuse me," said a cute blonde. "I didn't mean to bump into you."

"No worries."

The blonde pushed her bangs out of her eyes, but they fell right back. She didn't seem to mind.

"I don't think I've seen you around before," she said.

"I actually just got to town today."

"And you've already found this place? My kind of woman." She smiled then, a dimpled smile that made her eyes sparkle.

"I'll actually be working here," Susan said.

"Even more my kind of woman. Let me get your drink for you."

Susan agreed before thinking. She inwardly cursed. She wasn't looking for anything, she reminded herself. And she didn't need to let the first smooth talking butch to come along buy her a drink.

"Thanks," Susan said and turned away.

"Hey." The blonde grabbed her elbow. "Why not join us? We're safe, I promise."

Susan shook her head.

"No, thank you. But thank you for the drink."

She walked off and could feel the gaze of the blonde boring into her back.

CHAPTER TWO

Mel worked her way through the crowd back to the pool table she and Joey were running. She poured Joey a glass of beer and filled her own glass.

"Who were you talking to?" Joey asked.

"I have no idea. A new employee of this fine establishment, but I didn't get her name."

"She's a looker."

"Well, I don't need to worry about getting her vitals tonight. It's not like this is the only time I'll be here."

"True. Okay, well, we're out of opponents so rack the balls and I'll play you."

"Sounds good."

Mel was racking the balls for Joey to break when two young women approached them.

"We've been watching you two. You're really good."

"Thanks. You want to challenge us?" Mel said.

"No. We just want to watch, if that's okay?"

"Fine by me," Mel said. "Get yourself some glasses. We'll share our pitcher with you."

She watched as the women pressed their way to the bar and came back with glasses. She poured them each a glass of beer.

"My name's Mel," she said. "This is Joey."

"Hi. I'm Tonya," the dark-haired one said. She pointed to the blonde. "This is Carrie."

"Hi," Joey and Mel said in unison.

Joey and Mel played two more games while they chatted with the girls. Mel bought another pitcher, but just as it arrived, Joey announced she had to leave.

"Are you sure?" Mel said. She looked at her watch. It was only midnight.

"I'm sure. Some of us have a two-year-old we have to get up and deal with in the morning. I'll see you later."

"Good night," Carrie said. Then she looked at Mel. "She's really cute. Does she really have a two-year-old?"

"She does indeed. Little DJ. He's about the cutest kid ever."

"She doesn't look like the type that would have a baby."

"Actually, her wife had him," Mel said.

"That makes more sense. Still, I was hoping we could all get out of here and go party."

"You know," Mel smiled her best smile. "We could still do that, couldn't we?"

"I suppose," Carrie said.

"Sounds great to me," Tonya said.

"Where do y'all live?" Mel asked.

"We live in Somerset," Carrie said.

"Well, I live in town. We can go to my place. Let's go pick up some beers and we can head over."

They left the bar, and Mel pointed out her Chevy Z28. They pointed to Carrie's Prius. They got in their car and Mel pulled out of the parking lot, confident they were behind her. She drove to the liquor store and picked up a twelve-pack of Coronas. Then she got back in her car and drove to her house.

Mel was not a neat freak by any stretch, but at least she wasn't as bad as Joey used to be, she reasoned. She kept her place picked up and mostly free of clutter. And you certainly wouldn't find any day-old pizza in her living room. She did a quick scan of the room and found it met with her approval. While the girls took their sweet time, Mel hurried down the hall to her bedroom. Her bed was made with clean sheets. Right on. She was ready for the ladies now.

She walked back to the front room to find them standing there.

"Hey. The beer's in the fridge. Let me get some for you."

She got the beer and they all sat on the sofa.

"This is a nice place," Tonya said.

"Thanks. I've lived here for like ten years or so."

"Wow."

"So, what do you ladies do in Somerset?"

"We go to school there."

"College, right?" Mel was suddenly nervous.

"Of course," Carrie said.

"Just checkin'. You two look too old to be high school students, but I had to ask."

"Don't worry about it. We both went to high school in Orange County. We're old enough," Tonya said. She smiled, a slow, devilish smile that made Mel's boxers wet.

"I'm glad to hear that." Mel reached out a hand and played with a strand of Tonya's hair. It was soft and silky. She wondered what other parts of her were soft and silky. She was determined to find out.

Carrie moved from her place beside Tonya to the other side of Mel. Mel liked being in the middle. She was enjoying the way her night was turning out. She was reminded of the nights she and Joey used to cruise and pick up women. They all had a good, no strings attached kind of fun. And that's what she was in for that night.

Tonya got on her knees and cupped Mel's face. She bent to kiss her lips, and Mel felt a fire flare inside her when their lips met.

"Damn, woman," Mel said.

"I could say the same thing," Tonya said. She kissed her again, harder, and placed one of Mel's hands on her breast. Mel fondled her through her clothes but grew frustrated. She wanted to feel her skin. She started to unbutton Tonya's shirt when she remembered Carrie.

She turned to her and kissed her. Carrie's kiss was more apprehensive, but she soon relaxed into it. Mel ran her tongue along Carrie's lips until Carrie opened her mouth for her. Their tongues swirled around each other, and when Mel broke the kiss, they were both breathing heavily.

"God, I want you two," Mel said.

"You can have us," Tonya said.

"Yeah, just tell us what to do."

Mel finished unbuttoning Tonya's shirt. She folded it over the back of her couch.

"Now you two," Tonya said.

Mel lifted her golf shirt over her head and tossed it on the floor. She watched as Carrie took her shirt off and placed it with Tonya's. Mel sat bare-chested.

"Hey, no fair. I'm the only one with tits showing," she said. "Come on, you two, lose the bras."

They quickly did, and Mel was in heaven seeing those young, perky breasts. Tonya's were more than a handful, while Carrie's were a perfect fit. She held each of them in turn before she lowered her head to take one of Carrie's in her mouth. Carrie let out a low moan. Mel sensed movement and looked up to see Tonya with Carrie's other nipple in her mouth.

She reached over and kneaded one of Tonya's breasts while she continued to suckle Carrie. These women were hot. And they were only getting warmed up.

Mel took her hand back and ran it up Carrie's thigh. She had on a short skirt, so it was easy to do. She found a muscular leg with soft skin. She also felt the moist heat coming from her center.

She had to taste her. She unzipped her skirt and peeled it down her slim hips. Next, she took off her underwear the same way. She eased Carrie back on the couch and buried her face between her legs. She loved the flavor of Carrie's pussy. She tasted so sweet and young, and Mel couldn't get enough.

Mel stopped briefly when she felt Tonya standing next to her, un-buttoning and unzipping her jeans. Tonya pulled them down and Mel stepped out of them. Tonya then removed Mel's boxers. Mel went back to licking Carrie only to feel Tonya's fingers deep inside her.

"Oh, dear God," she moaned against Carrie. "That feels so good."

"Good."

Carrie had her knees over Mel's shoulders by then, and Mel slid her own fingers inside her. Carrie moved against them as Mel licked her clit until Carrie cried out and collapsed after her climax.

Tonya continued to move her fingers in and out of Mel, who was determined not to come before Tonya. She gently took hold of Tonya's wrist and withdrew her hand.

"Aw," Tonya said. She offered her hand to Carrie, who sucked Mel's juices off it.

"I insist on ladies first," Mel said. "Now, come on. Let's go to my room and we'll keep playing."

She led them down the hall to her room and turned to face Tonya.

"You are way overdressed," she said. "Let's get you out of those shorts."

Tonya stripped quickly and climbed onto the bed. Mel joined her. Carrie hung back.

"What's wrong, Carrie?" Mel asked. "Come on up and join us."

"I've already had my turn."

"What? Do you turn into a pumpkin at a certain time? You think you only get one turn? We're partying tonight, woman. And I plan to have you over and over again."

"Are you serious?" A small smile crept over her lips. "That sounds awesome."

"So get on the bed, sweetness. Let's do this."

Carrie lay back on the bed and Mel opened her legs again. She ran her hand over the softness she found there. She plunged her fingers inside her while she bent to taste Tonya. Her tongue rolled easily over her satin playground. She dipped inside her before moving her tongue back to her slick clit. She circled it several times before she lapped at it hard and fast, causing Tonya to scream as she came.

While Tonya came back to earth, Mel turned her complete focus back to Carrie, who had been writhing on her fingers. Mel moved them in and out, twisting her hand as she did so. Carrie's breathing got shallow, and she began to make little noises in the back of her throat. Mel withdrew her hand and swiped it across her clit, eliciting cries of ecstasy from her.

"What about you?" Tonya said. "Don't you get a turn?"

"I'm not through with you two yet."

"But we want at you," Carrie said.

"Fine," Mel said. "Go for it."

She lay back on the bed and relaxed. She was more than happy to have these two young women have their way with her. She was beyond ready for them. She knew she could hold off for a little while longer, but if she didn't have to, she wasn't going to complain.

Tonya kissed her hard on her mouth, and Mel raised her head to taste more of her. She loved the feel of their tongues against each other. Tonya broke the kiss and kissed lower until she was sucking on one of Mel's taut nipples.

Mel inhaled sharply at the sensation. She then felt Carrie's hand tentatively resting on her inner thigh. She looked down and saw Carrie gazing at her. The sight made her even wetter.

"You want to touch me, don't you?" Mel said.

"I can't decide. You're so beautiful. I might want to put my mouth on you. I already know you taste good."

"Well, I'd like to tell you to take your time, but I need you, so you're going to have to do something soon."

She watched Carrie's face disappear between her legs. She felt her tongue on her and groaned. She leaned back and closed her eyes. The feel of both ladies working their magic on her was heaven. She held Tonya's head in place and arched her hips to take Carrie's tongue deeper.

Tonya moved to Mel's other breast and sucked her nipple hard. Mel saw lights behind her eyelids, dim lights that grew brighter the closer she got to her climax. She felt Carrie move to her clit and knew it wouldn't be long. She closed her eyes tighter and grabbed hold of the sheet under her. She needed to come. She tried to hold off, but it was no use. The lights she was seeing grew bright as she rode one orgasm after another.

"You two know what you're doing," she said when her voice returned.

The two girls snuggled up against her. She held them both as sleep overtook them.

Mel woke up early Sunday morning. She looked from one young woman to the other. They appeared to be sleeping so soundly, it seemed a shame to wake them. She padded down the hall and got the coffee started. She wandered back to her room, and the girls still hadn't moved. She couldn't resist the sight of the two nubile bodies. She climbed onto the bed and buried her face between Carrie's legs while she ran her fingers over Tonya. Evidence of the previous night's orgasms greeted her.

She felt her own insides drip at the feel of the girls. Carrie tasted like heaven, and Tonya felt soft and warm and wet. She swirled her tongue around Carrie's swollen clit and dragged her hand over the length of Tonya.

The girls started moving, and Mel looked up to see them playing with each other's tits. That got her hotter. She rubbed hard on Tonya's clit and licked furiously at Carrie's. She heard them cry out together and slowed her actions, eventually stopping when she felt them quit shaking.

"Good morning to us," Tonya said.

"The coffee should be about ready," Mel said.

"Oh, no you don't."

Tonya kissed down Mel's body until she was between her legs. She licked her from one end to the other.

"You're wet and you taste wonderful," she said.

Carrie made herself comfortable at Mel's breasts. She suckled at one nipple then the other while Tonya licked inside Mel.

Mel was almost overcome with sensations. She was ready to come already, but told herself to hold off, that it would be worth it to wait just a little while longer. When she felt Tonya's tongue on her clit, she lost control. She felt herself soaring through the atmosphere as she reached her climax.

❖

Susan woke in her new house and stretched. She'd stayed out too late checking out Kindred Spirits. She'd decided it was a fun bar, and she was looking forward to working there. She'd seen a lot of different people there, all of whom were having a good time. However, her mind kept drifting back to the cute blonde who'd bought her her first drink there. She was charming and very easy on the eyes. Susan warned herself to stay away from her. She was sure she was trouble. Especially after she saw her leave with two young ladies. Susan was sure she was a player. And a player was the last thing she needed in her life.

She rolled over and checked the clock. Eleven o'clock! She'd overslept in a big way. She had hoped to get up early to get some unpacking done before she had to be at work, but that wasn't the case. She had to be at the bar by one to fill out paperwork and start training. She hurried in the shower, and it wasn't until she was drying off that she remembered she was in Maybon Tir, not Los Angeles. There would be no hour commute. It would take five to ten minutes to get to Kindred Spirits, tops. She relaxed and sat at the dining room table with a cup of coffee. She did have time to unpack some boxes, but decided to do that later. She just wanted to absorb her new life for the moment.

She felt the peacefulness of the land wash over her. An all-women's community was unique. One on the beautiful Central Coast of California was unique and breathtaking. Susan told herself she'd explore it a little more after her shift ended at seven that night.

She dressed leisurely and finally it was twelve forty-five. She checked herself in her mirror again. Short-shorts and a white T-shirt. That's what she'd been told to wear. She looked good. And there was a brief flicker in the back of her brain that if she saw the blonde again from the previous night, she might be interested. She shook the thought from her head. Susan wasn't interested, regardless of how the blonde felt. She grabbed her keys and headed out to her car.

Susan took a deep breath when she stepped outside her house, so grateful to be out of the smog-filled air of Los Angeles. The fresh air felt good and didn't burn. It was a nice change, to be sure. She drove to the bar and parked in the back parking lot. She used the back entrance and saw the office to her right. She knocked on the door.

"Come in," said a disembodied voice.

Susan opened the door.

"I'm Susan Maloney. The new waitress."

"Oh." The woman behind the desk stood. "I'm Leah, one of the owners. I believe you've been speaking to my wife. It's a pleasure to meet you. She speaks very highly of you."

"Thanks. I enjoyed corresponding with her, as well."

"Please. Have a seat." Leah motioned to a chair on the other side of the desk from her.

Susan sat.

"We have some basic paperwork for you to fill out before we can get you started," Leah said. She handed Susan a packet. "Go ahead and fill these out and then I'll take you out where we can see how much training you'll need."

Susan relaxed. This would be easy. The questions on the forms were easy. She wasn't at all nervous about her background check. She knew it would come back clean. She quickly finished the paperwork and handed it back to Leah.

"Great," Leah said. "Now let's go meet your coworkers."

CHAPTER THREE

L eah took Susan out to the bar, where she met Joanne, the afternoon bartender.

"Joanne's been with us since we opened," Leah said. "She pretty much gets the pick of shifts. She likes afternoons. You'll get a mix of shifts. Some nights, some afternoons. Now, do you tend bar, as well, or only waitress? Or did my wife ask you that and I should already know the answer?"

"I'm sorry. I don't bartend. But I can learn."

"Great. Joanne will start teaching you today since the place is so slow. There's really no need for a waitress. We thought there might be a few more people here."

"Oh, that sounds fine. I'd love for Joanne to teach me."

Leah left them alone, and Joanne handed Susan a black book. It was filled with cocktail recipes.

"Everything you need to know is in here," she said. "Sure, I'll show you drinks that get ordered today, but when you're on your own, refer to this book. It's a bible for us bartenders."

"Got it." Susan flipped through the book. It had drinks she was familiar with and some she'd never heard of. Still, she was undaunted. She thought bartending would be fun. And it would be a way to get more hours if waitresses weren't needed.

She shadowed Joanne all afternoon. Joanne finally let Susan make a few drinks. The patrons didn't seem to mind them, so everyone was happy. Joanne was very friendly, as were the customers. Susan once again thought how lucky she was to have landed in Maybon Tir.

It was six thirty, and she only had a half hour to go on her shift. She was cleaning glasses behind the bar when in walked the cute blonde from the night before. She took one look at Susan and broke into a dimpled smile.

She quickly crossed the bar to Susan. She extended her hand.

"We didn't get properly introduced last night. I'm Mel."

"Susan."

"It's a pleasure to meet you, Susan."

"I'm not sure I can say the same."

Mel withdrew her hand and stood up straight.

"Whoa. Where did that come from?"

"You're obviously a charmer and a lady's woman. The last thing I need in my life."

"Hey, I'm only trying to be a nice person welcoming you to a new town. I didn't say anything about charming my way into your life."

"No, but I know your type."

"Brrr," Mel said. "You're an icy one, aren't you?"

"Maybe I am. So what? If so, there's a reason for it."

"And what might that reason be?"

"None of your business."

Joanne walked up then.

"I see you've met Mel. She's a regular here so we treat her real nice."

"Okay," Susan said reluctantly.

"She used to be quite a skirt chaser back in the day," Joanne continued. "Back when she and Joey Scarpetti used to run together. Now Joey's a happy housewife with a baby boy at home. We hardly ever see her anymore."

"Is that who you were playing pool with last night?" Susan said.

"It was indeed. She left around midnight though. Had to get home."

"I bet you think that's disgusting. You probably think of her wife as a ball and chain or some such."

"Ouch. You really don't like me, do you? All this from a drink I bought you last night?"

"I just know your type."

"So you said. For your information, I love Joey's wife and kid. And I'm very happy that she's found someone like Samantha."

"Joey and Samantha are like the First Couple of Maybon Tir," Joanne said. "They're practically royalty."

"Well, I can't wait to meet them, then."

"Oh you will. Joey at least. She comes in here once in a while. Samantha you're more likely to run into out and about. She's not the bar type."

"So, anyway, even though you've decided to hate me on first sight," Mel said. "Can I get a half pitcher of Firestone Pivo?"

"Sure," Susan said with false cheerfulness. She grabbed a small pitcher from the refrigerator and filled it. She was proud of the amount of head she left on it. Joanne smiled and nodded. Susan grabbed a glass and gave both to Mel.

"That's five fifty," she said.

Mel gave her a ten-dollar bill.

"Keep the change," she said.

Susan looked at her incredulously. She watched Mel walk away and knew she had to pocket the change.

"Wow. She must really like you," Joanne said.

"Or she's trying to buy me."

"You seem to really dislike her. She's not a bad person. Trust me."

"I don't know. She strikes me as smarmy."

"Maybe in the good ol' days. But she's mellowed out with age."

"I can't seem to take your word for that. I don't know what it is about her, but she rubs me the wrong way."

"There are lots of women in this town who would love to have her rub them the right way." Joanne laughed. "At any rate, she's a regular here, so treat her nice."

"I'll do my best."

"Maybe have a beer with her after work."

"Oh, I don't think so."

"Come on. What would it hurt? Make peace with her. At least try?"

"I'll try. But I don't trust her."

"It's not like she's asking you out or anything. She's just relaxing and having a couple of beers. I'm sure pretty soon she'll be playing pool or something. I say you just go up to her after work and apologize for getting off on the wrong foot. I'm telling you, she's a good tipper and a nice person. She's good to have as a friend."

Susan sighed.

"Okay. I'll try. But the minute she hits on me again, I'm done with her."

"Again?"

"Yeah. She bought me a drink last night."

"Oh," Joanne said. "So you thought she was cute then, but not now?"

"I let my guard down briefly. I won't do it again."

"Yowza. Someone's been burned."

"I don't want to talk about it."

"Fair enough," Joanne said. "By the way, when do you work next?"

"Tomorrow night."

"It probably won't be too busy. Not until football season."

"Good. Maybe I'll learn more drinks then."

"Maybe. Oh, here's tonight's bartender and waitress."

Joanne introduced everyone to each other, then announced her departure.

"I'm out of here. I'll see you next time, Susan. Now, go play nice."

"What did she mean by that?" Lily, the bartender asked.

"I had a bit of a meltdown with that Mel woman."

"Mel? What did she do?"

"She's just too smooth for me," Susan said.

"Smooth?" Lily laughed. "You should have seen her in her prime years."

"That's what I hear. At any rate, Joanne thinks it would behoove me to make nice with her."

"It can't hurt. She's a regular here, after all."

Mel was almost finished with her half pitcher when she heard a cool voice behind her.

"Hey."

She turned to see Susan standing there.

"Hey yourself. You sure you're allowed to stand that close to me?"

"Don't be a jerk. I'm here to apologize."

Mel tried to fight the smile that threatened.

"Apologize? Really?"

"Yes. I was rude. Look, I have baggage, okay? I'm just getting out of an abusive relationship. But that's not your problem."

"I'm sorry to hear that, but don't we all have baggage?" Mel said.

"You? You were in a relationship? That surprises me."

"Hey now. I know you think I'm some lady charmer or something, but I'm not. I'm only human. I've been in relationships. They've ended. It's hurt. You're not alone, so please don't play the martyr with me."

Susan stood shifting her weight from one foot to another.

"Are you going to invite me to sit?"

"Sure. Have a seat. I'm going to go get more beer. Shall I get a full pitcher?"

"I'm not much of a beer drinker," Susan said.

"Oh, yeah. You're a lemon drop kind of woman. I'll get you one. Be right back."

Mel walked to the bar and placed her order. She turned to look at Susan and found herself being checked out. She turned back toward the bar and pretended not to notice. But she had. She believed deep down Susan wanted her. Something about "she doth protest too much" or something like that. But Mel told herself to move slowly with this one. She wasn't just going to fall into bed with her. She was going to make Mel work for it. But there was something different about Susan. Mel liked the idea of taking it slow and getting to know her. If only she could keep her hormones in check, she'd be in good shape.

She wandered back to the table and gave Susan her drink before she sat down with her beer.

"So, where are you from, Susan? And how did you end up here?"

"I moved here from LA. I ended up here because it's a community full of women on the Central Coast and I got a job here. Who wouldn't jump on that opportunity?"

"Oh, I don't blame you. I love it here."

"And how long have you lived here?"

"Oh, wow. Who knows at this point? I moved here right after college."

"And what do you do?" Susan asked.

"I work construction."

"That's rather vague. What sort of construction?"

"The crew I'm on works foundation to finish. So, I can do any type of construction needed."

"That's pretty cool. Is there enough construction around here to keep you busy?"

"Usually. This place is really growing. And when we're not working, my friend Joey and I can usually be found surfing."

"Joey. I've heard about her."

"Yeah? Good things I hope. I've never had a better friend."

"Well, I've heard you two were quite the forces to be reckoned with when she was single."

"True," Mel said. "I'll admit that. But that was a few years ago. She's an old married woman now."

"And you?"

"What about me?"

"Have you settled down?"

"I still haven't met the one yet, but I'm holding out hope."

"And until then?" Susan said.

"Until then I keep trying to find her."

"Were you trying to find her when you left with those two women last night?"

Mel arched an eyebrow.

"So, you were paying attention, huh?"

"I saw you. I was curious about you. You seemed like a smooth operator and I wondered if I was right. Then I saw you last night, and my feelings were confirmed."

"Hey, come on. Those two wanted to party. Who was I to say no?"

"It was nice of you to do your civic duty," Susan said.

Susan was so indignant, Mel had to laugh.

"Hey, look. I used to be a bit of a scoundrel. I admit it, but those days are gone. That doesn't mean I'm still not up for a little fun and games on occasion."

"Oh, I'm sure you are, Mel. I'm sure you're up for whatever comes along whenever it comes along."

Mel licked her lips. Susan intrigued her. Sure, she had Mel nailed, but only to a degree. And sure, Mel could tell her she desperately wanted to find a special lady and settle down and work on forever with her. But she didn't want to. She liked watching Susan getting so fired up over her. Clearly that had to indicate some form of attraction, didn't it? Regardless, Mel wanted to spend more time with her and get to know her better.

"You play pool?" Mel said.

"What self-respecting waitress doesn't?"

"Oh, my. Don't you sound confident?"

"I do okay."

"Shall we play for another round then?"

"Sure. I'm up for it," Susan said. "We'll lag to see who breaks?"

"Sounds good."

Mel went first and left the cue ball inches from the edge. Susan got the ball even closer.

"Rack 'em," Susan said.

"Gladly." Mel smiled. So far it seemed Susan had some skill. She'd find out how much in a minute. Mel was known for holding her own in a game of pool. She was feeling pretty cocky but warned herself not to go easy on Susan. She seemed to know her way around a pool table, as well.

Mel racked the balls and stood back while Susan broke them. Susan got three solid balls in on the break. Mel whistled softly.

"That was impressive."

Susan looked at her.

"I'm thirsty, but don't want to pay for another drink."

"Fair enough."

Susan ran the table, knocking in all the solids and then the eight ball without giving Mel a turn. Mel shook her head.

"Well, color me impressed," she said. "Want to go again?"

"What will we play for this time?" Susan said.

"Dinner?" It was out before Mel could stop herself. She watched as Susan visibly stiffened. "No strings attached. Just a new friend showing you around the town."

"Let's start with the drink you owe me. Show me you're no welsher."

Mel went to the bar and returned with another lemon drop.

"Satisfied?"

"Yep. So, dinner, huh?"

"Loser buys."

"You rack again," Susan said.

Mel felt her heart skip a beat. She didn't care if she lost. Susan was agreeing to go out to dinner with her. She wondered, if she played her cards right, how far she could take things with her. For the moment, though, she thought she'd just better focus on pool. If she got a chance to play, that was.

But the second game was only different from the first in that Susan ran the table with striped balls rather than solids.

"Hey, you two want to play doubles?" a woman asked.

"Hey, Noelle. That's up to her," Mel said.

"Sure," Susan said. "Why not?"

They took sips of their drinks, then waited while the newcomers racked the balls.

"Why don't you break?" Mel said, as she felt confident no one else would get a chance to play if Susan did.

"No. You take a turn."

"Fine, but I seldom actually run a table."

"Okay, then it'll be more fair."

"Gee, thanks for the confidence."

"Don't be silly," Susan said. "We're still going to win. And this way you finally get a chance to play."

"You're doing wonders for my ego."

"I don't think I'm saying things right."

"No." Mel laughed. "I think you're saying them exactly right. That doesn't mean I want to hear them."

Mel broke the balls and knocked in two stripes. She kept going until there was only one stripe left on the table.

Noelle took her turn but didn't knock any balls in. It was Susan's turn, and she easily finished the game.

"Wow, you two are good," Noelle said. "It reminds me of the Mel and Joey days."

"I don't think Joey was as good as Susan is," Mel said.

"Don't let her hear you say that," Noelle said.

"Maybe someday I'll get to play against her," Susan said. "That would be fun."

"Well, someone else put quarters up," Mel said. "Shall we keep going or do you have somewhere to be?"

"No. I'm up for keeping the game going. I'm really enjoying myself."

Mel smiled. Maybe she could melt the ice princess, after all.

"Oh," Noelle said. "We owe you drinks. Mel, I know what you drink. What about you?"

"I'd love another lemon drop," Susan said.

"Careful," Mel said. "Those things can go straight to your head."

"This isn't my first rodeo, cowgirl," Susan said. "I can hold my liquor."

"Okay. I'm just checkin' in with you."

The new duo racked the balls and Mel broke them. They won that game and the next. Mel lost count of how many games they'd won. She finally had to throw her cue on the table to show she was through.

"What gives?" said Susan.

"I need to get up for work in the morning. I can't play any longer. I need to get going."

Susan checked the clock.

"Oh, yeah. I can't believe it's after midnight."

"Time flies when you're having fun."

"I guess it does."

"So you admit you had fun?" Mel said.

"Yes. I admit it."

"And I was the perfect gentlewoman, was I not?"

"You were."

"Okay," Mel said. "So, fears dispersed?"

"Not completely. But mostly."

Mel laughed.

"I guess I can accept that. Do you want a ride home or are you okay to drive?"

"I think I'm okay."

"Well, I'll follow you to make sure you get home safely."

"You know you could just ask where I live."

"True. I could. But then I wouldn't know if you got home in one piece. This way I'll know. Now, come on. Let's get going."

Mel followed Susan to a cute little bungalow. She thought how perfect it seemed for her. She wished she would be invited in, but Susan just waved from the door and disappeared inside. At least Mel had shown some chivalry as well as having behaved so well all night. She knew she'd scored points with Susan. Now she just had to be patient and try to completely win her over.

CHAPTER FOUR

Joey was waiting for Mel when she arrived at the construction site the next morning.

"You're looking a little hangdog this morning," Joey said.

"Yeah. I was out a little late for a work night. But it was worth it."

"Yeah? Who's the lucky lady?"

"Nah. I was just at the bar shooting pool a little later than I should have been."

"Really? I'm a little disappointed. I do like to live vicariously through you."

"Well, to tell the truth," Mel said. "My partner at the table was the new waitress. The one I was talking to the other night."

"Yeah? The real looker?"

"Yeah. Her. She's so fine, Joey. You saw her. Her jet-black hair looks soft as hell, and her blue eyes are in such contrast to her hair. It's a combination I'm finding hard to fight. And she's a lot of fun when she lets her guard down."

"Okay then, I'm glad you got her to let her guard down. So, any plans to see her again?"

"I crashed and burned there. I didn't get her schedule. I should have. But I do get to take her out to dinner. I lost big time in a pool game. But no details were set up."

"It's something anyway. You'll get to see her again as long as she's working at Kindred Spirits."

"But not if she works afternoons only. Maybe she'll work a night shift sometime. Or maybe I'll waltz in just as she's getting off shift like I did yesterday. I don't know. I just know I need to see her again."

"Then it'll happen. Now, come on, let's get to work."

It was a hot summer day and the crew was pouring concrete. It was a thankless job, but one that Joey and Mel were particularly skilled at. They got it poured and sat in the shade to drink their water.

"How you feeling?" Joey said.

"Last night's catching up with me. I drank too much as well as stayed out too late."

"So, after work you just want to go home?"

"I'd like to try to catch some waves if you're interested."

"I am."

"Or we could grab DJ from day care early and take him to the park."

"Now, don't get me wrong. I love that little guy, but I'm already wiped and we're only halfway through our day. I think surfing would do me a world of good."

"Okay. Sounds good."

"Why don't you plan on coming over for dinner, too? I'll grill some steaks and we'll have a salad. It'll be cool and refreshing. And you'll be able to see the little man then."

"That would be great. Are you sure Samantha won't mind?"

"I'll text her right now and ask."

"Let's go. Back to work," Brenda, the forewoman, called. "Only two more hours. It's too hot to put in a full day."

"That's a relief," Mel said. "I'm frying out here."

"It's in the mid nineties," Joey said. "That's hot for us."

"Yeah, it is."

They went back to work framing walls. Time slowed to a crawl under the burning sun, but they got through it.

"That's it for today," Brenda yelled.

"Thank God." Mel said as she collapsed on the tailgate of Joey's truck. She immediately jumped back up. "Holy shit, that's hot."

"Why don't you go get your board?" Joey said. "I'll meet you at The Shack."

"You got it."

Mel drove home. She was barely able to keep her eyes open. But it had been worth it. Time with Susan was worth any sacrifice, she figured. She really had it bad for her. And she'd been on her best behavior the night before, so she was certain she'd made a good impression.

She slipped into her board shorts and tank top and grabbed her board. She put it in the back of her van and headed off to The Shack.

Joey was already there when she arrived.

"Come on. The waves are lookin' good, and I'm ready to cool off," Joey said.

They crossed the sand quickly as it was burning their feet and waded out into the water. They got on their boards and paddled out. The cool water felt good on Mel's legs.

"Oh yeah," she said. "This is what I'm talking about."

They caught several waves, and then, as the waves started to flatten out, they sat on their boards and bobbed in the water.

"You ready to head over to my place?" Joey said.

"Sure."

"Go ahead and store your board in your van. We'll take my car to my place. I'll give you a lift back after dinner."

"Sounds good," Mel said.

Joey checked her watch. "Samantha is probably home by now. I'm betting you can help feed DJ."

"Right on."

They arrived at Joey's house to find DJ in his high chair eating a banana.

"Meow!" DJ cried out.

"Hey, little buddy. How you doin'?" To his parents, she asked, "Is that his dinner?"

"No. He was just starving so I gave him it as a snack," Samantha said. "I'm afraid he's going to grow again."

"What does he get for dinner?"

"Steak, same as you and me," Joey said.

"How is that possible? Do you have to chew it for him first? Won't he choke?"

"No." Joey laughed. "I just cut it into really small pieces. Don't worry. I'm not out to kill my own son."

"I didn't think you would be. I just didn't know."

"You need to relax," Samantha said. "Sit down. Have a beer."

Mel went to the refrigerator and helped herself to a Corona. "Thanks."

She sat on a bar stool and watched Joey and Samantha in the kitchen while keeping an eye on DJ seated next to her.

"Can I get down?" DJ said, plain as day.

"I don't know. Let's ask your folks. Can DJ get down?"

"Yeah," Joey said. "You want to play with him while we see to dinner?"

"Sure."

Mel allowed DJ to grab her finger and lead her to the play room. She sat on the floor with him and played with building blocks. She pointed to letters on the side of the blocks and he identified them. She was convinced he was a genius.

"Dinner's ready," Joey said from the doorway.

"Did you know he can read letters?"

"Do you know Samantha is his mom? Of course he's a smart kid. And, yes. I knew that. We've worked hard with him."

"That's awesome."

Mel picked DJ up and carried him back to his highchair.

She sat at the table and enjoyed a fine meal.

"You seem in a better mood this evening than you were the last time you were here," Samantha said.

"Really? I must have been in pretty bad shape then, considering how tired and hungover I am today."

Samantha laughed.

"Ah. Just like the good old days."

"But unlike the good ol' days, she didn't bring her lady friend home with her."

"Oh, but you have one?" Samantha raised her eyebrows.

"I'm working on it." Mel felt her face heat up.

"Look at her blush," Joey said.

"Hey now, cut me some slack."

"You really like this woman?" Samantha said.

"She's really beautiful," Mel said. "So my interest was initially piqued. But then we had so much fun last night. We ran the pool tables at Kindred Spirits until after midnight. She was great."

"Well, then I wish you the best of luck with her. What's her name?"

"Susan."

"Susan? Have I met her?"

"I doubt it. She's new in town."

"How new?"

"Like two days new. Maybe three now."

"Wow. Well, it's nice of you to show her a good time." Samantha laughed.

"I'm trying," Mel said. "I'm trying really hard."

Susan woke Monday and stretched leisurely. It was eleven o'clock again, but she knew better than to panic now. She'd easily get to the bar by one. It didn't take her that long to get ready. Although, when she got out of bed and made her way to her kitchen, she looked at all the boxes all over the place and chided herself that she had to unpack someday. Wednesday and Saturday were her days off. She decided to do nothing on Wednesday but unpack and settle in.

She made her coffee and sat at the dining room table. She looked out the sliding glass doors at her backyard. She couldn't wait to do some landscaping either. So far she was really liking Maybon Tir.

Her mind drifted to the previous night at Kindred Spirits and on Mel…what was her last name? She'd have to find that out. No, she told herself. She wouldn't. It wasn't important. She sighed heavily. She couldn't deny her attraction to Mel. It was gut level and probably only good for one thing. She could have a fling, but did she want to have one with Mel? Why not? She was good-looking and seemingly out for one thing only. Maybe Susan should flirt with her next time she saw her. But who knew when that would be?

Susan got to work to find it as slow as the previous day. She spent most of her time studying the bartender's bible. She felt like she was learning lots of recipes, if only she'd be given the chance to mix them.

Around five o'clock, the place picked up and she actually wait-ressed for the last two hours of her shift. It felt good to be working and making tips. And once again, the patrons were all very friendly. She really liked her job. At seven o'clock, when her shift ended, she took off her apron and turned to the bartender.

"So, tell me. I need a place to get a bite to eat tonight. What's good?"

"If you just want a quick burger, I recommend The Shack. It's right across from the water. Food's good. Price is right."

"Thanks," Susan said.

She drove to the beach and easily found The Shack. She went inside and found an informal burger joint with music blaring from the jukebox. A woman walked up to her.

"Just sit anywhere you like," she said.

Susan sat by the window so she could watch the sun set over the ocean. It was still a little early for that to happen, but she wanted a good view, just in case. She asked the waitress if they sold alcohol.

"We only have beer and wine. Nothing harder."

"I'll take a glass of Chardonnay then."

"And to eat?"

"A Swiss bacon burger."

"You want fries with that?"

"Please."

The waitress walked off, and Susan sat back in her seat. She needed to get a grip on her eating. Both for financial reasons and sheer caloric intake. If she wanted to keep her figure, she'd have to stop eating like a pig. But not that night. She still hadn't been to the grocery store. She would have to find one so she could fill her fridge with healthy foods. She promised herself she'd get up early the next day to do that.

Her dinner came and she devoured it like the carnivore she was. She loved a good burger. Her ex-girlfriend, Dorinda, had tried to get her to go vegetarian, and she'd tried. But that was all in the past, and now Susan could eat whatever she wanted.

Susan shook her head. Thoughts of Dorinda were not welcome. She had been the wrong person for Susan and she knew that. Even though they'd had some good times. Susan told herself not to think about those. They were through and life went on. She had a new life and she was finally happy.

She paid for her dinner and walked out to the parking lot. She saw Mel getting out of a truck by a beat-up old van. She walked over.

"Hey," she said.

"Hey back," Mel said, all smiles. "What are you up to?"

"I just finished dinner."

"Me, too." Mel waved to Joey as she drove off.

"Huh?" Susan was confused.

"I had dinner at Joey's. We caught some waves after work then I went over to her place."

"Oh. Good for you. I'm sure you know how lucky you are to have such a good friend."

"I love that family. I feel like I'm part of it, you know?" Mel said.

"That's great."

"So, can I buy you a drink?"

"Sure. Why not?"

They walked into The Shack and took a table by the window again.

"Hey, Mel," the waitress said.

"How you doin'?" Mel said. "Can we get a Firestone Pivo and a...what do you drink besides lemon drops?"

"I'll have a Chardonnay."

"Did you work today?" Mel asked.

"Yep. I had an afternoon shift. So I studied cocktails some more. I did get to waitress a little this evening, though."

"Good."

"How was your day?"

"Hot. Fucking hot. Excuse my language, but it was brutal."

"I'm sure. I wouldn't have wanted to be outside in that sun today."

"No. The waves felt great this afternoon, but working in it? Not so much."

"Can I ask you a question without offending you?"

"Uh-oh. That sounds ominous. I suppose you can. I mean, you should be able to."

"If Joey was off work," Susan said. "Why wouldn't she be with her son instead of with you?"

"DJ goes to preschool. So he's learning stuff all day. Plus Samantha is there with him. Once in a while, Joey will pull him early, but it's kind of important that he keeps his routine."

"How old is he?"

"Two. And he's about the cutest two-year-old you'll ever see."

She pulled out her phone and showed Susan a picture of the little towhead.

"Oh wow, look at his blue eyes," Susan said. "He's a cutie."

"He looks just like his mama."

"She must be a very attractive woman."

"She is," Mel said. "Joey was hooked on her from first sight."

"But you weren't?"

"No. She's not really my style."

"And what is your style, Mel?" Susan said

"I'm beginning to wonder about that."

"Yeah?"

"Yeah. I try so hard, but always end up alone. I don't know if I have a type at all," Mel said.

"Well, I refuse to try. I want to be alone. I've done the relationship thing and now I'm single and happy."

"I've been in relationships, too. They don't seem to last long, though. I don't know what it is about me. It's like I wear a shirt that says, 'Hurt me.'"

"The thing about relationships, you leave yourself vulnerable. I don't plan to get near one again."

"What about casual dating?" Mel said.

"Maybe. I think I could do that."

"Well, we have a date for dinner, right? That'll be casual. No strings attached, right?"

"Yep. When is that, by the way?" Susan said.

"Friday night. I'll pick you up at six."

"Sounds good."

"Hey, I hate to do this, but it's getting late," Mel said. "Can I walk you to your car?"

"That would be great."

Mel put her hands in her pockets and walked next to Susan to her car.

"So, I guess this is good night," Susan said.

"I guess so," Mel said.

Susan leaned back against her car door. Strangely, she wanted Mel to kiss her. She wondered if she would or if she would have to kiss Mel first. Her stomach was fluttering like she was a school kid. She felt her legs quiver as desire rolled over her. She looked at Mel's green eyes and thought she saw a desire that matched her own. What harm was there in a kiss? She wasn't offering to marry Mel.

"So, I'll see you Friday night?" Mel said.

"Yeah. I'll see you then."

Susan watched Mel walk off and thought that she'd totally blown that chance. But she figured there would be more. Or at least she hoped there would be.

CHAPTER FIVE

Mel climbed into her van and watched Susan drive off. Damn, she was hot. And Mel wanted her in the worst way. But Mel wasn't sure she could just keep it casual with Susan. There was something about her that had Mel wanting to settle down and build that white picket fence. But Susan was gorgeous, and Mel wasn't about to turn down a casual fling, if that's what Susan wanted. Then why hadn't she kissed her? She got the distinct feeling Susan had wanted a kiss as they said their good nights. Mel wished she had. But she knew her hormones would be in overdrive if she had, and they were already fairly revved up.

Susan was long gone out of the parking lot when Mel finally came back to reality and fired up her old van. She drove to her house and parked out front. She walked toward the front door, her thoughts still on Susan. She almost missed the figure sitting on her porch.

"Who are you? What do you want?" Mel said.

The figure stood and walked toward her slowly.

"It's me, Mel. Tiffany."

"Holy shit. You scared me half to death. How long have you been sitting out here?"

"Not long. I came to town with some friends. We went by Kindred Spirits, and when you weren't there, I had them drop me off here. When you weren't home, I decided to wait."

"Well, it's great to see you. Come on in. Can I offer you a beer?"

"Sure."

"Do I need to get you back to your friends?" Mel said.

"There's no hurry."

Mel took in Tiffany's tight body and remembered fondly the days when they had sex on a regular basis. She wondered if Tiff would be willing to go for a tumble that night. Mel was certainly primed for it.

She handed Tiffany a beer and they sat together on the couch.

"Lookin' good, Mel," Tiffany said.

"Thanks. School's been good to you, I see."

"Thanks. It has been."

"I can't believe it's been over two years since I've seen you."

"Time has a way of slipping by, you know?" Tiffany said.

"Yeah, it does."

"I was really hoping you still lived here. I was afraid someone had snatched you up and moved you to a nicer place."

"Nope. I'm still single. But not for lack of trying."

"I'm sorry to hear that. But I bet you're still getting laid every time you turn around."

"I wouldn't go that far," Mel said.

"I would." Tiffany brushed her tits against Mel. "I wouldn't mind having a go with you tonight. You know, for old time's sake."

"You wouldn't, huh?" Mel said.

Tiffany took one of Mel's hands and put it on her breast.

"Remember now? Things got pretty hot between us back then."

Mel instinctively closed her hand over Tiffany's pert breast. She felt her nipple poke at her through her thin cotton top.

"Are you wearing a bra?" Mel said.

"Not necessarily." Tiffany grinned. "Easy access."

"Oh shit," Mel said. "I guess I'd forgotten how hot you really are."

"Are you going to take me, Mel? No one has fucked me like you in a very long time."

"Yeah?" Mel lowered her mouth and brushed her lips against Tiffany's.

"You're teasing me."

Mel laughed.

"You never were one for patience, young one, were you?"

"I'm not that young anymore."

"You're still impatient, though."

"I want you Mel," Tiffany said.

Mel eased Tiffany back so she was lying on the couch. Mel climbed on top of her and kissed her hard on her mouth while her hand slid up her shirt and closed over a perfect breast. She inhaled sharply.

"Damn, girl. I forgot how fine your tits were."

"Get my shirt off me so you can see them."

"That's right. You're a bit of an exhibitionist as well, aren't you?"

"You remember. I like to be seen. I won't deny that."

Mel pulled her shirt over her head and gazed at the beautiful tan tits on display. She noted appreciatively that Tiffany had no tan lines. She was gorgeous, a sight to behold.

"I have other parts I'd like you to see as well," Tiffany said.

"Again, patience, my dear."

Mel dipped her head and licked a nipple before taking it in her mouth. She felt Tiffany's hands in her hair, and it made her crazy to know she was pleasing her. It was as much for herself as for Tiffany, though. She loved the feel of the hard nipple pressed against the roof of her mouth. She sucked harder and took all of Tiffany's breast in her mouth. Tiffany groaned and Mel felt her crotch clench.

Mel finally released her grip and climbed off Tiffany.

"What gives?" Tiffany said.

"Come on." Mel offered her hand. "We're going to bed."

"Can't I get naked first?" Tiffany whined.

"Of course."

Mel sat back on the couch and watched as Tiffany slipped out of her skimpy shorts and pink thong. Tiffany tossed the thong over Mel's head. She laughed.

"I thought you might like that."

"Maybe I'll keep it as a souvenir," Mel said.

"Sure."

"Now, come on. If I don't get you to bed soon, I may just explode right here."

"That could be fun." Tiffany reached her hand between Mel's legs.

"Oh no, you don't." Mel grabbed her wrist. "Come on."

She led her down the hall to her bedroom.

"Too bad you don't have a four-poster bed," Tiffany said. "I do like to be tied up."

"I remember."

Tiffany lay on the bed and Mel knelt between her legs. Tiffany placed her knees over Mel's shoulders.

"Damn, you're gorgeous."

"Can you see okay?" Tiffany slid her hood back to make sure her clit was visible.

"You don't need to do that. You're big and hard as it is. I can see all of you."

"I love the way you're looking at me," Tiffany said. "It gets me so hot."

"I know. I see the cream coming out of you."

"Oh good."

Mel lowered her head and licked the length of Tiffany.

"You taste so good," she said.

Tiffany took Mel's head and guided her to her clit.

"Right there, baby. Get me off. I'm so close already just from being with you."

Mel was happy to oblige. She made Tiffany scream in no time.

"Do you still have your toys?" Tiffany asked, clearly just warming up.

"Which one do you want?" Mel said.

"The one that penetrates both holes. I love that one."

"You're so fucking nasty. I love it."

She went to the dresser and took out the toy, as well as some lube. She applied the lube generously to the small beaded end. She placed the toy between Tiffany's legs, which were spread wide.

"Please," Tiffany said. "Please. I'm so ready."

Mel easily slipped the fat end inside Tiffany's pussy, and she lined up the beaded end with her nether hole. Slowly, carefully, she slid it inside her.

"Oh, fuck yeah," Tiffany said. "Oh God, that feels good."

Mel pulled it out and slowly slipped it back in. She twisted it slightly.

"You like that, huh?"

"Yeah, I do."

Mel was incredibly aroused from watching Tiffany swallow the toy. She loved watching her stretch out to take both ends. She was so hot. She'd forgotten how much fun they'd had together. It had been so long.

Mel used her other hand to rub Tiffany's clit while she continued to move the toy inside her.

"Oh, shit," Tiffany said. "Oh, holy shit. I'm gonna come."

"Do it, baby. Come for me."

"Oh fuck, Mel. Oh, yes. Oh God, Mel."

She grabbed Mel and pulled her to her as she cried out her name. Tiffany finally released her grip on Mel.

"Can I take it out now?" Mel said.

"If you have to."

"I don't have to. Not yet."

"You should though," Tiffany said. "It's your turn."

"Yeah?"

"Yeah. I'm gonna eat you raw."

"I don't know about that."

"Well, maybe not raw, but I'm gonna eat you good."

Mel eased the toy out of Tiffany and laid it on top of her dresser. She stripped out of her clothes and climbed back into bed with Tiffany. She lay on top of her and relished the feel of their skin against each other. She kissed Tiffany hard, conveying all the need she was feeling in that kiss.

Tiffany slipped out from underneath her and rolled Mel onto her back.

"I'd forgotten how hot your body was," Tiffany said.

"Yeah? I'm not all old and out of shape by now?"

"Not even close."

Tiffany kissed down Mel's tight body until she came to where her legs met. She climbed between them and gazed at her.

"You're beautiful. Do you know that?"

"I don't know all that, but I'll take your word for it."

"You are." It was the last thing Tiffany said before she put her talented tongue to work on Mel's center. She licked deep inside her.

Mel pressed Tiffany into her. She felt so good. Mel arched her hips into her, needing more. Tiffany moved her tongue to Mel's clit, and that was all it took. Mel immediately came, clenching Tiffany to her.

❖

Susan woke early on her day off and went to the grocery store to stock up on items for her house. She got curious looks from many of the women in there, though several of them came up and introduced themselves. She was again amazed at the friendliness of the community. The store was just a few blocks from her house, walking distance really. But she drove that day due to the large amount of groceries she had to buy. The experience was pleasant, though, just as she'd imagined it would be.

It was another scorcher on the Central Coast, and Susan's bungalow was old enough not to have central air. Most of the older houses didn't have it, as it wasn't usually necessary. So, Susan had her windows open and fans blowing as she finally got around to unpacking some of the boxes and setting up furniture.

By midafternoon, Susan had had enough. She put on a swimsuit and a wrap and drove the short distance to the beach. She parked in public parking and took her towel and lawn chair down by the water. She put her feet in. It was cool but not unpleasant. Especially on such a hot day. She sat there looking out at the water when movement out of the corner of her eye caught her attention.

Down the beach a bit and out in the water were two figures bobbing. She raised her hand to block the glare. It was hard to tell from where she was, but she thought one was Mel. The other must be Joey, she thought. She watched the two as a wave formed and they stood on surfboards and rode the wave in.

She could tell plainly then that it was Mel, who had stood up and grabbed her board. As she turned to go back out, she paused and looked at Susan. Susan waved. Mel waved back. She seemed to say something to her partner before walking over to where Susan sat. Susan felt her heart skip a beat as Mel approached. Easy, she told herself. Calm down.

"Hey," Mel said.

"Hi there. That was pretty impressive."

"Yeah? It wasn't that big of a wave. But it was a fun ride."

"Is that Joey out there with you?"

"Yep. Looks like you'll finally get to meet her if you hang out long enough."

"I'm not going anywhere," Susan said.

"Great. I'm going to head out and catch some more waves now. I just wanted to say hi."

"Okay. Well, have fun."

"Can I buy you dinner tonight? Just at The Shack. After surfing?"

"Is that to make up for our bet?"

"No. We're still on for Friday night."

Susan fought not to let her relief show. Two dinners in the same week would be a real treat.

"Sure. I'll hang around. Though I don't have any clothes. I just wore a wrap over my suit."

"That's okay. It's The Shack. Bathing suits are welcome."

"Great. Well, get out there and catch some waves. I'll be watching."

The last words slipped out before she could stop them.

"Yeah?" Mel grinned at her.

"Sure. What else is there to do here?"

"Whatever." Mel was still smiling as she swam back out to meet Joey.

Susan thoroughly enjoyed watching Joey and Mel surf. They seemed to have some secret language they used to control the mighty ocean. It was poetic to watch. She was almost sad when they walked over later.

"Susan, this is Joey," Mel said.

Joey, huh? She was a looker, just like Mel. Only she was dark to Mel's blondeness, and her eyes were blue rather than green. But she could easily see why these two had been a deadly duo back in their day.

"Nice to meet you, Joey," Susan said.

"Nice to meet you, too. Hey, I've got to run. I'll see you tomorrow, Mel. Susan, it was nice meeting you."

They watched as she cut across the sand to the parking lot of The Shack.

"Why don't you just park here?" Susan asked.

"We like to leave these places open for the general public. Besides, it's not uncommon for us to have a beer or two after surfing. So, The Shack parking lot makes sense."

"Okay. Well, I'm parked here. Why don't you get in and we'll drive across the street?"

"You sure you don't mind? I'm kind of wet and salty."

"It's all good. It's not like I drive a Cadillac."

Mel laughed.

"You're a good sport."

She stowed her surfboard in the backseat and climbed in.

They walked into The Shack and grabbed a table by the window. Susan was good and ordered a salad.

"A salad? Are you a vegetarian?" Mel said.

"No!" Susan said harshly. "I'm sorry. My ex was militant about us being vegetarians so now I think I'm more of a meat eater than I've ever been. But it's too hot for anything but a salad today."

"Ah. Sorry about your ex. And I didn't mean anything by it. I was just curious. We have a lot of vegetarians and vegans in town."

"Oh. Well, I'm not one of them." She searched for a way to defuse the situation. "So, waves were good today?"

"Waves were great today. Did you enjoy watching?" She smiled.

"I actually did. I never did get the hang of surfing, though I'll admit I've tried."

"Yeah? Where?"

"Southern California."

"Ah. Lots of places there to surf."

"Yep."

Their meals came and they ate in comfortable silence. When their plates had been cleared, Susan didn't want the night to end.

"Can I buy you another drink?" Mel asked.

"That would be great."

The waitress brought their drinks.

"So, your ex wasn't the soft and cuddly kind, huh?" Mel said.

Susan laughed.

"That's a bit of an understatement. She was actually quite abusive."

"I'm sorry. You deserve better."

"Well, it was what it was. And now I know I need to stay single to stay happy."

"So you've said. That makes me sad."

"Why? You want to run off and marry me?"

Mel laughed.

"Not for me. For you. Everyone deserves to be happy."

"Look at you," Susan said. "You're single and you're happy."

"But I would love to have what Joey and Samantha have."

"They're a one in a million," Susan said. "A one in a million."

They finished their drinks, and Mel walked Susan out to her car. They stood in awkward silence. Susan tried to see what Mel was thinking, but Mel kept looking at the ground.

"What's so exciting down there?" she said.

"Huh?"

"You're awfully intent on the ground. I just wondered what was holding your focus."

"Sorry." Mel looked into Susan's eyes. Susan felt her heart flip-flop in her chest. She really wanted Mel and thought Mel wanted her, too. All the signs were there. And Susan had made it clear she wasn't looking for a relationship. Mel should be all over her.

"You've got the most beautiful eyes," Mel said.

"Yours are very nice, too."

Mel tucked a stray strand of hair behind Susan's ear. Susan grabbed her hand and kissed her palm. Mel stared hard into her eyes. She lowered her mouth and lightly kissed Susan.

"That was nice," Susan said.

"Yeah."

"I'd like another."

"I was thinking I should probably get going."

"What are you afraid of, Mel?" Susan said. "What's going on in your mind?"

"Nothing. I just think it's time for me to hit the road. I'll see you Friday."

Chapter Six

F riday evening rolled around and Mel was a nervous wreck. She really liked Susan and didn't want to do anything to screw up what might be blossoming between them. On the other hand, Susan had made it perfectly clear she only wanted a playmate. Mel told herself to think of her like she thought of Tiffany, but she couldn't do that. There was something about Susan. And then when she talked about her ex, all Mel wanted to do was hold her and keep her safe and protect her. She was in a fine mess. At any rate, she knew Susan wanted her, which was something. She told herself to relax and go with it. Let Susan set the pace.

She drove to Susan's house and knocked on her door.

"Come in," Susan called.

Mel let herself in.

"Have a seat in the front room," Susan called from down the hall. "I'll be out in a minute."

Mel sat with her hands firmly clamped in her lap. She waited patiently and stood in awe when Susan came into the room. She was wearing a light blue dress with a plunging neckline that left little to the imagination.

"You look amazing," Mel said. She kissed her on the cheek. "And you smell great."

"Thanks. You look very nice, too. The green of your shirt really brings out your eyes."

"Are you ready to go?"

"I am."

Susan grabbed her purse from the counter and they walked outside.

"I see you brought the nice car tonight," Susan said. "I was afraid you were going to pick me up in the awful van you drive to the beach."

"No. Only the finest for you."

"So, where are we going for dinner?" Susan said.

"I'm taking you to a steak house. I want to see the carnivore in you."

Susan laughed, a sound that was music to Mel's ears.

"Trust me, I won't disappoint. Point me in the direction of a ribeye and I'll be all over it."

"That happens to be my favorite cut of meat as well."

They arrived at the restaurant, and Mel got out of the car first and opened Susan's door for her.

"I see chivalry isn't dead," Susan said.

"Not on my watch, it isn't."

Mel rested her hand in the small of Susan's back and steered her toward the door. Just that little contact had her hormones racing. She could easily lose herself with Susan. She would have to fight to keep it casual.

They were seated in a corner booth at the back of the restaurant. It was dark and private and just what Mel wanted.

"So, about the other night…" she began after they ordered.

"You did nothing wrong. You were quite the gentlewoman."

"I'm glad I came across that way. I felt like a letch."

"How so?" Susan asked.

"I don't know. I had no right to touch your hair, for starters."

"Look. I'm the one that kissed your palm. And I asked for another kiss, and you were the decent one who called it a night. You did nothing wrong."

"Okay. That's a relief. It's just that…well…I don't know…"

"What? You can tell me," Susan said. "We're two consenting adults, Mel. And maybe I need to be a little more forceful in my wants and needs."

"What are you saying?"

"Look, you know I'm not looking for anything permanent. And I would imagine you're okay with that."

"Normally, I would be. But there's something different about you."

Susan sighed heavily.

"Look. I'd like to invite you back to my place after dinner. But you have to understand, it's not anything serious."

"I understand. But you have to understand that, while I can keep it casual as long as you want to, I'll be wanting more."

"I don't know then," Susan said. "You know I don't want anything serious, and I don't really think you're the settling down type. Even if you think you are."

"Well, let's just play it by ear." Mel wasn't going to blow a chance to take Susan to bed. She had dreamed of this. She'd be a fool not to jump on it.

Dinner came, and each of them oohed and aahed over how perfectly cooked their meat was. They shared a bottle of red wine, since they were having steaks, and Mel relaxed the longer the meal went on. The promise of making love to Susan's sweet body was almost too much to bear. She had wanted to leave the restaurant as soon as Susan had said she wanted to take her home. But the wine and food helped her relax.

When dinner was over and Mel had paid, she pulled Susan's chair out for her.

"See? You're a natural charmer," Susan said.

"No. I just know right from wrong."

They slowly crossed the parking lot. Mel was thinking of what lay ahead, and it took her a few steps to realize Susan seemed lost in her own thoughts as well.

"Penny for your thoughts," Mel said.

"Oh, just thinking. Wondering, actually, if you'll be as wonderful a lover as my imagination has built you up to be."

"Oh. No pressure, huh?"

"None." Susan laughed.

"I hope I'll live up to your expectations."

"I'm sure you will."

"So, as the old adage goes, your place or mine?" Mel said.

"I think I'd rather be in my own bed, if that's okay," Susan said.

"Sure. No problem."

"My house is a mess, though. There are boxes everywhere. So, just be warned."

"I'm not worried about that," Mel said. "My attention is going to be all on you."

"You say the sweetest things. I know there must have been years of practice that have gone into making you who you are today."

"I mean what I say. I'm not just full of lines like you seem to think."

"See? You really are, though. But you've been using them so long you don't think of them as lines anymore," Susan said.

"No. I mean it. My attention is going to be all on you. I've looked forward to this since the first time I saw you at the bar."

"So we both have high expectations, then."

"Not exactly. Maybe. I don't know. I think there's a fire burning between us. I don't see how that can't carry over to exquisite love making."

"Okay, we're here, so let's go find out."

Mel once again held Susan's door open for her. She took her hand and allowed Susan to lead the way to her front door. Mel was a nervous wreck. She really hoped she could live up to Susan's standards, but she'd never had any complaints. Still, she was totally into Susan so the pressure was on.

Susan fumbled with her keys.

"You nervous?" Mel said.

"A little."

She got the door open and walked in. Mel didn't take her eyes off Susan's sexy ass as she followed her in. Susan turned and Mel blushed.

"Busted," she said.

"It's okay," Susan said. "Can I get you something to drink?"

"No. I'm fine."

"Okay."

They stood awkwardly in Susan's front room. Mel finally reached out and took Susan's hands. She gently pulled her toward her.

"You're so beautiful," she whispered.

"And you're so cute."

Mel wanted to kiss Susan with every ounce of her being. But she wanted to draw it out, to make it last. Their kiss at The Shack had been brief yet wonderful, but she wanted this one to be special. She wanted this to be a kiss Susan would never forget.

Again, she brushed a stray strand of hair out of Susan's face. She left her hand there and cupped her jaw. Her thumb lazily stroked her cheek. She closed her eyes and lowered her mouth. The shocks that struck her when their lips met left her weak in the knees. She continued to kiss her as she added pressure with her lips. She ran her tongue over Susan's lips, and they parted and let her in. The feel of their tongues dancing together was almost too much for Mel. She was having a hard time standing as well as breathing. She broke the kiss and leaned her forehead against Susan's.

"That was some kiss," she said when she finally caught her breath.

"Yeah, it was," Susan said. "I want another. And another. Please and thank you."

Mel was happy to oblige. She kissed Susan full on the mouth again while she ran her hands up and down her back. She pressed Susan into herself and felt her heart race at the contact.

"I need you," Susan said. "I need you right now."

"Let's go to your room, then."

"Come on." She reached both hands behind her and Mel took them. She followed Susan down the hall to a large master bedroom.

Mel stood in the doorway and took in the room. The king-size bed in the middle of the room was unmade. It had purple satin sheets on it and a black comforter. The combination made her heart race. It seemed so Susan. She couldn't wait to see Susan's naked body on those sheets and to feel the softness of both.

Susan turned to face her, and Mel kissed her again. She could kiss her all day and all night. Her lips were soft and she tasted sweet. She could easily lose herself in those kisses. She fought not to. She forced herself to stay focused on everything about Susan.

She reached behind her and unzipped her dress. She slipped her hand inside the open material to feel the silky softness of her back. As she rubbed it, Susan moaned. She collapsed into Mel's arms.

"That feels so good," Susan said.

"You have the most amazing skin."

"You have the most amazing touch."

They kissed some more as Mel got Susan's dress down over her hips and to the floor. Susan stepped out of it. Mel placed her hands on Susan's hips and pulled Susan against her.

She stepped back to look at Susan in her matching lace underwear and bra. They were pale blue, just like her dress. Her breasts overflowed just slightly from the top of her bra. Mel felt her clit swelling at the sight of Susan. She wanted her more than ever. And the idea that she was about to have her threatened to short-circuit her. She could barely think. She told herself not to think, just to feel.

She eased Susan onto the bed and climbed on top of her, careful not to crush her with her full weight.

"You're so fucking hot," she said. She kissed her again and let her hand skim over Susan's semi-nude body.

"You need to get out of those clothes," Susan said.

Mel climbed off the bed and stripped down to her boxers and undershirt.

"All of them," Susan said.

Mel stepped out of her boxers and took her wife-beater over her head.

"Now look who's hot," Susan said. "Come here. Let me touch you."

Mel got back on the bed. She thought Susan would touch her belly or her chest, but no. When Susan said she wanted to touch Mel, she meant it. Her hand was immediately between Mel's legs.

"You're so wet and warm," Susan said.

"Easy there, sister," Mel said. She gently took hold of Susan's wrist and took it away. "You're not even naked yet. It's too soon for the fun to begin. And when it does, I get you first."

"Why's that?"

"Chivalry, my dear. Ladies first."

"We may just see about that."

"I don't know. I need you so desperately. I have to have you, and I have to have you soon."

She kissed her again as she drew her hand over the mounds overflowing the bra.

"Your breasts are so soft. Let's get you out of this bra."

Susan sat up and Mel deftly unhooked her bra. She tossed it onto the floor. Mel kissed Susan again, hard on the mouth before kissing down her neck to where it met her shoulder. She sucked on the hollow there and moved down until she had her face at one of Susan's breasts. She kissed the side of it. It was large and firm and Mel wanted to devour it.

"You have the nicest beasts," Mel said.

"Please. Oh, God, please touch it or suck it or something. Please, Mel."

Mel licked her nipple and watched it grow. She saw the areola pucker and knew she was as hot for Mel as Mel was for her. She took as much of Susan's breast as she could into her mouth and sucked as hard as she could. She ran her tongue over her nipple as she continued to suckle.

"Oh, dear God, Mel," Susan said in a high-pitched voice. "Oh yes. Oh, God, yes."

Mel continued what she was doing, though she tried to suck harder and lick faster.

"Oh, shit, Mel." Susan said. "I'm going to come."

"Mm hm," Mel said, not releasing Susan's breast.

Susan wrapped her legs around Mel and gyrated against her as she clung to her and cried out her name.

"Oh, jeez," Susan said when Mel finally released her breast. "That was incredible. I've never come from someone sucking on my nipple before."

"Good," Mel said. "Let's hope tonight will be a night of many firsts. Now, let's get you out of these panties so I can have my way with you."

"Don't I even get to catch my breath first?"

Mel smiled.

"If you insist."

"Come here, you." Susan pulled Mel to her and held her. Mel could feel Susan's heart racing. She waited until it was back to normal before she sat up.

"Okay, now that you've caught your breath, off with the undies."

"You like to be in charge, don't you?" Susan said.

"Not really. I just like to make sure the lady is taken care of first. That's really the only thing I'm in charge about."

"Well, one could argue that you already took care of me," Susan said.

"That was only the appetizer. It's time for the main course."

She slid down Susan's body and peeled off her underwear. Susan spread her legs wide.

"Okay, loverboi. Have at it."

"Oh, shit," Mel said. "You're beautiful. I don't even know where to start."

Susan reached down and ran her hands through Mel's hair.

"It's all yours tonight. Do whatever you want."

Mel was dripping in anticipation. She noticed Susan was, too.

She ran her fingers over the length of Susan, stopping to tease her opening. She lowered her head and ran her tongue over Susan's clit. She heard Susan's sharp intake of breath and smiled to herself.

"Oh yes, Mel. That feels so good."

"You like that?" Mel said. She licked Susan again and slipped two fingers inside her. She gently stroked her while she lapped at her clit.

"Oh, shit, Mel. You do know what you're doing." Susan said in between heavy breaths.

Mel was wet and ready for Susan, too. She was throbbing as she made love to her. She had to force herself to focus on Susan's needs and keep her own at bay. But damn, she wanted to come.

She slid another finger inside Susan.

"Oh, God, yes. Fill me, Mel."

Mel moved her fingers in and out as her tongue swirled over and around her slick clit. She licked frantically, urging Susan closer and closer to the edge.

"Oh, shit," Susan said. "Oh, Mel."

She pressed Mel's face into her and gyrated against her as the orgasms washed over her.

"Damn," Susan said when she finally caught her breath. "I lost count of how many times I came."

"Good," Mel said as she licked her lips. "You should be too busy to keep track anyway."

"I was," Susan said. "I've got to say, Mel, you didn't disappoint. You may have outdone my fantasies, even."

Mel blushed.

"Oh, my God. You even blush. Could you be any cuter?"

Mel felt the redness covering her skin deepen. She had nothing to say. She just wanted Susan to take her now. She lay down next to her. She kissed her hard on her mouth and ran her hand over her body.

"What do you think you're doing?" Susan said. "It's your turn now."

She playfully rolled Mel onto her back and straddled her stomach.

"I'm in the driver's seat now," Susan said.

"Far be it from me to protest if a beautiful lady wants to ravish me."

"That's just what I intend to do."

She slid down Mel's body and left a wet trail as she did.

"Jesus, you're wet," Mel said. "I feel the heat as you slide down me."

"Good. That's all you, loverboi."

Susan slipped off Mel and lay between her legs. She pried Mel's lips open and ran her tongue between them.

Mel shivered as the waves of heat rolled over her. She was going to come too soon. She just knew it. She tried hard to hold it in as Susan played her fingers over Mel's hard clit. Mel didn't think she'd ever been that hard before.

"You're so swollen. I like that. Do you want me to get you off, Mel?"

"Yes. Susan, please. Please. I need to come."

She felt Susan take her clit between her lips and run her tongue over it. She grasped the sheets and cried out as she reached her climax.

"I came too soon," Mel said. "I feel bad."

"Don't. It was hot. I enjoyed that you were so worked up and ready. No need to feel bad, okay?"

"Okay. Now get up here and let me hold you."

"Don't you think you should get going?" Susan said.

"Can't I stay the night?"

"I don't know that that's such a good idea."

"Susan—"

"Mel, please. Let's not make this awkward. We had fun. I'd like to have fun with you again. But for now, I don't think it would give you the right message if I allowed you to stay the night."

"Fine. I'm really sorry some woman did a number on you, but I'm not her." Mel grabbed her clothes off the floor. She dressed quickly and tried to keep her temper in check. "When will I see you again?"

"I work Sunday. One to seven."

"I'll stop by." She kissed Susan on the cheek and let herself out.

CHAPTER SEVEN

Susan woke Saturday morning with a smile on her face. Memories of the previous night flooded her brain. She found herself reminiscing about Mel's sparkling green eyes, the cute way she flipped her bangs, and her dimples when she smiled. Mel was a looker. And man, was she a skilled lover. It had been ages since Susan had had that many orgasms. One right after another. She stretched as she remembered how incredible Mel had made her feel.

She had nothing to do that day and no one to do it with. She decided she wanted to go to the beach and soak up some rays after she unpacked some more. And broke down the boxes that littered her house. She had a lot of work to do. She got out of bed and put a robe on then set to work.

Susan had the house fairly clutter free by two. She felt good about what she had accomplished. To reward herself, she slipped into her swimsuit and wrap and headed to the beach. The place was crowded, as it was a warm summer day with temperatures in the mid eighties. She couldn't find a parking place in the public lot, so took a page out of Mel's book and parked at The Shack.

She crossed to the beach and carried her beach chair all the way down to the water. Once again, she sat with her feet in the water to stay cool. She lathered herself in sunscreen and leaned her head back. She closed her eyes to relax.

"You look like you're getting too much sun," she heard from a distance as she fought to wake up. She saw Mel standing there. "Seriously, you should put a hat on. Your face is red."

"I put sunscreen on," Susan said. "What time is it?"

"It's just after five. What time did you get here?"

"Just after two." Susan was shocked that she'd fallen asleep for three hours. No wonder she was looking burnt. She hadn't reapplied once since she'd been there.

"Well, you got plenty of color for one day," Mel said. "Have you been asleep the whole time?"

"I think so. I didn't realize how tired I was."

"Late night?" Mel grinned.

It was then that Susan realized Joey was standing there, too.

"Hi, Joey," she said.

"Hi, Susan. Mel's right. It's time for you to pack it up and head inside. Maybe get some aloe vera for the burn."

"Have you guys been surfing?" Susan was surprised to feel the disappointment at having missed them.

"Nope. We've been playing with this little guy." Mel tugged on the hand of DJ to bring him around to where Susan could see him.

"Aw, hello," Susan said.

DJ hid behind Mel's leg.

"Hey, DJ, this is a friend of mine," Mel said.

DJ stayed hidden.

"He's awfully cute," Susan said to Joey.

"Thanks. His mom's a looker."

"I'm sure."

"We were just taking him home," Mel said.

"Okay. I think I'm going to head home, too."

"You want a wine or something first?" Mel said.

"Hey, Mel," Joey said. "We really need to get going."

"I'd love a glass of wine," Susan said. "Go ahead and take DJ home, Joey. I'll give Mel a ride when we're through."

"Sounds good," Joey said. "I'll see you tomorrow, Mel?"

"Yeah. I'll be over around noon."

"Okay. You two enjoy your evening. It was good to see you again, Susan."

"Good seeing you, too."

Mel and Susan entered The Shack and took what was rapidly becoming "their table."

"I'm glad we ran into you," Mel said.

"Me, too. How red am I, really?"

"Pretty red."

Susan excused herself and went into the restroom to see for herself. It was true. She was burned to a crisp. Aloe vera. She'd pick some up on the way home after dinner.

She walked back out.

"I'm glad I'm fried. This way you can't see me blushing from how embarrassed I am for falling asleep for that long."

"No worries. We've all done it."

"You have such a great tan, though. Surely you don't get sunburned."

"Not very often. You had a pretty good base going, too. I'm surprised you got that red."

"I'm hoping it'll fade."

"Maybe it will," Mel said.

They ordered their drinks.

"Are you interested in dinner?" Mel said.

Susan thought for a moment. She liked Mel. She wanted to sleep with her again. But she didn't want to give Mel any false hope for a relationship.

"I don't know if that's such a good idea," Susan said.

"Why not?"

"Look, Mel. You're adorable. You're charming. And you're fantastic in bed. But I'm not looking for a relationship and I'd hate to lead you on."

"You've made it quite clear that we're just fuck buddies," Mel said. "I'm not thinking of anything more. But I'd love to buy you dinner and take you home again. No strings attached."

"Are you sure?" Susan said. Her desire to have Mel again was overriding her common sense.

"I'm sure. Now let's get some menus and order."

After dinner, Susan took Mel back to her place. They closed the front door behind them and Susan pressed Mel against it as she kissed her with a need that came from her very core. Mel brought a knee up and Susan ground into it.

"Let's get to bed," Susan said. She stripped as she walked and was completely naked by the time they reached her room.

"Holy shit, you're hot," Mel said. "You've got the nicest body I've ever seen."

"Thank you. Now, let's get you undressed."

Susan pulled Mel to her and kissed her as she undid her shorts and slid them off. Next, she dragged her boxers down and Mel stepped out of them. They broke apart so Mel could take off her shirt and wife-beater. They stood together, naked.

Mel climbed up on the bed and pulled Susan on top of her, being careful not to hurt her sunburned areas. Their tongues played over each other as limbs tangled together. Susan loved the feeling of Mel's masculine arms and legs against her. She wanted her in so many ways. Susan disentangled herself and got on her hands and knees.

"I want you to take me like this," she said.

"You do, huh?" She could hear the excitement in Mel's voice. "I'd love to do that. I can get really deep that way."

"I know," Susan said. "I want to feel your fingers in my throat."

Mel laughed.

"I'll see what I can do."

First, Mel reached her hand around Susan and rubbed her clit. Susan lowered her head and bit her pillow. Christ, Mel made her feel so good. She knew she was going to come, and Mel hadn't even been inside her yet. She couldn't help herself. She was writhing against Mel's hand, humping it, as it were, determined to get off as soon as she could. She didn't have to wait long. Mel pressed hard against her clit one last time and held her hand there and Susan screamed into the pillow as the waves crashed over her.

When she trusted her arms again, she straightened them out and offered herself to Mel. This time, Mel slid her fingers inside as deep as they could go. Susan still needed more.

"Give me more, Mel. More fingers. Go deeper. Really fuck me."

Mel did as instructed, and Susan had never felt better. She felt full deep inside. It was an amazing feeling. Mel moved her hand in and out and Susan moved back and forth to meet each thrust. Soon she was lost in the rhythm, incapable of thought, only able to feel. She kept it up as long as she could until all her life force seemed to congregate in her center. She held it there, pulsating until all at once it burst forward, flowing over her body as she came over and over again.

When she had finished convulsing, she collapsed on her stomach.

"Damn," she managed to say.

"You are so fucking hot," Mel said as she flopped down next to Susan.

"Mm. You're not so bad yourself. Give me a minute and I'll be all over you."

"No worries. You don't have to if you don't want to."

"Bullshit. Tell me you just fucked me like that and it didn't turn you on."

"I'd be lying," Mel said. She grinned. "I just like the idea of you being too wiped to do anything."

"It'll never happen."

She rolled Mel over onto her back and kissed her hard on her mouth. She skimmed her hand down Mel's body and felt her muscles ripple at her touch. She moved her hand back up to her breast, which she cupped gently.

"You have the perfect sized breasts," Susan said.

"Yeah? I'm glad you like them."

"They match your personality. You know, all butch and outdoorsy."

"Okay…"

Susan laughed.

"Don't worry. It's a compliment."

She teased Mel's nipples briefly before running her hand down to where her legs met. She slipped it between them and Mel spread them for her.

"Oh, Jesus," Susan said. "Just feel how wet you are for me."

She dragged her hand all over Mel before sliding her fingers inside. In and out, she moved them. She saw Mel grabbing hold of the sheet.

"You like that?" Susan said. "Does that feel good?"

"Oh God, yes."

"I want to make you come for me."

"Yes. Oh God, yes."

"Are you close, Mel? What do you need?"

Mel closed her eyes and gritted her teeth. Susan knew she was close. She moved her hand faster, and Mel finally cried out when she came.

Susan lay down next to Mel and allowed Mel to take her in her arms. They lay like that peacefully until Susan felt her eyelids grow heavy.

"I think you'd better go," she said.

"Yeah, I figured that was coming," Mel said. She dressed and turned to leave. "I'll see you tomorrow."

"Yep. See you then. Oh, do you need a ride?"

"No, I'll walk. Thanks, though."

Mel showed up at Joey's at noon the next day. She was looking forward to a day in the waves. She'd enjoyed playing with DJ the day before, but surfing sounded like a great way to clear her head.

"Hey, Mel." Joey answered the door. "How was your night last night?"

"Same as the night before."

"Yeah? So you and this Susan may be getting serious?"

"No. She kicked me out again."

"Really?" Joey said. "Maybe it's for the best. Maybe she's got some deep, dark secret that's keeping her from a relationship. Maybe she's a werewolf or a serial killer or something."

"Yeah. Those are likely. Whatever. She got burned in her last relationship and is now sworn off them. Sound familiar?"

"Sounds very familiar. But then Samantha came into my life and I was willing to take a chance again. Maybe she just needs to realize you're a good person to take a chance with."

"Yeah? Well, how long is that going to take?"

"I can't answer that, my friend. I wish I could, but I can't."

"Whatever. Let's hit the waves."

They surfed for three hours. Mel felt great after a day in the sun and water. The waves had been great, and Mel was relaxed and ready for a shower when she and Joey got out of the water.

"You want a beer or something before we head home?" Joey asked.

"No. I'm good. I need to take a shower and head over to Kindred Spirits. You want to come with?"

"No. I need some family time."

Mel showered and dressed in khaki cargo shorts and a black golf shirt. She hoped Susan would think she looked good. Man, she had it bad for Susan. She wondered what she could do to get Susan to see she wasn't just another smooth talker. She hoped to figure that out sooner rather than later. In the meantime, she'd simply enjoy the sex. Because the sex with Susan was out of this world.

She entered the bar to see quite a crowd. She wondered what was going on. She saw Susan waitressing, so took a seat and waited for her to come over.

"Half pitcher of Firestone Pivo?" Susan said when she got to Mel's table.

"Exactly. Thank you."

"Coming right up."

When she brought the beer, Mel motioned to the empty seat across the booth.

"Take a load off?" she said.

"I can't. Too busy."

"Can I buy you a drink when you're off duty?"

"Sure," Susan said. "That would be great."

Mel put quarters on the pool table to challenge Noelle, the woman currently running it.

"Oh, Mel. Come on. I've been having so much fun," Noelle said.

"Sorry. I need something to do to pass the time."

She beat Noelle soundly and then accepted challengers. She kept herself busy between pool and watching Susan make her rounds. She looked so fine in her short-shorts and tight white T-shirt. Mel's palms sweat at the thought of rubbing her hands all over Susan's body.

Finally, seven o'clock rolled around. Susan came over and collapsed in the booth across from her.

"Wow. What a day."

"Why is it so crowded?"

"I don't know," Susan said. "But I'm glad it was. I made bank on tips today."

"Good for you." Mel hadn't really considered how much tips meant to Susan or any of the other waitresses. She always tipped them well if they did a good job, but thought of it more as a way of saying they'd done a good job and not so much how it meant financially to the recipient.

"So, are you totally into this pool game?" Susan said.

"No. I don't even have a challenger at the moment."

"Good. Let's get out of here. I need a hot soak and some fun time."

Mel's heart skipped a beat. She was always up for fun time with Susan.

"Sounds good to me."

"Wait a minute," Susan said. "How many nights in a row will this be?"

Mel was crestfallen. She didn't want Susan to say no. She needed her. She had feelings for her like she'd never had before.

"Three," she said softly.

"Okay. I don't mind sleeping together as often as we can. But we need to check in periodically so we both are clear on where we stand."

"Look," Mel said. "You know what I want. I know what I want. But we both know that's not going to happen. So we play by your rules. I'm clear on them. Even though I'd never abuse you like your ex."

"I have such a hard time believing someone with your reputation would want to settle down."

"Stranger things have happened."

"I suppose."

"I'd like to stop by the liquor store on the way to your house," Mel said.

"Okay. I'll leave the door unlocked. I'll be in the tub, so you can let yourself in."

"Sounds good."

Mel showed up at Susan's house bearing a six-pack of beer and a bottle of Chardonnay. She was ready to relax with Susan. She was really enjoying spending all this time with her, though she wondered how good it was for her psyche. She felt like Don Quixote chasing windmills. But she was determined to keep trying. Hopefully, someday she'd wear Susan down.

She put the beer and wine in the fridge and wandered down the hall to find Susan reclining in a claw-foot tub.

"Nice bathtub," Mel said.

"Isn't it the best? I love it and have been dying to try it out."

"Well, you look very comfortable. Can I bring you a glass of wine?"

"That would be great. Thanks."

Mel returned with wine for Susan and a beer for herself.

"Cheers," she said. She looked around for a place to sit. There was only the toilet. She closed the lid and sat there.

"Are you enjoying the show?" Susan asked.

"Very much. Is that okay?"

"It's fine. I just don't know how comfortable I want you to get, you know?"

"Look, you invited me over. You're in the bath. I think we both know what happens next, so why shouldn't I watch you bathe?"

"I suppose you have a point."

"I'd be happy to help if you'd like," Mel said.

"No, thanks. I'm fine. But you'll have to excuse me now while I take my shower."

"I could join you."

"Please do."

Mel could hardly believe her ears. She hurried into the bedroom to shed her clothes and then went back to the bathroom. Susan was already in the shower. Mel stepped in with her. She took the soap in her hands and lathered them up then ran her hands all over Susan's body. Susan stood with her arms above her head and let Mel wash her.

"Damn, you're fine," Mel said as she washed down Susan's front. She paused to make sure her breasts were extra clean.

Susan reached for Mel and pulled her to her. She kissed her hard on the mouth. Mel's head grew light as the kiss deepened. She continued to scrub Susan's body. She finally reached between her legs and cleaned her carefully. She dipped her fingers inside and stroked her walls briefly then brushed them over her clit.

Susan held tightly to Mel as she shuddered in her arms.

"Oh, my God. You know just how to please a woman," Susan said. "Let me guess. Years of practice?"

Mel blushed.

"I think the important thing is that I'm learning to please you. That's what matters."

"Nice dodge, Mel. Okay. Let's rinse off and get out."

Mel stepped out first and held a towel for Susan. She stepped into it, and Mel wrapped it around her.

"Thank you," Susan said.

Mel was doing everything she could to prove she was a gentle-woman not in search of a one-night stand, even though that's what Susan wanted. Or rather, she wanted a string of one-night stands. Still, Mel held out hope that she could win her over.

They made their way to the bedroom and fell into bed together. Mel kissed Susan and ran her hands all over her body.

"I swear, your body was made for me to love," she said.

"You think so, huh?" Susan smiled.

"I do."

"Well, do with me what you will, stud."

Mel placed her hand between Susan's legs and rubbed her clit.

"Oh, God. No pretense tonight, huh?" Susan said through heavy breaths.

"Not a one. You're so wet and ready for me. Why shouldn't I just go for it?"

"Oh. No reason. God, Mel. Don't stop."

Mel continued to rub Susan's clit until Susan dug her fingernails into Mel's back. She screamed out incoherently. Mel smiled to herself, proud that she could have that effect on Susan.

"So, you want to play quick and dirty tonight, huh?" Susan said.

"Sure." Mel laughed.

Susan moved so she was between Mel's legs. She licked her clit and slipped her fingers inside her.

"Oh, shit," Mel said. "I'm so full. How many fingers are in me?"

"Four," Susan said. "Now give it to me baby. Let yourself go. I want you to come for me."

She didn't have to ask twice. Mel felt the ball of heat forming in her core. She felt it explode, sending heat waves throughout her body as the force of the orgasm hit.

She lay there until she could catch her breath.

"I guess it's time for me to go," she said.

"I guess it is."

"Can I leave my beer here?"

"I don't know," Susan said. "That seems awfully commitment-esque."

"Look. Quit harping on it," Mel said. "I get it. No commitment. Jesus Christ, woman."

She grabbed her beer from the fridge and left.

CHAPTER EIGHT

Susan lay awake in bed after Mel left. She hadn't needed to be so pissy. Susan just had to protect herself. She had been hurt badly by Dorinda, and she had no intention of getting hurt again. Dorinda had been emotionally, verbally, and sometimes physically abusive, and she didn't want to set herself up for more pain. Sure, Mel was being the perfect gentlewoman for the moment, but Susan knew her type. She just wanted Susan to fall for her, and she'd be on her way to woo some other poor, unsuspecting femme. It said a lot about Mel's character that she'd been rude when she'd left.

Susan rolled over and willed herself to go to sleep, but sleep was hard to come by. She should have been very relaxed after the orgasms Mel had given her. But she couldn't sleep. She got up and made herself some warm milk. She sat at the kitchen table and thought about the pros and cons of getting serious with Mel. She shook her head when she realized what she was doing. The fact that she was even considering it was wrong. Mel would just as soon break her heart as look at her. Susan would keep her distance emotionally. Too bad Mel was such a good lover. Susan might have been able to keep a physical distance, too.

She went back to bed and fell into a restless sleep. She woke the next morning feeling tired and cranky. She made herself a pot of coffee and sat on the back patio as she drank it. The fog hadn't burned off yet, so it was chilly, but the birds were singing, which cheered her spirits.

She wondered if Mel would show up at work that day. She hoped so, because she enjoyed the sex they had. On the other hand, she wasn't impressed by Mel's temper tantrum. Maybe if she apologized for it, they could get past it and have some fun that night.

Susan went to work. It was a slow day in the early part of her shift, so she studied the bible some more. Things started picking up around three o'clock so she grabbed her tray and set about waitressing. She kept her eye on the door, though, hoping Mel would come in. Her shift was ending and there had been no sign of her. Oh, well. She supposed that was for the best. She did a quick sweep around the bar and picked up empty pitchers and glasses before she grabbed her purse to leave for the night. She walked out the back door after one more glance around the bar for Mel.

Her mood souring by the minute, she found herself in the parking lot of The Shack. It had been her intention to drive home, but some unknown force had pulled her there instead. She looked around the lot but didn't see any sign of either of Mel's cars. Disappointment flooded her. She told herself to get a grip. She wasn't that into Mel. She was just looking to get lucky. That was all there was to it. Mel was a good lay. Nothing more.

She drove home and made herself dinner. She drank a couple of glasses of wine and considered getting a cat. That occupied her mind for a matter of time before it turned back to Mel. Why the hell couldn't she keep her out of her mind?

She poured herself another glass of wine and took it into the bathroom. She set it on the shelf and stripped off her work clothes. She drew a nice warm bath and slowly sank into it. It felt good. Nice and relaxing. She sipped her wine as she soaked and let the tension of the day fade away.

Susan dragged the loofa over her and let the scented water take her away. She closed her eyes and relaxed. Unbidden and unwelcome, thoughts of Mel returned. Mel with her fabulous fingers and her talented tongue. Mel who could make her come so powerfully and so easily with barely a touch.

She spread her legs and slipped her hand between them. She was warm and slick, just as she'd expected. She dragged her hand over herself and felt her clit swell. She slid her fingers inside and explored there briefly. She withdrew her fingers and played with her clit. It grew larger as she rubbed it. She allowed herself to fantasize that it was Mel touching her, coaxing the orgasm out of her. She finally came, screaming Mel's name.

Disgusted with herself, she climbed out of the tub and dried off. She poured another glass of wine and plopped down in front of the television. Something would take her mind off Mel. She just knew it.

❖

"She said that?" Joey said as she packed up her tools from the day's work.

"She did. She said 'commitment-esque.' Is that even a word?"

"Apparently, it is now."

"Yeah, well she thought leaving my beer there was too much like a commitment. How is that possible? If we're going to keep hooking up, even no strings attached, what's the harm in my beer being in her fridge for when I come over?"

"Look, Mel. Maybe she's seeing people other than you. And maybe it would be weird to have beer in her fridge when she doesn't drink it."

"What? How could she have time to see someone other than me?"

"Come on, Mel. She said no commitment. You're both free to see who you'd like."

"Oh yeah?" Mel said. "You think she'd be okay if I showed up at Kindred Spirits and left with someone besides her?"

"She'd have to be."

"I don't believe it, Joey. I think she's into me and is too scared to admit it."

"Well, your thoughts on the matter really don't count. It's what she's saying, and you need to respect her wishes."

"Shit." Mel sat on Joey's tailgate. "I've got it bad. What am I going to do?"

"That's a really good question. What are you going to do? Are you going to go by the bar tonight to see her?"

"I feel like she'd see me as a pathetic puppy if I did that. And I don't feel she deserves to see me after her attitude last night."

"You know, Mel, maybe you need to swallow your pride here. I mean, what's more important to you? Seeing her or teaching her a lesson of some sort?"

"I don't know. I want to see her," Mel said. "But it really pissed me off."

"Then maybe take a day away from her. Maybe don't go over there after work today."

"That sounds like a good idea," Mel said. "I'm going to head home and order a pizza."

Mel did just that. She opened a beer and ordered a pizza. Thoughts remained on Susan, no matter how she tried to turn them off. She watched television until she couldn't keep her eyes open any longer, then crawled into bed alone and lonesome.

She awoke the next morning bright and early. She had survived the night without Susan, she thought wryly. She quickly dressed and headed for the jobsite.

"Hey, you. You look the most rested I've seen you in weeks. You must have finally gotten some sleep last night," Joey said.

"I did. I went home, had a pizza, drank a few brews, and crashed. It was nice. And I woke up in my own bed. Overall, it wasn't a bad experience."

"Good. See? You don't need Susan."

"No, but I sure as hell want her. I'm going to go by the bar tonight."

"You are, huh?"

"Yeah. I figure why not? After having a night to think about it clearly, maybe I owe her an apology."

"What for?"

"For my outburst."

"Suit yourself," Joey said. "I would just go about it like nothing ever happened. But you do what you need to."

"So you're saying I shouldn't say I'm sorry?"

"I'm not getting involved in this one. You do what you feel is best."

"Shit. Maybe you're right. I don't know."

"Okay," Joey said. "You've got all day to work it out. Now, come on, let's get to it."

Mel spent her day completely focused on her work at hand. She never once let her mind drift to Susan. At the end of the day, she was feeling proud of herself.

"Good for you," Joey said. "I'm glad you were focused or we could have really fucked up this house."

"No doubt." Mel laughed.

"And now that the day's over? What are you thinking?"

"That I'm going to go home, take a shower, and swing by Kindred Spirits. I'm hoping to get there just as she gets off work."

"Sounds like a plan. Good luck. I'll see you tomorrow."

"See ya."

Mel stripped out of her filthy work clothes as soon as she hit the door to her house. She got in the shower and washed away the dust and grime of the day. As she showered, she thought back to her shower with Susan. That had been most enjoyable. She really wanted another shot at her.

She dressed in shorts and a T-shirt and headed to the bar. It was six thirty, almost time for Susan to get off. She walked into the bar and immediately caught sight of Susan making her rounds. She watched her short-shorts sway as she walked. She watched her muscular arm hold up a tray of drinks. And she heard her easy laughter even over the noise of the patrons.

Mel took her seat at a booth and waited. It wasn't long before Susan approached her from behind.

"Hi," Mel said.

It took a moment for recognition to register on Susan's face.

"I'm sorry. I'm on autopilot. I didn't even see you come in. Can I get you a half pitcher?"

"Please."

She made her way through the crowd, picking up empties as she did. She returned momentarily with Mel's beer.

"Thanks," Mel said. "Can I take you to dinner after work?"

"I don't know," Susan said.

"Nothing fancy. Just like The Shack or something."

"Sure. That'll be nice."

"Great. I'll enjoy my beer while I wait for you."

Susan was back in a half hour. She sat across from Mel with her lemon drop.

"I hope you don't mind. I needed a drink after my shift."

"No worries. I still have a little beer left. What was so bad about your day?"

"Nothing, really. It was just really busy. My feet hurt, and I need a moment before we head out to dinner."

"Did they at least tip you well?"

"They did."

"Right on. I know how you depend on that."

"I really do."

They finished their drinks and walked out to their cars.

"Do you want to ride with me or take separate cars?" Mel said.

"I think we should each take our own cars."

"Okay. I'll see you there."

Mel arrived before Susan, and she leaned against her car and waited. She saw Susan pull up and crossed the parking lot to meet her.

"You okay?" she said. "You look tired today."

"That's what every girl wants to hear." Susan smiled.

"Sorry. I didn't mean it in a bad way."

"It's okay. I haven't been sleeping well."

"I'm sorry to hear that." Mel bit her tongue. She'd love to offer to help Susan sleep better, but wanted to play it cool.

"It's okay. I'll be fine. Now, come on. I'm starving."

Mel opened the door for Susan and they were assaulted by loud music coming from the jukebox. A group of kids were dancing around it. She steered Susan as far away from them as she could in the little restaurant.

They took a table and looked at their menus.

"Hi, Mel!"

Mel looked up to see Tiffany standing there in her short-shorts and tube top that barely covered her perky breasts. She hadn't even realized she'd glanced over her whole body before responding.

"Hey, Tiffany. What are you doing here?"

"We just came over looking for fun. What are you doing?"

"Tiffany, this is Susan. Susan, this is Tiffany."

"Hi, Tiffany," Susan said stiffly.

"I used to babysit her when she was a kid," Mel said.

"Yeah?" Susan arched an eyebrow.

"But I'm not a kid anymore," Tiffany said.

"Clearly," Susan said.

"It was good to see you, Tiff," Mel said. "But we need to order dinner."

"Oh, yeah. Well, I'll be over there if you need anything." She winked at Mel.

"Isn't she a bit young for you?" Susan said.

"Yep."

"And yet you sleep with her?"

"Once in a while. Nothing serious. As a matter of fact, she showed up at my house a few nights ago. I hadn't seen her in a couple of years. She goes to school in Somerset."

"Well, she looks like she'd love nothing better than to take you home tonight. Should I excuse myself?"

Mel fought the urge to laugh. Susan was jealous. It was great.

"No. I'm here with you."

"Maybe the three of us could have some fun," Susan said.

"Or just you and I could."

"I just thought I'd throw that out there in case you were into those sorts of things."

"Are you?"

"Not really."

"Okay. Then the answer is no. We'll have dinner and then I'd like to take you home."

"I'd like that, too," Susan said. "Just the two of us."

"Exactly."

CHAPTER NINE

Mel followed Susan back to her place, her stomach aflutter with anticipation. Her palms itched. She felt like a kid on a first date. She cautioned herself to remain calm, to be cool, to be herself. Forget about the fight, she told herself. Tonight is a new night.

Susan parked in her driveway, and Mel parked in front of her house. She walked up to meet Susan at the front door. Susan fingered the buttons on Mel's shirt.

"I can't wait to get you inside," she said.

"The house or you?" Mel said.

"Ah. Good question. Both."

"Were you going to open the door for us?" Mel said.

"I suppose I should."

As soon as the door closed behind them, Susan was in her arms. She pressed herself into Mel's body and filled her arms. Mel's hormones soared. She moved her tongue into Susan's mouth and moved it all around. She pulled her against her as close as she could get her.

They broke apart, breathless. Susan took Mel's hand and led her down the hall to the bedroom. They frantically stripped out of their clothes and fell onto the bed, wrapped up in each other.

"Dear God, I want you," Mel said.

"Take me, then. I want you, too."

Mel ran her hand all over Susan's body. She covered every inch from her cheek to her ass and back again. She kissed her hard again. She was committing her taste and every inch of her to memory. She had another taste to memorize as well. But that was coming. She was determined to make her wait.

Susan was squirming underneath her. She held her head as she kissed her. She suddenly broke the kiss.

"So are you into that?"

Mel stopped short. She stared at Susan and blinked.

"Into what?"

"Threesomes and stuff. I mean I saw you leave the bar that first night with two women. Is that normal for you?"

Mel rolled over onto her back and folded her hands on her belly.

"I've had a few of them. It's not the norm, by any stretch."

"I'm not sure I believe you."

"Why did you ask me if you weren't going to believe my answer?" Mel said.

"I don't know. I think you would have taken that girl home tonight with us if I'd given the okay."

"If it was what you wanted, I would do it. For you. Not for me."

"I'm not so sure about that."

Mel rolled over and looked into Susan's eyes.

"Look, do you want this tonight or not?"

"I don't know, Mel."

Mel sat on the edge of the bed. She reached down for her clothes.

"Wait." Susan placed a hand on her arm. "Who you've been with before me shouldn't matter to me."

"And who I'm with now shouldn't matter, either, if there's no commitment." There. She'd said it.

Susan was silent for a moment.

"You're right. Of course," Susan said.

"Okay. I'm glad we got that out of the way."

"And it won't matter to you if I go home with someone else."

"You say that like it's a fact. You know it'll bug me. Because I really like you. But it can't matter. You're right."

Susan ran her hand up and down Mel's arm.

"Now, can we get back to what we were doing?"

"That's up to you," Mel said. "You're the one that called it off."

"Okay, well, I'm sorry. Come back to bed."

Mel climbed back on the bed and kissed Susan hard again. She kissed down to her breast, which she took in her mouth and sucked hard. She flicked her tongue over her hard nipple and felt it grow. She released her grip and kissed lower until she was between her legs. She placed Susan's knees over her shoulders and lowered her head. She licked inside her and tasted the flavor that was only Susan's. She dipped her tongue in as far as it would go before she moved it to her slick, swollen clit. She licked circles around it, which she knew made Susan crazy.

"Please. God, please. I need to come, Mel."

Mel smiled to herself as she lapped the tip of Susan's clit and felt her press her head into her. Susan screamed, a guttural scream, as she rode the orgasms Mel provided.

Susan relaxed back against the bed and fought to catch her breath.

"Damn," she said. "You're so fucking good."

Mel dropped her head again and enjoyed the taste of Susan's climaxes as she licked all over her.

"Oh, no. Not again," Susan said.

"Oh yes," Mel said then went back to work. It didn't take any time for Susan to come again and again.

"Okay. I give," Susan said. "I've got no more."

"You sure?"

"Positive." Susan took hold of Mel's arm and pulled her up next to her. She kissed her gently.

Mel lay back and pondered the soft kiss. She hoped to God she was going to get a turn. She was horny as hell after loving Susan.

"You ready for your turn?" Susan finally said.

"Oh, yeah. I need you so bad right now."

Susan teased Mel between her legs. She circled her clit and her opening.

"Please," Mel said.

"What?" Susan feigned innocence.

"You're killing me."

"Yeah? You need more?"

"God, yes."

Susan slid her fingers inside and stroked Mel's walls before she moved her fingers to Mel's clit and pressed harder. Mel pulled Susan to her and kissed her with all her need. She moaned into her mouth as the orgasm washed over her.

She lay back and basked in the euphoria, but only briefly. She knew she had to go. She hated leaving and longed to hold Susan while she slept. But rules were rules. She sat up.

"I need to get going."

"Yeah."

Mel dressed and started down the hall.

"I don't work tomorrow," Susan said.

"Okay. Then I won't stop by the bar."

She fought the urge to ask for Susan's number. Or to ask what she was doing so maybe they could get together. She simply left.

Susan fell into a sound sleep and awoke the next morning sleepy but satisfied. Mel had really done a number on her the night before. She had the whole day ahead of her and no plans. She was kind of bummed she wouldn't see Mel later, but figured it would be good for both of them, even though Mel seemed to be content with the casual thing. Which Susan knew she would be. She just had to get past the trying to impress her. And the no strings attached thing was certainly working for Susan. She was getting a lot of great sex without any emotional ties.

She got up and had her coffee, forced herself to do some chores, then sat on the back patio contemplating how best to spend the rest of her afternoon. It was one o'clock when she gave up the fight and put on her swimsuit and headed for the beach. She was addicted to it. She wouldn't deny it.

Susan found a parking spot by the play structure and crossed the sand to the water. She put her chair and feet in it and leaned her head back to soak up the rays. She set her phone alarm for an hour and a half so she wouldn't get fried again. It went off and woke her from a light sleep. She sat up and looked out toward the horizon. She was hoping to see a couple silhouettes out there, but she saw no one. She tried to deny the disappointment in her gut, but couldn't. She thought maybe it was too early for Mel and Joey, but that didn't matter. She wasn't going to stay any longer. She'd had enough sun for one day.

She crossed the sand back toward her car. As she passed the play structure, she heard happy squeals.

"Meow, push me again," a young child cried out.

"Okay, okay. Hold on tight."

Susan recognized the voice. It was Mel. She wondered if it was DJ she was playing with. She walked around the structure and saw her pushing a child in a swing. Thank God she'd had sense enough to put him in one of the little kid swings.

She stood quietly just out of sight and watched the interaction. Mel seemed to be having as much fun as DJ.

"Now the swide, Meow."

The little boy was adorable, as was Mel. She helped him climb the steps, then waited at the bottom for him to come down. By that point, Susan was in plain sight, but Mel was too absorbed in DJ.

"Again," DJ cried. Mel repeated the process. She was so cute. Susan felt a tug on her heartstrings. Maybe Mel wasn't a horrible person just looking for a good time. Maybe she'd been serious about wanting to settle down. But was that what Susan wanted? Suddenly, she was unsure. If she got together with Mel, maybe someday they could have a kid. Whoa. She was getting way too ahead of herself. She still had a heart to protect. A very fragile heart.

At that moment, Mel caught sight of her standing there.

"Hey," she called to Susan.

"Hey," Susan said. She walked over to Mel and DJ.

"DJ, you remember my friend, Susan, right?" Mel said.

"We're pwaying," DJ said.

"I know. I was watching. Is Mel fun to play with?"

DJ nodded emphatically. He took Mel's hand.

"Come on."

Mel looked apologetically at Susan.

"Sorry. Duty calls."

"That's okay. I don't mind watching you two. I think you're awfully cute."

"Aw. Thanks."

Susan wandered around to the other side of the structure where she found Joey sitting on a concrete wall, watching Mel and DJ. Susan unfolded her beach chair and sat next to her.

"They seem to be having fun," she said.

"Yeah. That's the downside of having Mel for a best friend. I have to wait my turn for time with my own kiddo."

"She really loves him, doesn't she?"

"She really does."

They sat in silence for a few moments.

"She really likes you, too," Joey said.

Susan sighed. If only life was so simple. Two people like each other and live happily ever after. She knew better.

"You know, I'm not a horrible person incapable of feelings," she said.

"I didn't say anything about you being a horrible person."

"I just don't want to get burned. You've got to admit, Mel's a bit of a party boi."

"I admit Mel's had a great run. But she's ready to settle down," Joey said.

"But I'm not."

"That's too bad. You're blowing a great chance with a good woman."

"You don't think I can see that?"

"I don't know," Joey said. "Can you?"

"Mel's sweet and kind and funny and great in bed"

"TMI."

"Sorry. But she's a catch and now I see that. I just don't know that I'm ready to open my heart and take a chance."

"Well, I'm here to tell you that while she's crazy about you, I don't know how much longer she's going to wait around."

"Nobody's telling her to wait around," Susan said. "She's free to do whatever she wants and still have sex with me. There's no commitment between us. I'd think she'd like that."

"She's tired of one-night stands. She wants more."

Susan watched Mel chase DJ around the structure. DJ was squealing in delight. Mel was laughing. Susan's heart started to melt.

"I see the way you look at her," Joey said.

"What? I find her attractive. I've never denied that."

"It's more than that. Whether you know it or not. Your face tells a different story."

"I think it's probably time for me to go."

"Aren't you going to say good-bye to Mel?"

"I probably should, huh?"

"It would be nice," Joey said.

Susan couldn't decide if she liked Joey or not. Sure, Mel was her priority over Susan, but did she have to be so snarky? Susan walked over to where Mel and DJ were digging in the sand box.

"I'm going to head home now," she said. "It was nice seeing you."

"You, too. Hey, can I come over a little later? I'll bring a couple of steaks to grill."

"Yeah. That would be nice. See you around six?"

"See you then."

Susan walked away smiling. Damn it! She could feel the wall slipping again. She needed to put it back in place. Firmly. So no one could get through it, least of all Mel. She reflected on her conversation with Joey. It felt good to know Mel really liked her. And if she was honest with herself, she really liked Mel. She just owed it to herself to keep her at arm's length. But what if Joey was right and Mel quit coming around? How would she feel then?

She got home and slipped into a tub filled with lavender and vanilla salts. The warm water and soothing scents had her fighting to keep her eyes open. She allowed her mind to drift back to Mel and DJ at the beach. They were so cute together. It was easy to see DJ worshiped her, and it sure appeared the feeling was mutual. She finished washing off, rinsed, and wrapped a thick towel around herself. She thought about greeting Mel wearing just the towel, but then decided against it. She dressed in a long blue denim skirt and a yellow peasant blouse.

It was five thirty. She had a half hour left alone with her thoughts. Not ideal. It seemed all she did these days was argue with herself over Mel. What happened to the idyllic life in Maybon Tir she'd imagined? She'd been nothing but frustrated since she moved and it was all because of Mel. It wasn't easy not to let her in. As a matter of fact, it was a constant battle.

The doorbell rang and startled her out of her reverie. She checked her watch. Not quite six, but close enough. She opened the door to find Mel with her arms full.

"Sorry if I'm too early," she said. "The store didn't take as long as I thought it would."

"No worries. Come on in. What the heck did you bring?"

"Well, along with the steaks, I thought we'd have garlic bread and a salad, so I brought all the fixings."

"Sounds delicious."

"And the best part is, you do nothing. I'll take care of all of it."

"There's nothing I can do?"

"You can open the wine and a beer for me, if you don't mind."

"I don't mind at all."

She took a glass of wine and a beer out to the patio to join Mel, who was firing up the grill.

"It's a beautiful evening for a barbecue, don't you think?" Mel said.

"It is. Thank you for doing this."

"No problem. Let's go inside and I'll throw together a salad."

Susan stood and sipped her wine as she watched Mel chop lettuce, carrots, and tomatoes. She was a natural, and Susan couldn't wait to taste the salad.

"Oops. We almost forgot the garlic bread," Mel said. "Do you mind if I leave you in charge of that while I throw the steaks on?"

"No problem." Susan was happy to help. She felt bad that Mel was doing all the work in her house.

She took the garlic bread out just as Mel walked in with the steaks.

"Medium rare, right?" Mel said.

"Exactly."

They sat at the table and Mel raised her beer.

"To beautiful nights."

Susan thought that seemed safe enough. She raised her glass and clinked it against Mel's bottle.

Dinner was delicious, and afterward, they took their drinks out to the patio to look at the stars.

"It's nice that the fog didn't roll in," Mel said.

"It really is. I like it when it stays warm into the night."

They sat quietly sipping their beverages until a chill came into the air.

"So much for a warm night," Susan said. "Let's go inside."

They went into the kitchen and Mel set her beer down. She took Susan's wine and set it next to it. She moved close to Susan and stood inches away from her, looking into her eyes.

Susan found it hard to breathe with Mel that close. She felt the electricity between them. It was undeniable. Mel lowered her mouth, and Susan closed her eyes and braced herself for the contact. Her knees were already weak and they hadn't even kissed yet. When Mel's lips brushed hers, Susan reached her arms around Mel's neck and pulled her close, urging her to prolong the kiss.

They kissed for what seemed an eternity, but was actually only a few minutes. It was a long, slow, easy kiss that had Susan craving more. She stepped back and took Mel's hand. She led her down the hall to the bedroom.

"I need you and I need you now," she said.

"I'm all yours," Mel said.

Susan balked briefly at the comment, then went back to peeling Mel's clothes off her. Soon Mel stood nude in front of her.

"My God, you're gorgeous," Susan said.

"Your turn," Mel said. She took Susan's blouse over her head, then reached around and unsnapped her bra with one hand. She ran her hands over Susan's breasts. "You're so beautiful."

Susan stepped out of her skirt and underwear. She loved the feeling of being naked with Mel. She moved closer and pressed her body into Mel's. She relished the feel of their skin together. She kissed Mel and Mel held her against her and ran her tongue over Susan's lips until Susan opened her mouth and let her in.

Mel fell back on the bed and pulled Susan on top of her. They continued kissing as Mel skimmed her hands all over Susan's body.

"I love the feel of your touch," Susan said.

"I love touching you."

"That works then."

"Yeah, it does."

Mel kissed down Susan's neck and chest until she reached Susan's breast. Susan shivered as she felt Mel's warm breath on it. She took Mel's head in her hands and lowered it to her nipple. Mel sucked hard on it and ran her tongue over it.

Susan arched into her.

"Yes. That's it. Oh, yes."

Mel moved her hand down between Susan's legs. Susan spread them wide to offer her easy access. Mel plunged her fingers inside Susan.

"Yes. God, that feels good," Susan said. She slid her own hand down there and rubbed her clit while Mel moved in and out of her. Together they took her to a screaming orgasm.

"Thanks for the help," Mel said.

"Sorry. I couldn't wait."

"It's all good. I thought it was hot."

"Yeah? Good. Now you lean back and get comfy. I'm going to make you feel so good."

"My pleasure," Mel said as she lay back and spread her legs.

Susan climbed between them and licked every inch of her. She dipped her tongue inside, then dragged it to her clit. She sucked it into her mouth and flicked it with her tongue. Mel pressed Susan's face into her, and Susan knew Mel was close. She licked harder and Mel cried out before relaxing back against the bed.

They lay there in silence for a few minutes before Mel sat up.

"I should get going."

Susan reached out a hand and rubbed Mel's back.

"Why don't you stay?"

CHAPTER TEN

Mel was shocked. Her heart fluttered in her chest. Could it be possible? Was Susan admitting that she was ready to get serious?

"Are you sure?" she said.

"Sure," Susan said. She propped herself up on an elbow. "Maybe I've been wrong about you."

"About me?"

"Yeah. Maybe you aren't just out looking for one thing."

"I told you I wasn't," Mel said.

"I know. But I didn't believe you."

"What about you? What about your need to keep your heart protected?"

"Maybe if I keep it too protected I'll miss a good chance for happiness."

"Maybe, huh?" Mel climbed back on the bed. She leaned over Susan and kissed her. She covered her with her body and brought her knee up between her legs. She pressed it in to her. Susan moved against it and Mel felt how wet she still was.

"God, that feels good," Susan said.

"You're so wet."

"It's what you do to me."

"Good." She kissed her again and wedged her hand between her knee and Susan. She guided her fingers inside her and spread them as wide as she could.

"Oh, God," Susan said. She dug her nails into Mel's back and cried out as she came. "I didn't know I had any left in me."

"I knew I could coax at least one more. Now let's get some sleep."

Mel held Susan as they drifted off.

Morning came, and Mel woke to find Susan still asleep in her arms. She hadn't been dreaming. Susan had let her sleep over. She looked so peaceful there. Mel couldn't decide whether or not to wake her up for playtime. Then she saw the clock.

"Oh, shit," she said. "I'm late."

Susan opened her eyes.

"Huh?"

"Sorry, babe. I just realized I've got to get going. I'll stop by the bar tonight?"

"Sounds great."

Mel kissed her good-bye and left. She pulled up on the jobsite to find Joey strapping on her tool belt.

"I was just wondering if you were going to make it," she said.

"Yeah. I overslept."

"And you're in the same clothes you wore yesterday."

Mel felt a slight blush creep over her face.

"Did you have a sleepover?" Joey said.

"I did."

"No shit? The ice princess melted?"

"She's starting to."

"That's awesome," Joey said. "Good for you."

"Yeah. I'm still not convinced, but letting me stay over was a huge start."

"Now that she's letting you in, don't you dare go backing off," Joey said.

"Oh, I'm not. Don't worry. I just need a little more proof that she's willing to be mine."

"Like what?"

"I don't know. But I'll know when it happens."

"Man, I hope you don't fuck this up."

"I won't."

Work went well, but Mel was tired and excited for the day to come to an end. She couldn't wait to see Susan. She and Joey sat on Joey's tailgate at the end of the day.

"So, I don't suppose you want to come over for dinner tonight?" Joey said.

"No, thanks. I'm gonna go home, shower, then hit the bar. You want to go with?"

"No. I'm going to go home, shower, and get dinner prepped." Joey laughed. "Times have changed, huh?"

"Yeah. I just hope I've finally found what you and Samantha have."

"I hope so, too. You deserve it."

"Okay, I'm out of here."

"Hey. Before you go, you two want to come over for dinner this weekend?"

"Sure. She doesn't work Saturday. I mean, I'll ask her, but I don't see why not."

"Great. And yeah, I need to run it past Samantha, too."

"Sounds good. I'll catch you tomorrow." Mel said, then drove home for a nice, hot shower. Her mind never left Susan. Thoughts of her were welcome now and pleasantly occupied all her time. She was thrilled that Susan had opened herself up to her. She still urged herself to go slow, to not scare Susan off. But she didn't want to seem so aloof as to appear disinterested.

It was six o'clock when Mel walked into Kindred Spirits. The place was dead, and Susan was behind the bar with a book in her hand.

"Whatcha reading?" Mel asked.

Susan looked up and smiled at her. It was a bright, radiant smile unlike any she'd given Mel to date.

"I'm reading a book that has recipes for cocktails in it. Thrilling stuff, huh?"

"Well, if it's teaching you, then it's worth it."

"Can I get you a half pitcher?"

"Yes, please."

Susan brought Mel's beer to her. Mel gave her a twenty. When Susan brought the change back, Mel was unsure of what to do.

"I feel like I should tip you, but I kind of feel weird about it."

"I agree. It would be odd. Don't worry about it. Just take me to dinner tonight."

"You've got a deal."

"I've been jonesin' for some crepes. And I love that restaurant. How does that sound to you?"

"Sounds great. I love that restaurant, too. So, has it been this slow all day?"

"I'm afraid so," Susan said. "I've been practicing cocktails as people come in. I think I'm doing okay. I just wish there were more people to practice on."

"I'm sorry. Hey, Joey invited us over to their place Saturday for dinner. How does that sound to you?"

Susan's eyes grew wide, and Mel wondered if she'd blown it.

"Too soon? Too much?" She said. "Talk to me."

"No. Sorry. None of the above. It will be great. I need to meet this wonder woman Samantha, anyway."

"Wonder woman?"

"Whoever could tame Joey would have to be a wonder woman." Mel laughed.

"Yeah, she is a really great woman. I think you'll like her."

"Okay. Then let's plan on it," Susan said.

"Are you absolutely sure? There's no pressure."

"I'm sure."

Susan reached her hands across the bar and grabbed Mel's.

"I'm way sure," she said.

At exactly seven, Susan took off her apron and grabbed her purse.

"Let's get out of here," she said. "I'm starving."

"Okay. I'll meet you at the restaurant."

"Well, meet me at my car first," Susan said.

Mel followed her out the back door to her car.

"Since it's not dark, I didn't think you needed walking to your car. Sorry if that was a mistake."

"No," Susan said. "I feel perfectly safe here. I just wanted you out her for this."

She pulled Mel to her and kissed her hard on the mouth. Mel felt her crotch clench.

"That was nice," Mel said.

"I needed it."

"So did I."

"Okay," Susan said. "I'll meet you there."

Mel kissed her again, then walked over to her own car and fired up the engine.

They arrived at the restaurant at the same time and parked next to each other. The lot was practically empty.

"What's going on with this town?" Mel said. "It's like a ghost town today."

"Maybe people are on summer vacation."

"I suppose that could be true. Well, at least we'll get a good seat."

Mel was surprised when Susan took her hand. She glanced over at her and Susan simply smiled at her. They walked into the restaurant and the hostess raised her eyebrows.

"Oh my, I declare. Mel O'Brien has a girl?"

"O'Brien, huh?" Susan whispered.

They were seated at a table in the middle of the restaurant, right by a large white fountain.

"Yep, O'Brien," Mel said. "What of it?"

"It fits you," Susan said. "It's as cute as you are."

"Why, thank you," Mel said. "And you? What's your last name?"

"Maloney."

"Ah. Another good Irish gal. No wonder I like you so much."

"We are quite a pair, aren't we?"

"I like us," Mel said.

"So do I."

They looked over their menus, and Mel was grateful for the break in conversation. She didn't want to say too much, to scare Susan away when she was just starting to open up to her.

Susan perused the menu as her heart raced. She'd gone from being in a relationship to being single and then back to being in a relationship in the time it took most people to change their clothes. Or at least that's how it felt. Whatever happened to staying single? She couldn't fight it. When it's right, it's right, and with Mel it felt more than right. And she'd almost admitted that to her. It was way too soon for that as far as Susan was concerned.

She found a crepe she wanted and set the menu down. Her hand shook as she picked up her glass of water.

"You okay?" Mel said.

"Yeah. I'm fine. Why?"

"You seem to be shaking pretty bad. You sure you're all right?"

"Positive. I'm just hungry. Low blood sugar, you know." She lied. She was nervous about where the conversation almost went. She took a deep breath, and when the waitress came by, ordered a lemon drop. She figured that would calm her nerves.

They discussed their days while they ate dinner. Then talk turned to DJ.

"He's so cute," Susan said. "I know I've probably said that a million times, but he really is cute."

"Well, wait until you meet his mama. She's really pretty, too, like I've said."

"And you should see yourself when you play with him. You're absolutely adorable."

"I'll admit I feel like a two-year-old as well when I play with him. He's so much fun."

"And Joey really trusts you with him, doesn't she?" Susan said.

"She does. She knows I love that little guy like he was my own."

"That's wonderful, Mel."

Dinner was through, and they walked out to their cars hand-in-hand.

"So, what now?" Mel grinned.

"Aren't you tired?" Susan teased her. "Long day and all that?"

"I'll sleep when I'm dead."

Susan laughed.

"Okay, in that case, I suppose you can follow me back to my place."

"Thanks." Mel leaned in and kissed Susan lightly on the lips. "I'll see you there."

Susan kept glancing at her rearview mirror as she drove home. She knew Mel knew how to get there, but she still liked seeing her behind her. It made her smile to know Mel wanted to come over all the time. She wondered when she'd get to see Mel's place, but figured it didn't matter. She enjoyed sleeping in her own bed, so for now the arrangement worked beautifully for her.

She walked up to the front door and unlocked it, then stood waiting for Mel to come up the drive. When she got out of her car, Susan's heart skipped a beat. The first thing Mel did was brush her bangs out of her eyes, only to have them fall back in. Susan smiled. Mel really was adorable. She didn't make that up. Then there was her easy swagger when she walked. Like she was the most relaxed person on earth. She was easy to watch. That was for sure.

"You waiting on me?" Mel asked when she finally reached Susan.

"I was just admiring the view."

"Oh yeah?"

"Yeah."

"Well, let's get inside so I can get a full view to admire, as well," Mel said.

Susan entered and held the door for Mel. She closed it behind her and leaned against it. Mel placed a hand on either side of her head and leaned in to kiss her. The kiss was soft and tender at first, but grew more passionate as it went on. Soon, Mel's body was pressed flat against Susan's. Susan liked the feel of it. She snaked her arms around Mel's neck and held her close.

"Shouldn't we get out of these clothes?" Mel said.

"Not yet. First, let's have a drink and sit on the couch together."

"Are you sure?"

"Mel," Susan said. "If we're going to be an item, we're going to have to do something once in a while besides just make love."

"That's fair. That's cool. Let me just check my libido."

"No worries about that. We'll end up in bed tonight, Mel. I just want to chat with you or maybe make out with you on the couch first."

"Right on. I get what you're saying."

"And," Susan said, "I have beer and wine for us."

She grabbed a beer out of the fridge for Mel and poured herself a glass of wine. She brought them both over to the couch where Mel looked quite at home.

"So what do you want to talk about?" Mel asked.

"I don't know. Your hopes and dreams, maybe? Surely you didn't spend your whole life hoping to work construction."

"Well, when I was in college, I thought I'd be a marketing genius."

"Yeah? What happened?"

"Joey and I opted to move to Maybon Tir instead. There wasn't really a need for a marketing genius at the time. And we met Brenda, our forewoman, and she was looking for help, so we hired on with her. The rest, as they say, is history."

"Okay. But what about when you were a little girl? What did you want to be then?"

"Oh, that's easy. I wanted to be an astronaut."

"That's so sweet," Susan said. "I bet you were an adorable little girl."

"Whatever. My folks made me wear dresses until I was in junior high. Then they gave up."

Susan laughed.

"I bet that drove you crazy."

"It totally did. I hated dresses."

"I loved them," Susan said.

"I bet you did. And I bet you looked damned good in them."

"I still do."

"I know. I've seen you in one."

"Oh, yeah. I suppose you have, haven't you?"

"Yes, ma'am. So I know you wore dresses and were cute as a bug's ear. But what else? What did you want to be when you grew up?"

"I wanted to be a teacher."

"That's noble," Mel said. "So, what happened?"

"I was waitressing to put myself through college. College got too expensive, and I was making enough money waitressing that I didn't think I needed to go on and become a teacher. I was having fun and making money. It was a win-win."

"So you were going to school in SoCal? Were you from there as well?"

"I'm originally from San Diego."

"Nice," Mel said.

"Yeah. That's why Maybon Tir was just a perfect choice for me. It's much smaller, of course, but it's right on the beach. And it's a women's community. Again, win-win."

"Yeah. Maybon Tir is a little slice of heaven."

"That it is."

Susan put her empty glass on the coffee table.

"You ready for bed?" she said.

"I am."

"Okay, then, let's go."

Once in the bedroom, Susan turned and wrapped her arms around Mel.

"I enjoyed just talking with you tonight."

"Me, too," Mel said. She ducked her head and nibbled Susan's neck.

"It's important that we get to know each other."

"Mm hm."

Susan finally gave up talking and allowed herself to simply feel. Mel was sending white-hot chills throughout her body with her kisses and bites. She quit long enough to strip Susan out of her clothes before she went back to it.

"Hey," Susan said. "We need to get you naked, too."

"Not yet. Holy fuck. I need you so fuckin' bad, Susan. Let me take you first."

"Not until you're naked."

"Shit," Mel said. She pulled away from Susan and quickly undressed. When she was naked, she stood and took Susan in her arms.

"I love the feel of our bare skin against each other," Susan said.

"No shit. Let's lie down. I have to have you now."

They lay on the bed and Mel climbed on top of Susan. She kissed her hard on her mouth before moving down her body. She stopped to take a full breast in her hand. She kneaded and played with it and watched as her nipple grew. She took the nipple in her mouth and sucked as hard as she could. Susan tangled her hands in her hair. She loved the sensations Mel created within her. She felt her very core tighten as Mel continued to play with her nipple.

Mel released her finally and kissed down her body to where her legs met. She climbed between them and ran her tongue all over her. Susan could barely breathe, her need was so great.

"Get me off, Mel. Please. I need to come."

Mel continued what she was doing, and Susan felt the tightness inside her burst loose, and waves of electricity shot through her veins to every inch of her. She lay breathless as Mel kissed back up her body and held her close.

"Damn, I love making love to you," Mel said.

"You sure are good at it," Susan said. She was a little unsure about the term "making love." Were they that serious? She wasn't sure, but didn't want to ruin the mood, so said nothing about it.

"It's my turn to please you now," Susan said. She kissed Mel and tasted her own orgasm on her lips. She ran her hand down between Mel's legs. She found her wet and ready. "Holy shit, you're ready for me."

"Always, baby. I want you all the time. If I had my way, we'd never get out of bed."

"Wouldn't that be fun?"

Susan slid her fingers inside Mel and stroked her. Mel met each thrust as Susan moved her fingers in and out. She continued fucking her, picking up speed as she went, and Mel finally cried out.

"You're a lot of fun to mess around with," Susan said.

"I thought it was more than messing around."

"Well, it is. But in bed we mess around, you know?"

"Yeah. I guess so."

"Now, you'd better get to sleep. You have to get up in a few hours."

Susan lay awake after Mel fell asleep wondering if she'd handled the terminology of their sex as diplomatically as she'd wanted to.

CHAPTER ELEVEN

"Do you want to hit the waves?" Joey asked Mel as they put away their equipment Friday afternoon.

"I was actually thinking beer and pool sounded good. You up for that?"

"Sure. I can handle that."

They loaded their cars and drove to Kindred Spirits. Mel was excited, as usual, about seeing Susan. Even though they saw each other every day, it was always new and fun. She was nervous as a schoolgirl going into the bar filthy dirty after work. But she was thirsty, and Joey only had so much time before she'd have to go home. Mel would shower later. Maybe she'd even be able to convince Susan to join her.

They walked in the bar, which was slightly crowded, and found a booth by the pool tables. Susan was there immediately.

"A pitcher?"

"Please," Joey said.

"How's your day been?" Mel asked.

"Crazy. I'll be right back."

"Man, this is going to be a drag," Mel said.

"What is?" Joey asked.

"Being here and not being able to talk to her."

"Hey, loverboi, I thought we were here to shoot pool. Sure, you can talk to her as well, but maybe this way you'll be able to keep your head on the game."

"Yeah, you're right. Let's play."

Susan brought the pitcher over and set it on the table.

"Keep a tab open?" she said.

"Yes, please," Mel said.

"Will do." And she was off again.

Mel and Joey started a pool game. Soon, people were putting quarters on the table to challenge the winner. After a while, they were asking to play doubles. Joey and Mel kept control of the table. They drank pitcher after pitcher of beer and always stopped the game to try to talk to Susan, who never had time for more than a "hey."

Time passed quickly, and eventually Susan was sitting at their booth with them, sipping a lemon drop. Mel took a quick break from shooting to go over and kiss Susan.

"I'm glad you can finally relax," she said.

"Me, too. You two plan on playing for a while?"

"I suppose so. Why?"

"Because I'd love a few more of these."

"Then enjoy them and watch us clean the floor with these poor suckers."

The night went on with drinking, pool games, and much merriment. When Mel checked her watch again, it was already eleven thirty.

"Whoa. You'd better get goin', Joey. You're gonna be late."

"No shit! I'm out of here. I'll see you both tomorrow?"

They nodded. She kissed Susan's cheek and left the bar.

"You ready to take this home?" Mel said.

"Yeah, but I'd better get a ride with you."

"Really? Okay. I have my van, though, and it's thrashed."

"I don't mind," Susan said. "I just don't feel safe driving."

"Okay. Well, let's go then."

They left the bar hand-in-hand and Mel felt such a sense of pride that Susan was hers and hers alone. They climbed into the van.

"You weren't kidding," Susan said. "This thing is a mess."

"It's my work van. I use it for working and surfing and that's it. I'm not used to escorting lovely ladies in it."

"Yeah. That's what the Z28's for."

"Exactly."

"So, speaking of dives. When do I get to see your place?"

"Now, wait a minute," Mel laughed. "Who says my place is a dive?"

"I'm just hazarding a guess."

"Well, easy does it, sunshine. I live in a nice place and keep it fairly clean."

"Fairly clean by whose standards?" Susan said.

"Anybody's."

"Okay. So, when do I get to see it?"

"Whenever you want. Except tonight. Because we're already here and it's late and I want you."

"Fair enough. So, tomorrow then?"

"Sure thing. Now let's get inside."

They walked into the house, and Mel pulled Susan into her arms.

"You turn me on so much," she said. "I need you now."

"You sure know how to woo a lady," Susan said.

Mel laughed.

"What can I say? At least I'm honest."

"Yes, you are."

Mel stepped back and looked down at herself.

"Oh, crap. I forgot. I'm filthy from the jobsite. Let me take a shower and I'll meet you in bed. Unless, of course, you want to join me?"

Susan smiled, a slow, seductive smile.

"Now that sounds like just what the doctor ordered."

Mel took her hand and led her to the bathroom. They stripped out of their clothes and climbed into the shower. Mel stood letting the warm water run over her. Then she traded places with Susan so the water could play over her curves. Next, she pressed Susan into the wall and kissed her hard. She pulled away only to lather her hands and run them over Susan's body. Every inch, every curve, was covered in a soapy lather. She slipped her hand between Susan's legs and dipped them inside. Susan was so ready for her, and the soap helped keep things slippery down there. Susan moved against her until she grabbed hold of Mel's shoulders and cried out as she collapsed against her.

Mel stepped out of the way and let Susan rinse off and get out of the shower. Mel finished her shower, dried off, and padded down the hall to the bedroom. She found Susan fast asleep. She smiled to herself. Susan was a beautiful woman. She carefully slid under the covers, pulled Susan close, and fell asleep.

They awoke the next morning with nothing particular to do until six, when they were going to Joey and Samantha's. Mel rolled over and cuddled with Susan.

"No hurry getting out of bed is there?" She ran her hands up and down Susan's body.

"Not that I can think of."

"Excellent." Mel kissed the back of Susan's neck and brought a hand up to cup her breast. She teased her nipple. "I can think of at least one good reason to stay in bed."

Susan rolled over onto her back and looked at Mel with a sparkle in her eye.

"Yeah? And what might that be?"

"Someone was asleep when I got to bed last night."

"Yeah. I'm sorry about that."

"That's quite all right. It had been a long day. But I have plans for us now that we're both wide awake."

"I like the sound of that," Susan said.

Mel slid her hand between Susan's legs. She gasped.

"Dear God, I love how you're always ready for me," she said.

"Always," Susan said.

Mel teased Susan's clit and felt it grow at her touch. She finally brushed over it with her fingers, and Susan screamed as she came.

"Now I get to make up for last night," Susan said.

She climbed between Mel's legs. She licked at Mel's clit as she slipped her fingers inside. She moved her tongue in rhythm with her fingers, and soon Mel was bouncing on the bed, meeting each of Susan's thrusts. In no time, she was pressing Susan's face to her and crying out as one orgasm after another rolled over her.

They lay together in bed, basking in the afterglow when Mel sat up.

"I'm starving. You want to go get some breakfast?"

"What time is it?" Susan said.

They looked at the clock. Eleven o'clock.

"Wow. Time flies," Mel said.

"Yeah, it does."

"I tell you what. Why don't you put on your suit and we can drive over to my place and get my trunks? Then we can have lunch at The Shack and then head over to the beach?"

"That would be great. What a wonderful way to spend the day."

"I'd have to agree."

"Will you be bringing your surfboard?" Susan said.

"I doubt it. Why?"

"I thought it might be fun to have you teach me how to surf."

Mel laughed.

"Are you serious?"

"Yes."

"Great then. I'll bring my board. Now, come on, sweetness, get your suit on."

Mel put her clothes on while Susan got dressed. When it was time to leave, they climbed back in the van.

"Are you sure your house doesn't look like this van?" Susan said.

"I'm positive. Just wait and see."

Susan was excited to see where Mel lived. She believed you could tell a lot about a person by the way they kept their home. She expected Mel to be slightly messy, but not overly so. She was shocked when she walked in to a tidy house.

"Do you have a maid?" Susan said.

"Funny. No, I don't. It's not that hard to keep the house up. I'm the only one living here, so as long as I pick up after myself, things don't get too bad. And I clean it about once a week or so, you know, vacuum, dust, and stuff. Like I said. It's not that hard."

"Well, color me impressed. I thought your house would be a little more thrashed than it is."

"Okay, well, now that you've seen it, you can relax on the couch without fear of a rodent joining you." She laughed. "Can I get you something to drink?"

"No, thanks. I'm fine. You just go change so we can hit the beach."

She made herself comfortable and waited for Mel. She fought the urge to walk down the hall and help Mel change into her suit. The thought of her naked and that close got Susan wet. But if they were going to have any time at the beach, they needed to get going.

Mel finally emerged, and Susan took in the sight of her in board shorts and tank top with a sports bra underneath. All her finely toned muscles were on display, and Susan's palms itched to touch her.

She got off the couch and crossed the room to where Mel stood.

"You ready?" Mel said.

"I suppose." Susan ran her hands up and down Mel's muscular arms.

"Either we get going or we get busy," Mel said. "It's your choice."

"Okay, okay. Let's get going."

Mel grabbed her board and they were off. It was only a few blocks to the beach. Susan enjoyed how easy things were with Mel. They chatted amicably as they drove. There was sexual tension there, to be sure, but outside of that, it was just nice to be with her.

They parked at The Shack and crossed over to the water. It was a beautiful day with highs in the mid eighties. Susan felt it was the perfect day to learn to surf.

"Have you ever body surfed before?" Mel asked.

"I've tried."

"Okay. Um, boogie boarded?"

"No."

"Okay. So we've got our work cut out for us. We're going to start with you surfing on your stomach."

"Fair enough."

"First thing is let's get out to where the waves break. It's going to be a little deep. When it starts getting deep, you can get on the board and I'll hold on to you."

"Sounds good. Should I be nervous? Because I'm not."

"No, you shouldn't be. This should be fun."

"Great. Let's do it."

They walked out until the water was waist deep. Then Mel helped Susan up onto the board. She lay flat on her stomach and Mel held the back of her board and swam with her. Mel finally declared they were where they needed to be. She bounced in the waves while she turned Susan toward the shore and instructed her.

"You wait. I'll tell you when to start paddling."

"Okay."

"And when I tell you to, it's just like swimming, okay? You move your arms the same way."

"Got it. Is it time yet?"

"Yes," Mel said. "Paddle, paddle, paddle."

Susan paddled. She paddled fast and furiously. She paddled like her life depended on it. She rose up on top of the wave and then it was gone.

Mel grabbed the board and pulled it back out.

"That's okay," she said. "You can't expect to catch your first wave."

"That seems like an awful lot of work," Susan said.

"Oh, but it's so worth it when you catch one."

"Okay, then. Let's try this again."

Mel kept her gaze on the sea, and Susan took the opportunity to allow herself to really take her in. She was a sight for sore eyes, to be sure. She had high cheekbones, a square jaw, and those eyes. Susan melted every time they looked at her.

"Okay, get ready."

"Ready." Susan was shaken from her reverie.

"And paddle!"

Susan paddled as fast and hard as she could, and suddenly, she felt like she was flying. She stopped paddling and just held on. It was such a freeing feeling. It was simply amazing.

The board slowed as it got to the shallow water by the shore. Susan picked it up and walked out as far as she could. She tried to climb on it, but found herself lacking the coordination. Mel swam over to her and helped her. They made their way back out.

"So, what did you think?" Mel asked while they awaited the next wave.

"It was awesome! I want to do it again and again."

They spent the next couple of hours surfing. Susan was a natural, or so Mel said. Either way, Susan had a wonderful time.

"I'm starving," Mel said. "You want to grab a bite?"

"What time are we supposed to be at Joey's?"

"We have a few hours. We're not supposed to be there until six. What do you say we split an order of fries at The Shack? Just something to tide us over."

"Sounds good to me," Susan said.

They crossed to the parking lot, and Mel stowed her surfboard. Then she took Susan's hand and led her inside The Shack. Susan ignored the curious glances. Clearly, it had been a while since Mel had brought a date there. Whatever. It didn't bother Susan. She was proud to be Mel's. Mel was a good woman. And a better lover.

They ate their fries, then Mel dropped Susan off at her place to get ready while she headed home with the promise to be back in half an hour.

Susan stared at her closet and tried to decide what outfit to wear. She was determined to make a good impression on this Samantha woman. She didn't know why, but she felt the need for her approval. This was uncommon for Susan, but it was how she felt, so there you go.

She chose a denim skirt with a blue blouse. She checked herself out in the mirror. Perfect. Not overly dressed, but she looked nice. She paced in the front room while she waited for Mel. She couldn't believe how nervous she was.

Susan opened the door the minute she heard Mel's knock.

"Wow," Mel said. Were you standing right by the door?"

"Pretty much. Oh, Mel. I'm so nervous. I never should have agreed to this."

The shock on Mel's face made Susan feel awful.

"What? Why? You've met Joey. It's hard to find anyone more laid-back than she is. And, trust me, Samantha is a sweetheart."

"What if she doesn't like me?"

"Who? Samantha? Please. What's not to like?"

She pulled Susan to her and stroked her hair.

"Baby, you just relax, okay? It's going to be fine."

"I hope so."

"It will be. Now, we'll need to stop by the liquor store to get some vino and brewskis. We should get going."

They made their stop and bought both red and white wine, as well as a twelve-pack of beer, and were standing on Joey's doorstep at precisely six o'clock.

Samantha opened the door in a mid-calf length yellow sundress. Susan immediately knew she'd made the right choice in attire.

"Hey, Samantha." Mel hugged her and kissed her cheek. She stood back and offered her hand to Susan. "This is Susan."

Samantha gathered Susan to her in a warm hug.

"Susan. What a pleasure to meet you. I've heard so much about you."

"It's so nice to meet you, too," Susan said. She felt mesmerized by the sheer sweetness of Samantha. She was a warm, kind person.

"Joey's in the playroom with DJ," Samantha said. "Why don't you two go in there while I check on dinner?"

"Would you like some help?" Susan said.

"Oh, no thanks, hon. You go in with them. I'll only be a minute, I promise."

Susan took Mel's hand, and they walked into the next room, which was a child's paradise. They found Joey sitting on the floor rolling a ball back and forth with DJ. DJ was clearly enjoying himself. And then he saw Mel.

"Meow!" he cried. He hurried over to give Mel a hug. Mel bent and picked him up.

"How you doing, tiger?" Mel said.

"Good."

"Right on. You remember Susan, don't you?"

DJ buried his face in Mel's shoulder.

"Oh, my. Someone's shy tonight," Joey said. She stood up and offered her hand to Susan. "Susan. It's great to see you."

Just then Samantha walked into the room.

"What's goin' on?" She reached out and ran a hand along DJ's arm. "What's with you?"

DJ grabbed tighter to Mel.

"I think someone's got a crush," Joey said.

"Can you blame him?" Mel said. She managed to disentangle herself from his little arms and took his hand. "Do you want to play?"

He dropped her hand and went to Joey, who picked him up.

"I think he just needs to relax for a few. Are you hungry, champ?"

He shook his head.

"Okay, well, the grown-ups are going to chat now, so you keep yourself busy. I'm going to put you down now."

She set him on the ground, and he went behind a giant castle in one corner of the room.

"That's a great castle," Susan said. "Where did you get that?"

"Mama," DJ said.

Susan looked from Joey to Samantha.

"I'm Mommy and she's Mama," Samantha said. "And Joey built the castle for him. He loves it."

"I guess. What kid wouldn't?"

She looked over and caught a slight blush on Joey's cheeks. Oh my, she thought. Mel and Joey together in their single days must have broken a lot of hearts.

"Can I get everyone a drink?" Joey said.

"I'd love a glass of the Chardonnay," Susan said.

"I'll take a brewski," Mel said.

"I already have a glass of Pinot," said Samantha. "Would you mind bringing it in?"

"No problem." Joey kissed Samantha's cheek as she walked past her.

The atmosphere was very relaxed, and Susan wondered what she'd ever worried about. Dinner was delicious. The company was wonderful, and Susan saw a side of Mel she'd never really seen. Mel treated Joey and Samantha like family. It was very much like a family gathering, and Susan thoroughly enjoyed herself. She was sad when the evening came to an end.

"I do hope you'll come over again," Samantha said as they were leaving.

"I'd love that."

"Great. Don't be a stranger." She kissed Susan on the cheek, and Susan and Mel walked out to the car.

"That was so much fun," Susan said.

"Yeah? You really had a good time?"

"I had a blast. They're great people, Mel. They're amazing people. You're lucky to have them in your life."

"Tell me about it," Mel said. She drove them back to Susan's house. They got out of the car and went inside.

"I'm really full and kind of tired," Susan said.

"No worries," Mel said. "So am I."

"Hold me tonight?"

"Gladly."

CHAPTER TWELVE

Sunday was slow at the bar. Susan was bullshitting with Joanne. She studied the bible, too, but had a pretty decent grip on drinks by then. Her phone rang. She ignored it, as was the rule when working. It rang again. And again.

"Someone's really trying to get ahold of you," Joanne said. "You think it's Mel?"

Susan shook her head.

"Believe it or not, we've yet to exchange phone numbers."

"Well, next time it rings, why don't you answer it? No harm, no foul. I won't tell anyone."

The phone rang again. Worried it might be important, Susan slid the phone out of her pocket. She checked the face of it. *Dorinda.* She slipped it back in her pocket.

"No one important," she said.

Dorinda didn't give up, but Susan didn't want to talk to her. She thought maybe she'd answer the phone if Mel was with her. Maybe.

Mel showed up at five o'clock and the place was still dead. She sat at the bar where she and Susan could talk.

"How was your day?" Susan said.

"It was nice. Joey and I took DJ to the park. Then Samantha came and got him so Joey and I could surf for a while. All in all, it was a win day. How was yours?"

"Dead. But interesting."

"Interesting? How so?"

"Dorinda's been calling me all day."

"*The* Dorinda?" She saw Mel's eyes turn cold.

Susan nodded.

"What the fuck did she want?"

"I don't know. I haven't answered. I thought I'd wait until I was with you. You know, for moral support."

"That's fine. Or I'll answer it and tell her never to call you again."

"I wonder if I should let you do that. I mean, what could she possibly want from me?"

"You're going to have to answer it to find out."

Just then, Susan's phone went off again.

"I'm not going to answer it until I'm off work," she said.

"Fair enough. Can I get another half pitcher? I've got a feeling I'm going to need it."

Seven o'clock rolled around, and Susan made herself a lemon drop and joined Mel on the other side of the bar. As soon as she was seated, her phone rang again.

"Are you going to answer it?" Mel said.

"Yes." She squeezed Mel's hand for good luck and answered the phone. "Hello?"

"Susan? Is this you? It's Dorinda. I've been trying to call you all day."

"I was at work. Can't take calls at work. You know how that goes. What's do you want?" She kept her voice cool, disconnected.

"You moved to Maybon Tir, didn't you?"

"Yes."

"Okay, do you remember my aunt Lucinda? She's the one you helped so much when she had breast cancer a few years ago."

"Of course I remember her."

"Well, she's moved to Maybon Tir, too."

"That's great. You'll have to give me her number. I'd love to see her."

"That's just it. I was hoping you'd want to do more than just see her."

"How so?" Susan said.

"Susan, you're the closest thing to family she has," Dorinda said.

"What is this all about?"

"Susan, she has cancer of the bladder. She's on hospice. She's not expected to live six months."

"Oh, shit," Susan said. She leaned into Mel for support. She and Lucinda had gotten so very close while she helped care for her. She couldn't imagine the poor woman suffering again.

"Will you help us out?" Dorinda said. "Will you help take care of her?"

"Of course I will," Susan said.

"Great. I'll be in town tomorrow. So will her brothers and sister. We'll organize a schedule then."

"I work one to seven," Susan said.

"Fine. We'll meet right after seven then."

"Okay. Where?"

Dorinda gave her the address, which she wrote on a bar napkin, and Susan said good-bye. She turned to Mel with tears in her eyes.

"What's going on?" Mel asked.

"It's Lucinda," Susan said. "She's Dorinda's aunt, but is also a dear friend of mine. She's living here with bladder cancer. Dorinda wants to know if I'll help provide care for her."

"And you said yes?"

"Of course. How could I not?"

Mel didn't say anything.

"Look, I'm doing this for Lucinda, not Dorinda, okay?"

"If you're sure about that."

"I am."

"I really don't want you having any contact with Dorinda, babe. I don't think it's healthy," Mel said.

"I'm sure I won't. Everyone is getting together tomorrow after seven to set up a schedule of who does what for Lucinda when."

"Can I go with you?"

"Is it that important?" Susan said.

"Yes."

"Then you can go."

"Thanks. Now. Want another drink?" Mel said.

"I think I'm ready to head home. You coming with?"

"You know it. Do you want to stop for dinner along the way?"

"I'm not really hungry," Susan said.

"Oh yeah, I guess not. Sorry. I'll just order a pizza when we get there."

Mel sat eating pizza and drinking beer while Susan sat quietly on the couch next to her. She was so sad about Lucinda. She was kind, loving, funny. She deserved a long life. Susan knew she couldn't be more than fifty-five. It just wasn't fair to lose her so soon.

"Hey, babe," Mel said. "I'm really sorry to hear about your friend. That's gotta be harsh."

"Thanks. It is."

"And I'm sorry I freaked at the bar. I just don't want Dorinda hurting you again."

"She won't. I won't let her. Besides, I have you now."

"Yes, you do. Don't ever forget that," Mel said.

"I won't."

Susan leaned into Mel. Mel wrapped her arm around her and held her close.

"I just wish I knew her better so I'd know if I could trust her," Mel said.

"I'm the one you have to trust," Susan said. "And I should hope by now you know you can."

"I do know that, baby. That's not what I meant. I trust you implicitly. But I don't trust her not to hurt you. And now that you're not together anymore, will she quit picking on you? Or will it continue?"

"I don't really expect to have much contact with her," Susan said. "I figure I'll see her tomorrow and that'll be it. She'll go back to LA, and I'll be here to help with Lucinda."

"I hope that's how it goes down," Mel said.

"It will."

❖

Mel was fuming inside. She didn't want to let Susan near Dorinda. She was proud of her for wanting to take care of Lucinda, but why did she have to be in the same room as Dorinda? At least for the meeting, Mel would be there to keep her safe, but what about after that? What if Dorinda didn't just poof and go back to LA? Mel didn't like Susan setting herself up for the verbal and mental abuse she knew Dorinda could dish out.

"Hey, babe? Why don't you go take a bath?" Mel said. "I'm sure it'll make you feel better."

"Will you come scrub my back?"

"You know it."

Mel opened another beer and sat on the couch while she waited for Susan to call her. Mel couldn't get her mind off this Dorinda chick. She'd never seen her before and didn't know if she was ready to see her now. But she had to. She didn't trust that woman alone with Susan.

"Hey, baby?" Susan called from the bathtub.

"Coming." She walked in and saw Susan in a bath full of bubbles, with only the tips of her breasts showing.

"You look divine," Mel said.

"Thanks."

She ran her hand over Susan's nipples.

"Mm," she said.

"I thought you were going to scrub my back," Susan said.

"How about I scrub your front and your back for no extra charge?"

"I like the sound of that."

"Are you sure?" Mel asked. "I mean, if you're not in the mood after today, I totally understand."

"Thank you," Susan said. "But I think reaffirming that I'm alive and in a happy relationship is just what I need tonight."

"And I'm just the one to help you with that."

"I thought you might be."

Mel kissed Susan. It was a soft, loving kiss that said enough without too much. Susan reached up and stroked Mel's cheek.

"You're so wonderful," she said.

"Thanks, babe. I think you're pretty wonderful, too."

Mel was true to her word. She scrubbed Susan's back before lathering her hands to wash her front. She teased her nipples, then her breasts, lightly washing their fleshy undersides. Then she moved her hand lower, over her soft belly until she found where her legs met. She slipped her fingers inside her, and Susan leaned back to allow her greater entrance. Mel stroked her hard and deep and felt Susan close around her fingers as she came for her.

"Oh, my. That was nice," Susan said.

"Why don't you rinse off and meet me in bed?" Mel said.

"That sounds wonderful to me."

Mel stripped out of her clothes and climbed into bed. She waited as patiently as she could for Susan to join her.

Susan finally came into the room, looking fresh and clean and smelling delicious.

"I almost feel bad getting you dirty again," Mel said.

"Oh, please don't. I'm actually looking forward to it."

"That's good to hear. So, come on in. The water's fine." Mel flipped back the covers on the bed.

Susan slid in next to Mel.

"You smell so good," Mel said.

"Thanks. That's why we girls use all those froofy things in the bath."

Mel nuzzled her neck.

"Well, I'm sure glad you do."

She kissed around to Susan's mouth and planted one on her lips. It was deep, passionate, and soulful. It made Mel's toes curl in its intensity. She pressed herself into Susan, needing more contact. She wanted to feel at one with her. And she did.

Susan broke the kiss and lay there panting.

"That was some kiss," she said.

"Yeah, it was."

"I almost came just from kissing you."

"Then why did we stop?" Mel said.

"It was too much. Too overpowering, really."

"I thought it was wonderful."

"It was. I was just scared, I guess. I've never climaxed from a kiss before, and I was so close. It scared me a little."

"Fair enough."

Mel kissed her softly then. Their lips barely met.

"And see?" Susan said. "Those kisses make me crazy as well."

"Maybe it's just us," Mel said. "Maybe it's just that we kiss so great together."

"That's got to be it."

Mel kissed her again and this time drew her hand along the length of Susan's body. She felt her shiver and grinned.

"What?" Susan said.

"I just love how you respond to me."

"A woman would have to be dead not to respond to you."

Mel laughed but continued to move her hand. She ran it over Susan's mons and she spread her legs for her. Mel slid her fingers between her legs and teased her clit. She made slow, gentle circles around it while Susan begged for more. She finally pressed directly onto it, and Susan cried out her name.

"Damn, Mel," Susan said. "I can't get over what you do to me."

"I like doing things to you."

"Lucky me."

Mel kissed Susan again before kissing down her body. She stopped to lick a nipple and admire it as it grew hard. She sucked it briefly then kissed down her belly until she came to where her legs met. She climbed between them and made herself comfortable. She licked from one end of Susan to the other. She loved her flavor. The taste of her made her dizzy. She plunged her tongue inside Susan and ran it around as deep as it could go. Susan arched off the bed and gyrated in time with her.

Mel was becoming more aroused with each passing second. She wanted to make Susan come and then she wanted to come herself. She could feel a big one building inside her, and she looked forward to riding the crescendo.

She moved her tongue to Susan's clit and licked at it fervently. She felt Susan's hand on the back of her head. She could barely breathe from being pushed into Susan, but still she persevered. Moments later, Susan screamed again as she reached another climax.

Mel kissed up Susan's body until she was lying beside her. They were both breathing heavily.

"Oh, my God," Susan said. "Just wow."

"Yeah? I'm glad you enjoyed that."

"Oh yeah, I did. I don't know if I'll ever catch my breath."

"I hope so," Mel said.

"I know. Your turn is next. And don't worry. I'll give you what you deserve."

When she was breathing normally, Susan got out of bed.

"Hey. Where are you going?" Mel said.

"You just be patient. I'm going to make you feel things you've never felt before. Now close your eyes."

Mel kept her gaze on Susan.

"I mean it. Close your eyes. Don't you trust me?"

Mel reasoned this was as good an exercise in trust as any, so she closed her eyes. She kept them closed until she felt Susan's weight back on the bed.

"Can I open them now?"

"Sure," Susan said.

Mel did and was surprised to see Susan holding a toy in her hand.

"Is that for me?" Mel said.

"It is. If you don't mind, I mean. I'd love to use it on you."

"I don't care what you do at this point, babe. I'm about to explode."

Susan turned the toy on. Mel watched the length of it twist and turn.

"How does that work, exactly?" Mel said.

"That part moves inside you while the dolphin vibrates against your clit. It's amazing, trust me."

"I do. Let's get started."

Mel spread her legs and Susan pressed the tip of the toy against her opening.

"Please. I can't wait," Mel said.

Susan eased it inside her and Mel moaned.

"Holy shit, that feels good. I feel it moving in there."

Susan drew it back out.

"What? Why?"

"Relax, lover. I'm not through."

She pushed the toy back in, all the way until the dolphin was buzzing against Mel's clit.

"Yes, baby. Holy fuck, yes. That's what I'm talking about. Oh, shit!"

Mel cried out and rode wave after wave of orgasm.

"Holy, shit," she said after she had floated back to Earth. "That was amazing."

"Good, baby. I always want you to feel good."

"Yeah? Well, you outdid yourself that time."

"Right on. Now, we should get some sleep. You've got to be at work early tomorrow."

"Right. And you have a big day tomorrow."

"I don't want to think about it."

"I'll be right there with you," Mel said.

"I do appreciate that."

"Of course," Mel said. She stopped just before she said the three words she wanted to say but was sure Susan wasn't ready to hear.

CHAPTER THIRTEEN

Susan readied herself for work and tried to ignore the boulder that was in her gut. The last person she wanted to see was Dorinda. She'd found such happiness with Mel. Granted, it was still new, but she was happy. Mel was an honest to goodness good person. Dorinda was anything but.

She got through a very slow workday by checking her watch every fifteen minutes. Finally, it was four thirty and Mel and Joey came in.

"I brought reinforcements." Mel smiled.

"Is she going with us?"

"No," Mel said. "She's just here for moral support until we leave."

"Well, I appreciate it. I can use all the support I can get."

"How are you doin'?" Mel said.

"Not good. I mean, I'm hanging in there, of course. But I'm a nervous wreck."

Mel reached across the bar and took both her hands in hers.

"It'll be okay, babe. She's just going to set up a schedule of who helps when, right? Then she goes back to LA and is out of our lives again."

"I hope that's how it goes down," Susan said.

"And I'll be right there with you."

"Oh, Mel. What would I do without you?"

"That's not something you need to worry about."

Joey and Mel drank beer until it was time for Susan's shift to end. She came around to their side of the bar.

"Thank you so much for being here," she said to Joey. "I really do appreciate the support."

"No problem. I'm out of here. Good luck."

She left and Mel took Susan's hand.

"You ready to do this?"

"I guess so."

"We'll need to take your car since I bummed a ride with Joey."

"No problem."

Mel took Susan in her arms and stroked her hair.

"It's going to be fine," she said. "Honest. We'll get through this."

"I know. Come on. We should get going."

They arrived at the address on Susan's napkin.

"I know this place," Mel said. "I knew the previous owners."

"Well, it's Lucinda's place now."

They got out of the car. Mel took Susan's hand.

"You ready?"

"I am."

They walked up to the door and knocked. Dorinda opened the door and stood there, her long, dark hair pulled back in a ponytail. Her brown eyes red-rimmed and puffy. She hugged Susan to her.

"Susan. I'm so glad you agreed to do this."

"You look horrible, Dorinda," Susan said. "Is she okay?"

"As okay as she can be. She's in a lot of pain. We just got her to sleep. I hate to see her in that kind of pain."

"I'm sure. Oh, Dorinda, this is my girlfriend, Mel. Mel, this is Dorinda."

Mel extended a hand to Dorinda, who instead hugged her.

"It's so nice to meet you," Dorinda said.

Mel stepped back.

"I've heard a lot about you," Mel said.

"Oh, don't believe everything you've heard. I'm not a total monster."

Susan cleared her throat. She believed Dorinda to be nothing short of a monster.

"Shouldn't we get down to business?" she said.

"Sure," Dorinda said. "The family is gathered in the living room. Follow me."

They followed Dorinda down a short hallway to a large, open room decorated in sixties style furnishings. Lucinda was born too late to be a true hippy, but she was certainly one at heart. Susan smiled. She had missed Lucinda, but had written her off when she left Dorinda.

At the far end of the room, by the sliding glass doors that led to the backyard, was a hospital bed. The small emaciated body in it couldn't be Lucinda, could it? Susan fought tears forming in the back of her eyes. She squeezed Mel's hand hard, and Mel wrapped her arm around her and pulled her close.

"Are you okay?" she whispered.

"I don't know."

"Okay," Dorinda said. "Now that we're all here, let's get started. Susan, Mel? You want to take a seat, please?"

They sat on the only open sofa left. Mel held Susan's hand, offering comfort Susan was glad to take.

"As most of you know," Dorinda said. "Lucinda is on hospice. She will have nurses and home health aides coming here to do a lot of the work with her. They'll manage her medicines and keep her clean. Things like that. What I'm looking for is for us to just be here for anything else she needs. Just so she's not alone. She's given us all so much love and happiness throughout our lives. It's only fair that we be here at the end for her."

"Now, the only one here who lives in town is Susan, and she'll help as much as she can, but it's really only fair that the family pull the bulk of the weight. As you know, I've taken a leave of absence to be here with her."

Susan felt cold in the pit of her stomach. She didn't want Dorinda to be here. She wanted her to go back to LA. She didn't want to see her on a regular basis. She felt Mel squeeze her hand again. She tried not to show her amazement and disappointment.

"So I'll be here twenty-four, seven, but I'll need some breaks. This is where you all come in. Also, I just think it's important for her to have family around her as the disease progresses. With all this in mind, here is the schedule I've come up with. What do you all think?"

She unveiled a white board that had names, days, and times written on it. The family was mostly etched in on the weekends. Susan was listed for Monday, Wednesday, and Friday afternoons.

"I can't do any of those days except Wednesday," Susan said. "I work Monday and Friday afternoons."

"Okay. That's good to know. What time?"

"One to seven."

"Let's see then. Can you come here from seven to eleven? Maybe feed her dinner and hang out with her?"

"Sure. I can do that."

"Okay." She changed the white board to indicate Susan's schedule.

"Does anybody else have any questions or concerns?"

No one said anything.

"Meeting adjourned then." Dorinda laughed. The sound seemed sacrilegious in the room where Lucinda lay dying. Susan stood. Lucinda's brothers and sister came over to talk to Susan.

"Thank you so much for helping out," her sister said.

"My pleasure. I love Lucinda."

"You were such a big help when she had breast cancer."

"I was just happy I could be there. And I'm happy I can be here now."

"Thank you so much," one of Lucinda's brothers said.

"I am just so happy she lives in Maybon Tir so I'm able to help," Susan said.

She visited for a few more minutes before Mel whispered in her ear.

"You about ready to go?"

She nodded. They left the house, and the tears that had been threatening fell freely.

Mel held Susan as she cried. They stood on the front lawn, but Susan didn't seem to care who saw, and Mel was only aware of Susan. Nobody else was around as far as she was concerned.

"Are you going to be able to do this?" Mel asked when Susan's sobs had finally mellowed.

"Yes. I have to."

"But you don't. She's not your blood."

"She may as well be. I love her so, Mel. I just have to hold it together. It's going to be painful to see her that way. But they need me, so I'll do this."

"If you say so. But I honestly don't think anyone would think less of you if you bailed."

"That would leave Dorinda with total care during the week. That's not fair to her."

"Again. Who are you doing this for?"

"Lucinda. I swear."

"Okay."

"That doesn't mean I can't feel bad for Dorinda providing full-time care for her."

"No. It doesn't mean that. I guess."

"Please," Susan said. "Let's not fight about this."

"Look, I've heard about her and didn't like her. Now I've met her and don't like her. I'm sorry I'm not more sympathetic to her plight."

"Think more about me and my needs, please. I love Lucinda. This is the last I'll get to spend time with her. I'm grateful that I will be with her in her time of need."

"I suppose I need to remember that. I'm glad you'll get time with her, too. I just know it's going to be rough for you, and I hate to see you going through that," Mel said.

"But you'll be right here for me, right?"

"To the best of my ability. I'll even come over with you if you want."

"We'll see about that. I might just want some time alone with Lucinda, if that's okay."

"That's fine, babe. Whatever you need. You hungry?"

"A little."

"The Shack?"

"Sure," Susan said.

They started their dinner in silence, Mel worried about Susan and Susan apparently lost in her own thoughts.

"Do you want me to stay the night?" Mel said.

"Yes, please."

"Okay. Just checking."

"I need you now more than ever, Mel."

"I'm here for you, babe," Mel said. "I'm not going anywhere."

"So, what did you think of Dorinda?" Susan said.

"I didn't like her." Mel was honest. "I got really bad vibes from her."

"Really? And she was on her best behavior."

"You can't hide evil," Mel said.

"Well, I suppose I have prejudiced you toward her."

"I suppose you have, but still, I felt like she was fake and I hate fake people."

"To her credit, she really does love Lucinda," Susan said.

"Is she capable of loving anyone but herself?"

"Good point."

"And what did you think of her taking a leave of absence to be here?"

"Oh, my God. I did not like the sound of that. I wasn't expecting it and almost withdrew my services when she said that. But again, this is for Lucinda, not Dorinda."

"Yeah. I just hope Dorinda knows that."

"I'm sure she does," Susan said.

"I'm glad you are."

"What? You think this is some twisted scheme to get me back? Mel, Lucinda is dying. No one's faking that."

"Oh, I know. I just think Dorinda may have plans for you. Just be on guard."

"I'm not interested," Susan said. "I have you."

"Yes, you do. Now, let's get out of here."

Mel paid their tab and drove home to Susan's house. She took her hand as they walked to the door.

"You know, I mean what I'm saying. I support what you're doing. I just don't trust Dorinda. But I'll be here every night when you get home, waiting to hold you or love on you or whatever you want."

"I'll be getting home late, babe. It'll be after eleven."

"I don't work Saturday. So Friday shouldn't be a problem. Monday night, you may have to wake me when you get home."

"Or maybe Mondays we can just stay at your place. We'll see."

"Yeah. We've got options."

They were in the house and Susan poured herself a glass of wine and brought Mel a beer. Susan sat next to Mel, who wrapped her arm around her.

"How you doin'?" Mel said.

"I'm okay." Susan snuggled deeper against her. "This isn't going to be easy."

"No. No, it's not."

"I couldn't even walk over to look at her tonight, Mel."

"That's okay. She was asleep."

"But I have to be able to face her."

"You will, baby."

"She just looked so tiny on that bed," Susan said.

"I'm sure she did. She's sick. Very sick. I'm sure she's wasted away, baby. You need to brace yourself for that. I wish I could at least go with you tomorrow, but I'll be working."

"It's okay, lover. This is something I have to do. And I do need to do it alone."

"Okay, babe. You about ready for bed?"

"I am."

"Is it just going to be a sleeping kind of night?"

"Hell no. I need you to make me feel alive again. I need to remember I'm not the one in that bed. And I need to know I'm yours. Safely and securely yours. No worries about Dorinda. I want you to own me tonight, Mel."

"Gladly."

Mel placed Susan's glass and her empty beer bottle on the table and kissed Susan hard on the lips. She climbed on top of her there on the couch and ran her hand over her full breasts, heaving under the tight white shirt she wore. She closed a hand over one breast as she continued to kiss her. She ground her pelvis into her.

"Oh, God, Mel," Susan moaned. "Take me to bed. Please."

Mel climbed off her and offered her a hand. They went down the hall, stripping off clothes as they walked. They were both naked when they fell onto the bed together, and Mel lay back and pulled Susan on top of her. The feel of her hot skin against her own fanned the fire that already threatened to burn out of control.

"Holy Jesus, you feel good," Mel said. She ran her hands up and down Susan's sides, before guiding her toward her so she could take a breast in her hands and suck on the nipple. She sucked it deep into her mouth and ran her tongue all over it. She finally released it and was getting ready to flip Susan over onto her back when Susan kissed her mouth, chest, breast, and stomach. She pried Mel's legs open and climbed between them.

She licked at Mel with a need that matched Mel's. Mel pressed her face into her and ground her hips, finally finding much needed release.

"Your turn now," Mel said.

She kissed Susan and tasted her own orgasm on her lips. She slid her hand down her body to where her legs met. She found her clit slick and hard. She dragged her hand over it briefly before slipping her fingers inside. She moved her fingers in and out while Susan arched her hips to greet each thrust.

Mel moved her thumb to Susan's clit and rubbed it while she fucked her and Susan cried out. It was a guttural cry that let Mel know she'd done her job and done it well.

She took Susan in her arms.

"That was wonderful," Susan said. "Thank you."

"Mm. My pleasure."

"Thank you, Mel. For everything."

"It's the least I can do," Mel said. "I really do like you, Susan."

"I really like you, too, Mel."

And that was enough for Mel. For then.

CHAPTER FOURTEEN

Susan woke the next morning when Mel did. She said good-bye to her and tried to go back to sleep, but her mind was restless. She would be taking care of Lucinda in a few hours. She needed to be rested. She wondered what all it entailed. She envisioned mostly visiting with Lucinda, which would be easy and she would assume, natural, since they'd done that so many times before. But things were different now. When she'd had breast cancer, there'd been no guarantee she'd pull through it, but now there was a guarantee she wouldn't.

She checked her clock. Seven o'clock. Five hours until she had to be there. What was she going to do with her time? She decided to take a drive down to the beach and just relax there for a while. She'd let herself commune with nature, which would hopefully calm her nerves. She sat there, just beyond where the waves ended their journey to the shore and contemplated her life.

She had moved to Maybon Tir to escape drama, specifically in the form of Dorinda, but drama in general. She'd promised herself to remain single and free. It hadn't taken her long to meet and fall for Mel. Which wasn't really a bad thing, she admitted. Mel was good people. And really seemed to care for her.

But now, up shows Dorinda, out of the blue, needing her help. And she couldn't say no. She loved Lucinda and was truly happy to spend the last of her days with her. Sure, she was scared. She'd never dealt with death before. But she would put on her brave face and deal with it. But she did wish Maybon Tir could be her safe place once again.

She packed up her chair and towel and walked back to her car. She took a deep breath of the cool morning air before driving home to shower and get ready. She took a long, hot shower and tried to resurrect the sensations Mel had created the night before, but it was no use. She was preoccupied. She was unsure of what lay ahead of her and that was very disconcerting to her.

Susan showed up at Lucinda's house at exactly twelve o'clock. She knocked on the door and Dorinda answered it, looking much more chipper than she had the day before. She wore a halter top and short-shorts. There was very little left to the imagination, but it didn't attract Susan. She'd seen it all before and knew the person wasn't worth the goodies those clothes hid.

"Hi," Dorinda said.

"Hi. How's Lucinda?"

"She's great. We just finished lunch. Come on in."

Susan braced herself for what she was about to see. She followed Dorinda across the room to where Lucinda lay on the hospital bed. She had shrunk so much. The bed looked way too big for the tiny figure lying there.

"Lucinda!" Susan said and bent over to hug her.

"Oh, my dear, sweet Susan. I had no idea you lived here or I would have contacted you long ago."

"I haven't been here that long."

"Oh. Okay. Well, let me look at you."

Susan stood up straight.

"You look wonderful. Looks like you may have put on a pound or two. Which you desperately needed."

Susan smiled. She knew Lucinda was right. She'd been too skinny at the end of her relationship with Dorinda. It was stress and fear.

"Thanks," she said.

"How long are you here today?" Lucinda asked.

"I'm here till five."

"Oh, wonderful. We'll have such a nice visit. As long as I can stay awake, anyway. Dying seems to take a lot out of me."

Susan didn't have any idea how to respond. She looked to Dorinda for help.

"It's the pain and all the meds that knock her out."

Susan nodded.

"Speaking of her meds, she's had her morphine for now, but if her pain gets out of control, you can give her a bolus."

"A what?"

"Sorry. A bolus. Here."

She walked Susan over to where an array of pill bottles stood on a table.

"This is an extra pill she can have every fifteen minutes if her pain is bad. She won't be due for her regular dosage until four, and I plan to be home by then. These go under her tongue."

"Got it," Susan said, though she was decidedly uncomfortable about giving medication.

"Look at it this way," Dorinda said. "She's still on pills. When it gets worse, they'll put an IV pump in her. So she's still holding her own. That doesn't mean she doesn't hurt, but at least the pain is mostly controlled with her pills."

"So, where are you going?" Susan said.

"Out to get groceries. There are some here. You can make a sando or something if you're hungry."

"I'm fine."

"And she should be, too. I guess you two will just get to hang out while I'm gone. Thanks for being here, Susan."

"No problem. I'd do anything for Lucinda."

Susan wanted to make it clear she wasn't there for Dorinda. She hoped she got the point across.

"Okay, well, I'll be back," Dorinda said. She hugged Susan tightly. "It's so good to see you again."

She was out the door before Susan could say anything.

"Looks like someone might still be sweet on you," Lucinda said from her bed. Susan had briefly forgotten she was being watched.

"I can't imagine that," she said. "Our breakup was anything but pretty."

"Still, you can't fight what's in your heart," Lucinda said.

"Well, there will be no reconciliation, if you must know. I'm seeing someone new."

"You are? Now there's something that'll brighten my mood. Tell me all about her."

Susan sat in the chair next to the bed.

"What do you want to know?" she said.

"Everything. Child, you're like blood to me. If there's a woman out there who can make you happy, I want to hear every detail."

"Okay, her name is Mel O'Brien. She's gorgeous. She works construction. She's just great."

"Okay. Well, that gives me the skeleton. You're going to have to flesh it out for me. Where did you meet?"

"At the bar I work at."

"Oh. You got a job at a bar? That's fantastic."

"Yeah, only, being the newbie, I get all the afternoon shifts which are pretty slow. So tips aren't really what they should be. Of course I'm hoping that'll change when football season starts. I expect Sundays to be jumpin' then."

"Oh good, honey. I hope that's the case. So this Mel of yours, what does she look like?"

"She's got short blond hair that she can't keep out of her eyes. Her eyes are green, and her smile lights up the room."

"Sounds like someone's got it bad," Lucinda said.

"You could say that. But it's new, so we still need to wait and see if it's there for the long haul."

"Well, I hope for your sake it is."

"Me, too. Thanks, Lucinda. I sure have missed you."

"I've missed you, too. We sure were close back then. You were so young and so full of Dorinda. I was scared for you. It wasn't right to be that into one person. You practically worshipped her. And she let you. That was what was wrong."

"Yeah. It's nothing like that with Mel. We just hang out together and enjoy each other's company. She asks me what I want to do and stuff, doesn't just tell me what to do or how to feel. She's a real special person."

"That's great to hear, Susan. Really great. Hey, hon? I'm starting to hurt. Could you give me a pill, please?"

Susan looked at her and saw her eyes clouding in pain.

"Sure. Just a second." She walked over to the table. Which bottle was it again? Shit. She looked at all of them, confused.

"Susan? Could you hurry, please? Oh, shit. It hurts."

She found one that said prn for pain. She thought that sounded right. She put one in her hand and took it to the bed.

"Is this the right one?" She held up the pill for Lucinda. Lucinda seemed to struggle to open her eyes against the pain.

"Yes."

She opened her mouth and Susan placed it under her tongue. She leaned back, stiff with pain. Susan watched as she slowly relaxed as the pill worked its magic.

When Dorinda got home, Lucinda was asleep.

"Do you need help with the groceries?" Susan said.

"No, I'm fine. You can just relax."

"Well, I was wondering, since she's sleeping and all, could I just leave a half hour early?"

"Sure. No problem. Get out and enjoy the sunshine. Let me tell you, Susan. I totally get why you chose to move here. It's beautiful. And it's all women."

"Yeah. It's a special place, all right."

"I'm thinking of retiring to here."

Susan felt a knot in the pit of her stomach. She forced a laugh.

"Isn't it a little soon to be thinking about retirement?"

"It's never too soon. Maybe I'll win the lottery and not have to work another thirty years before I retire. Wouldn't that be great if I could move here soon?"

"You'd probably really like it here," Susan said. "Now, I'm going to take off. I'll see you Friday night."

Mel was sitting at the bar drinking her beer when she saw Susan walk in. Her face was tight and the color had drained from it. She crossed the room and pulled Susan into her arms.

"Baby? Are you okay?"

"Oh, my God. I hate Dorinda. I just hate her."

"What happened?"

"She's all talking about retiring and moving here or winning the lottery and moving here. I don't know, Mel. I don't want her here. I don't want her anywhere near me."

Mel led her to the bar and signaled for a lemon drop.

"You know, babe. You don't have to do this."

"I know. But my time with Lucinda when Dorinda wasn't there was great. We had a really nice visit. As a matter of fact, were your ears burning?"

Mel laughed.

"No. Why? Should they have been?"

"Yep. I told her all about you."

"Well, that took two minutes. Then what?"

"We just visited. It was so wonderful. I've missed her so, Mel."

"Good. I'm glad you got some good time with her today. Not all days are going to be good, you know," Mel said.

"I know. So, I'm grateful for the ones that are."

They sipped their drinks.

"So Dorinda wasn't there most of the time, huh?" Mel said.

"No. She went to the store. She must have run other errands, too, because she was gone four hours. I'm not complaining, though. It was nice without her."

"What are you going to do about the evenings when she's there with you?"

"Deal with it, I guess."

"You sure you don't want me going with you?"

"I'm sure."

"Okay."

Mel ordered another half pitcher for herself and a lemon drop for Susan.

"By the way, Joey invited us over for dinner tonight," Mel said. "I told her I didn't know how you'd be feeling."

"That sounds wonderful. What time?"

"I'll text her."

Plans were made for Mel and Susan to be at Joey's at six. Susan seemed nice and relaxed when they left the bar.

"One car or two?" Mel said.

"Better take both. Neither of us wants to leave our car here, do we?"

"Not if we don't have to."

They arrived at Joey's house at precisely six o'clock.

Samantha opened the door and greeted Susan with a hug and a peck on the cheek.

"So good to see you again. Come in. Come in."

Mel followed Susan in and was also given a hug.

"I do like to see you with the same woman more than once," Samantha said.

Susan stared at Mel, who just blushed.

"It's nice to have a woman who'll stay with me," Mel said.

Samantha turned to Susan.

"I understand you have a sick friend. I'm so sorry to hear that."

"Thank you," Susan said. "She's actually on hospice. She has less than six months to live."

"That's got to be so hard for you."

"It is. But I'm glad to be able to spend some time with her before she goes, you know? I'd hate to get a phone call telling me she was gone and me not having the chance to say good-bye."

"I get that," Samantha said. "That makes perfect sense."

"Why don't we try to take her mind off it for now?" Joey entered the room carrying DJ.

"Excellent plan," Samantha said. "You guys go get settled in the play room and I'll bring the drinks."

Mel held Susan's hand.

"You doin' okay?" she said.

"Yeah. Mostly."

"Good. You let me know if you need to leave, okay?"

"Okay. Thanks, Mel."

They visited with Joey and Samantha, and Susan soon seemed much more relaxed. Dinner was served and the conversation was light and easy.

"So, how are you liking Maybon Tir?" Samantha said.

"I like it a lot. It's beautiful and everyone is so friendly. And, of course, there's Mel. I really think I've found a slice of Paradise to live in."

"That's wonderful. We want more women to move here. We want to be as self-sustained as we possibly can. We need to be a little bigger to afford certain things. But we want special women here. Like you."

"And Lucinda. You'd all really like her if you could have met her."

"I'm sure we would have," Samantha said.

"I'd invite you to meet her now, but I think it would be too much for her."

"Oh, I'm sure it would. She's so lucky to have you, though."

"Thanks. I think I'm the lucky one. I just wish I didn't have to interact with my ex."

"Oh yeah, how'd that go today?" Joey said.

"It was horrible. She's talking about retiring here. Or winning the lottery and moving here. I don't want her anywhere near me."

"I'm sure you don't."

"So I take it it was a bad breakup?" Samantha said.

"The worst," Susan said. "She was emotionally and mentally abusive. Sometimes even physically."

"I'm sorry."

"Thanks. And just when I thought she was out of my life for good and I'd moved on, poof, she's back."

"Now how does she fit into all this?" Samantha said.

"Lucinda is her aunt," Mel said.

"Oh. I see. I'm so sorry, Susan."

"Thanks."

Dinner ended and Joey and Mel put DJ to bed. Then they met their girls on the patio.

"What a beautiful night," Samantha said.

"It was a wonderful night," Susan said.

"I was referring to the clear sky and cool temperature," Samantha said. "But you're right. It was a lot of fun having you two over again. I can't tell you how happy I am to see Mel with someone who's really right for her."

Mel cleared her throat before she and Joey stepped up and took their seats.

"I don't care if you heard that, Mel O'Brien. It's the truth," Samantha said.

"Thanks," Mel said. She felt awkward and uncomfortable being the subject of the ladies' conversation. She sat down and finished her beer. She contemplated another one, but checked her watch. It was after ten.

"We should probably get going, babe."

"Okay," Susan said.

They rose and hugged Samantha and thanked her for a great time. Susan hugged Joey, but Mel just said good-bye with a promise to see her in the morning.

"Follow me to my place?" Mel said.

"Oh, really? We're staying there tonight?"

"Why not? I mean, if it's okay with you."

"It's fine with me. I'll see you there."

CHAPTER FIFTEEN

Mel was torn. She wanted Susan in the worst way. And after Susan had broken out a toy the other night, she wanted to show off some of her own. But Susan might be tired. She was probably emotionally exhausted after the day she'd had. Mel told herself to take it easy and not be disappointed if Susan wasn't in the mood.

She waited for Susan to get out of her car, then walked with her to the front door. When they were inside, she pulled Susan to her for a hug. She stroked her soft black hair and wondered if she should kiss her.

Susan stepped out of the embrace.

"Are you tired?" Mel said.

"Not really." Susan took her hand and led her to the couch. "I'm actually kinda amped."

"You are?" Mel stifled a yawn.

"Ah. But you're not."

"I'm fine. Trust me."

"Okay. If you say so. I think we should play. I think that would help me sleep and maybe put you to sleep. If you can stay up for it."

"I can always stay up and play with you."

Susan leaned forward and kissed her. It was a deeply passionate kiss that made Mel's crotch clench. She returned it in kind and finally had to break it off to catch her breath.

"That was insane," she said.

"It was magical."

"Yeah. It really was."

"Take me to bed, Mel," Susan said.

"Gladly."

Mel showed Susan to her room and undressed her slowly and deliberately. She nibbled every spot her hands left bare. Finally, Susan was naked and wet. Mel eased her back on the bed. She stripped out of her own clothes and climbed on top of Susan.

"Damn, you're fine," Mel said.

"So are you. I love the feel of your body on mine."

"So, I was wondering…" Mel said.

"Yes?"

"Would you like to try one of my toys tonight?"

"One of?"

"Yeah."

"Sure. Surprise me, lover."

Mel went to her drawer and pulled out a purple toy.

"That looks interesting," Susan said. She took it from Mel and ran her hand over the length of it and then over the shorter end of it. "How does this work?"

"It's a strapless strap-on," Mel said. She climbed back on the bed.

Susan spread her legs, willing to take whatever Mel offered. Mel slipped the shorter part of the toy inside herself and guided the longer part inside Susan.

"Oh, God, that feels good," Susan said.

"Fuck yes, it does."

Mel moved her hips back and forth, driving the toy deeper inside Susan with each thrust. Susan arched her hips and met her every time. Mel was close to the edge. She felt herself shuddering, trying to fight to keep from coming. She hoped Susan was close, because she didn't know how long she'd be able to hold out.

Her question was answered when Susan arched her neck and threw her head back and cried out. Mel was so relieved, she let herself come immediately after her. She collapsed on Susan, the force of her orgasm having exhausted her.

"Oh, my, God, that was wonderful," Susan said.

"Yeah, it was."

"I could lie back and let you fuck me all night, Mel. What other toys do you have?"

Mel went to the top drawer of her dresser. She moved the toy she'd used with Tiffany out of the way. She wasn't sure how to broach that other hole with Susan. She decided on her Wild Orchid toy. She went back to the bed and kissed Susan hard on her mouth. She kissed down until she took a nipple in her mouth. While she suckled, she brought the vibrating toy up and pressed it against her opening.

"Oh, God, don't tease me. Please, Mel. Please give it to me."

Mel slipped the long shaft of the toy inside her while the short shaft moved against her clit. She pressed hard, then released, then pressed hard again. Susan writhed on the bed, begging for release.

"Oh, sweet Jesus, I need to come. Please, get me off, Mel. Oh, God, please."

Mel shoved the long shaft as deep as it would go and turned the shorter shaft on high. Susan's head was moving back and forth on the pillow.

"Oh, yes. Oh, yes. Oh. God. Mel. Yes!"

Mel held the toy in place while Susan rode out her orgasms. When she quit thrashing, Mel withdrew it and set it on the nightstand.

"So, you liked that, huh?" Mel grinned.

"Holy fuck. Did I ever. That toy was amazing. I think you should bring it with you every day in case you spend the night at my house."

Mel laughed.

"We'll save it for nights spent here," she said. "Unless you want me to buy you one of your own."

"You'd do that for me?"

"Of course. Just say the word."

"Please do."

"Consider it done."

Susan's shift was close to ending Friday evening when Joey and Mel walked in. They got a pitcher of beer and sat at a booth. The place was full and Susan was busy waitressing. She wished she could sit and talk with them, but there was no time. When her shift finally ended she walked over to their booth.

"I wish I could stay and chat with you two," she said.

"Can't you at least have a drink?" Mel said.

"No. I need to get going."

"Okay. Wait here, Joey. I'm going to walk her to her car. I'll be right back."

Mel took her hand and walked out the back door with her.

"You be careful," she said.

"I will."

"You want to come to my house or you want me to go to your house and wait for you?"

"Leave your front door open. I'll come to your place."

"Okay."

Mel kissed her good-bye. Susan watched as she walked back into the bar, then braced herself for another dose of Dorinda. She arrived and was anxious to talk to Lucinda and see what kind of day she'd had. Dorinda let her in and she walked straight to Lucinda's bed.

"How are you today, Lucinda?" she said.

"I had a good day. Not a lot of pain."

"That's great." She kissed Lucinda's cheek. "Can I get you anything?"

"I just finished dinner. Why don't you just sit down and we can visit?"

"Great. Will you be going somewhere, Dorinda?"

"No," Dorinda said. "I'm going to stay in tonight."

Susan wanted to ask what she was doing there, then, but she didn't want to seem like she didn't want to spend time with Lucinda.

"Oh. Okay," she said. "What will you be doing then?"

"Actually, Lucinda and I were talking and we were thinking it might be fun to play cards and then watch *Charade*. It's on TV tonight. As I recall, you really like that movie."

Susan's heart stopped. Yes, she liked that movie. It was one of her favorites. Who didn't love Cary Grant and Audrey Hepburn? But the thought of watching it with Dorinda again made her skin crawl. The last time they'd watched it together, Dorinda had had too much to drink and ended up backhanding her. Just the thought of it had Susan fighting back tears. Of course, Dorinda hadn't remembered it the next day, but Susan would never forget.

"I haven't seen that movie in so long. And I absolutely love it," Lucinda said.

How could Susan deny Lucinda? She hated Dorinda for doing this to her. She didn't like the position she'd put her in.

"Sure. If that's what you want, Lucinda," Susan said. "So what kind of cards shall we play?"

"Gin rummy," Lucinda said.

"Sounds good," Dorinda said.

Susan watched Dorinda get the cards. Maybe she'd changed. She seemed to really care for Lucinda. And that made Susan feel good.

They played cards for an hour or so, during which Dorinda showed ceaseless attention to Lucinda and her needs. Susan realized she wasn't going to be the only one who missed Lucinda when she was gone. She actually felt sorry for Dorinda.

The conversation was lively as they recalled happier times. They laughed and joked and had a really good time. It felt good to be able to laugh and enjoy herself with Lucinda and Dorinda.

When they finished playing cards, it was time to watch the movie.

"Why don't you grab a seat and I'll make some popcorn," Dorinda said.

"Can I get you anything?" Susan asked Lucinda.

"I'm fine for now," she said. "Just keep those pills ready in case I need them."

"Of course," Susan said.

Susan sat in the chair next to Lucinda's bed. She reached out and held Lucinda's hand.

"Oh, honey, it's so nice to have you around again," Lucinda said.

"I've really missed you," Susan said.

Dorinda came back into the living room.

"Susan, why don't you come over here so you can get some popcorn?" she said.

"I'm fine here."

"No, dear," Lucinda said. "Go sit there and have some popcorn. Surely you're hungry after work?"

Susan was hungry and the popcorn smelled delicious.

"But I'd rather sit here with you," she said.

"Please, hon. I insist. I'm fine."

Against her wishes and better judgment, Susan moved over and sat on the love seat next to Dorinda. Dorinda turned on the television and they settled in to watch the movie. Susan helped herself to the pop-corn, happy to put something in her empty stomach. At one point, she reached her hand in the bowl at the same time Dorinda did. Their fin-gers brushed and Susan pulled her hand back as if bit by a snake. She had felt currents run through her hand. What the hell was that about?

"Relax," Dorinda said. "Jeez. I don't bite."

"I'm sorry."

"I'm just teasin'. But you should relax. You seem really uptight."

"I'm fine."

"What's going on over there?" Lucinda said.

"Nothing," they said in unison. Susan's stomach tightened. She just wanted out of there. And she still had three more hours in her shift. Thank God for the movie, so she wouldn't have to talk with Dorinda.

Dorinda offered her some more popcorn.

"No, thanks. I'm good."

"Are you sure?"

"I'm positive."

They settled back to watch the movie. Three quarters of the way through it, Lucinda cried out in pain.

"Please. I need a pill."

Susan was at her side while Dorinda went to get her medicine. Susan held her hand while Lucinda arched her back and writhed in pain.

"Hurry!" Susan said.

"I am."

And then Dorinda was beside her, offering her a pill and a glass of water.

"It was time for her usual dose," Dorinda said.

"I hope we didn't miss her actual due time, did we?" Susan was pissed but didn't want to show it.

"No. She could have gone another five minutes."

"Okay."

Lucinda still had a death grip on Susan's hand, but was no longer arched off the bed. She seemed focused on taking deep breaths. Her eyes were cloudy but Susan didn't know if that was from the pain or the meds.

"That's it, Lucinda," Dorinda said. "Breathe with me. In and out. In and out."

"Should we give her a bolus?" Susan said.

"Not until we see if this works."

Waiting seemed cruel to Susan. But Dorinda was a cruel person. No, she told herself. Not anymore, she wasn't. She was thinking of the old Dorinda, not this new one she was seeing. Still, she vowed to herself not to ever let Lucinda get close to getting her meds out of her system. It was unfair to her. Lucinda had never done anything to anyone. She was always caring and loving, and now that she had to rely on others, Susan was determined that, on her shift, she'd never be in pain.

They waited until Lucinda had drifted off to sleep.

"You want to finish the movie now?" Dorinda said.

Susan forgot they'd paused the movie.

"I'm not really in the mood."

"Look." Dorinda took her hands. "This is part of taking care of her. She's not always going to be in good shape. You need to be able to handle it when she's in pain. You just get her some meds and wait with her until they kick in. You have to be able to deal with that."

"I can." Susan took her hands back. "That just came on so suddenly. I can do this. You can count on me."

"Okay. I'm glad. Because she really enjoys seeing you. She gets confused sometimes. She knows her schedule, but the meds fuck with her head. She was asking if she was going to get to see you yesterday. I had to explain it wasn't your day. She really loves you, Sus."

Susan didn't like Dorinda's familiarity. But she was too tired to deal with it then.

"Can I go home?"

"Yeah. Sure. We'll see you Monday?"

"I'll be here."

The drive back to Mel's led past Kindred Spirits. Susan checked the lot and saw Joey's truck was still there. She pulled in.

It was easy to find the deadly duo. They were running the pool table, as usual. Mel was about to take a shot. She walked up behind her and ran her hand up her inner thigh. Mel jumped and turned around. She laughed.

"Hey baby. That's one way to get my attention."

"I thought it might work."

Mel checked her watch.

"You're off early."

"Yeah. Rough shift."

"You wanna talk about it?"

"Maybe when we get home," Susan said.

"Do you want to leave now?"

"Oh, no. I could use a stiff drink."

"Or at least a lemon drop," Joey said.

Susan laughed. It felt good to be with Mel and Joey. She didn't have to be on edge all the time. She could just relax and have fun. She questioned again about her hours volunteering, but reminded herself she was doing it for Lucinda, who clearly needed her help. It wasn't going to be fun, but it was worth doing. She felt guilty for even thinking about quitting.

Joey returned from the bar with a lemon drop for her.

"Thanks," she said.

"My pleasure. Sorry you had a rough time tonight."

"Well, it's not fun caring for a dying person."

"I'm sure it's not. That's nothing I've dealt with before."

"Me, neither."

"What's with all the serious faces?" Mel walked up and joined them.

"Is it my shot yet?" Joey said.

"Not yet, but it will be in a second."

"Sweet."

Joey walked away from the booth. Mel took Susan's hand.

"I'm glad you're here now," she said. "I was missing you."

"I was missing you, too."

"I wish you'd let me go with you when you go over there."

"I don't know," Susan said. "It's hard to explain. It's like a really personal thing. And personal time with Lucinda. I'll have to take you sometime. She really wants to meet you."

"And I'd like to meet her. Although I'm not so keen on spending any more time with Dorinda."

Susan sat there looking at Mel. Did she dare tell her about Dorinda's movie choice for the night? And about their hands meeting in the popcorn bowl? She really wanted to, but she didn't want Mel to worry. She was Mel's. All Mel's. Wasn't she?

"Again with the serious face," Mel said. "What's on your mind?"

"Nothing. I'm sorry. I'm going to go get another drink."

"No. You stay here. I'll go get it."

They spent another hour at the bar before Joey pleaded parental duties.

"You have no idea what time a two-year-old will wake you up. And how hyper they are. I don't know how they do it, but I've got to be ready," she said. "I'll see you guys later."

"You ready to hit it?" Mel said.

"Yeah. Let's go."

They got to Mel's house.

"You want to tell me what happened tonight?" Mel said.

"It was just Lucinda," Susan said. "She had a fit of pain. I think Dorinda forgot to give her her morphine on time, but I can't prove anything. It was terrible. She was in so much pain. It killed me to see her like that. And the meds don't take effect right away, you know? So we had to watch her in pain for a while."

"I'm sorry, babe." Mel pulled Susan into an embrace.

"Would you mind just holding me tonight?" Susan said.

"Of course not. If that's what you need."

"I do."

And Susan fell into a fitful sleep with Mel's strong arms around her.

CHAPTER SIXTEEN

Susan woke the next morning in an empty bed. She was disoriented at first and then remembered they'd crashed at Mel's place the night before. She was horny as hell, though. Where was Mel?

She looked at her clothes in a pile on the floor, but opted not to put them on. She was going to find Mel and have her way with her. She found her in at the kitchen table, sipping coffee.

"Well, don't you look nice?" Mel said.

"Come back to bed, lover. I need you."

"Would you like some coffee?"

"Maybe later. For now, I only want you."

She took Mel's hand and placed it between her legs.

"See? I'm ready for you."

Mel withdrew her hand and licked her fingers clean. She followed Susan down the hall to her room.

"Show me a new toy," Susan said.

"How do you know I have any other toys?"

"I can tell. Don't lie to me. Bust 'em out."

"I don't know, babe. You may not be into any of the other ones I have."

"Let's see."

Susan walked over and opened Mel's top dresser drawer. She stood back in awe.

"Oh, my God. What a collection you have. I'd never dreamed you'd have so many. And such a variety. Oh wow."

Mel turned bright red.

"You're so cute when you blush," Susan said.

"Okay, okay," Mel finally said. "You've seen them. Now, do any of them appeal to you?"

"I want this one." She grabbed the fattest dildo Mel owned.

"You sure you can take all that?"

"I sure want to try. Now come to bed and fuck me with this thing."

Mel took the toy to the bed. She climbed in next to Susan who lay there with her knees bent and her legs spread.

"Do you like what you see?" Susan said.

"I do," Mel croaked. She took the tip of the toy and ran it along Susan's opening. "Hold on. Let me get some lube."

"I won't need it."

"Are you serious?"

"I am," Susan said. "At least try it without the lube. If we need some, we can always use it later."

"Okay. If you insist."

She played with the toy against Susan again. Susan moved around, rubbing herself onto the huge dong. Mel slipped the tip inside.

"Oh, damn, that feels good. Give me more, lover. Fill me up."

Mel slipped the toy farther inside her.

"Is it all the way in yet?" Susan said.

"No. It's about halfway. How are you doin'?"

"More, Mel. I want you to fill me with that bad boy."

Mel slid the toy in until Susan had swallowed all but the base. She took in back out and slipped it in again.

"Yes. That's what I'm talking about. Fuck me, Mel."

Susan was staring at Mel's eyes, which were focused on her pussy.

"You like what you see?" Susan said. "Does it look hot?"

"Fuckin' A it does."

"Take a picture."

"What?" Mel said.

"Take a pic with your phone. I wanna see."

"Okay. If you insist."

Mel did as she was asked and showed the picture to Susan.

"Look how spread out I am. That's awesome," Susan said.

"You're a lot kinkier than I expected," Mel said.

"I don't think this is kinky. Whips and chains. Now that shit's kinky. Now finish fucking me before I take matters into my own hands."

Mel went back to moving the toy in and out of her, thrusting it as deep as it would go. She bent over and licked Susan's swollen clit, and in no time, Susan was crying out Mel's name.

Mel tried to withdraw the dildo, but it was stuck.

"You've got a grip on that thing," she said. "We'll have to give it a minute before I can slip it out of you."

"That's okay. It can stay there. Now come here and let me have you."

Susan kissed Mel hard on the lips. She needed to prove to herself that Mel was the only woman in her life. The thought made her pause. Of course Mel was. Why would she need to prove it? She shook the thoughts from her head and allowed herself to simply please Mel. She ran her hand down her body to where her legs met. She slid her fingers inside as deep as they would go before pulling them out. In and out, she moved them until Mel was begging for release. Susan dragged her fingers over Mel's clit, and Mel let out a guttural moan that let Susan know she'd been successful.

Susan rolled over onto her back. Mel pried her legs open and took the toy out of her.

"That was awesome," Susan said. "Now I think I'm ready to go back to sleep."

"Is that the kind of day today's going to be?" Mel said. "A lazy kind of day?"

"Mm. I don't know. Lie down with me?"

"I'm pretty much awake, but I suppose it wouldn't hurt to lie down for a few."

Susan woke two hours later to find Mel snoring next to her. She loved Mel's snores. They were loud enough to let her know she was breathing, but soft enough to not require earplugs. Mel was so hot lying there that it took every ounce of self-control not to ravish her again.

Just then Mel's eyes opened.

"Hey, babe," she said.

"Hello again."

Susan rolled over so her breasts pressed into Mel's.

"Hm. Is someone ready for round two?" Mel said.

"Always with you."

Mel played with one of Susan's breasts.

"I like that."

"Aw, come on," Susan said. "You know you're hot."

"I know you think I am. That's all that matters."

They made love again, and after, Mel seemed restless.

"Hey, babe, I love what we're doin' and all, but I'm not the type of person who likes to lie around in bed all day. What do you want to do with the rest of our day?"

"I want you to teach me to surf again."

"That sounds great."

"Okay," Susan said. "Get dressed for the beach and then we can go to my place so I can get ready."

She lay back on the bed and watched her sexy Mel slip into board shorts and a tank top.

"You ready?" Mel said.

"Let's go."

Mel was glad that Susan was in a better mood that morning. She had seemed so upset when she first got to the bar the night before. Mel sensed there was something Susan wasn't telling her, but she had to trust her. She just hoped Dorinda wasn't being a raging bitch to her. She wished Susan would open up a little more, but she hadn't, and there was nothing Mel could do but be there for her. Maybe over time, she'd have more to say.

It was a hot day in Maybon Tir. Temperatures were in the mid nineties, which meant the beach was packed. Susan and Mel had to sandwich their chairs between two large groups.

"This isn't ideal," Mel said.

"It's because we got such a late start," Susan said. "I'm sorry about that."

"I wouldn't have missed it." Mel winked. "And it wouldn't have mattered when we got here. Someone would have to have set up camp right next to us. Fortunately, it doesn't look like too many people are surfing, so your lessons should go unimpeded."

"Unimpeded, huh? That's a big word."

"Well, you know what I mean."

"I do. You're just so cute."

Mel could feel the heat start at her neck and creep up her face. She turned away under the pretense of searching the waves for the perfect breaking spot. When she felt the blush fade, she turned back to Susan.

"Okay, kiddo. Let's paddle out there."

"Kiddo? I'm at least your age." Susan laughed.

"Sorry. It's a term of endearment," Mel said. "Now, let's go."

They got to the deeper water and Mel helped Susan onto the board. They went a little deeper to where the waves were breaking. Mel held onto the board as she waited for the perfect wave for Susan to catch. When she saw it approaching, she turned the board so Susan faced the shore.

"Get ready," Mel said.

"I am."

Mel gave her a shove.

"Paddle! Paddle!"

"I am."

Mel watched as the wave took over and Susan rode it to shore. Susan quickly paddled back out to Mel.

"That was awesome," she said.

"It was a beautiful ride. I think you might be a natural."

"I don't know about that. When do I get to try standing?"

"Not for a while. We might try knees next week."

"Fair enough."

They surfed for another couple of hours. Mel was thrilled to see Susan enjoying it so much. Obviously, it was one of her favorite activities and she was happy to share it with Susan, who took to it like a pro.

"So, what now?" Susan said.

"I'm starving. How about heading over to The Shack?"

"That works for me. I swear I could eat a double cheeseburger."

"There's no way."

"Bet me?"

"You're on," Mel said. "What's the bet?"

"Who comes first tonight."

"You got it."

They went to The Shack and grabbed their favorite table. They'd barely been seated a minute with Dorinda walked up.

"Hey, you two," she said. She sat in an empty chair. "Do you mind if I join you? I feel so lost here. I don't know a soul. I was so happy to see you two walk in."

"What are you doing here?" Susan said.

"Mark is with Lucinda today. I enjoyed my day off at the beach. Then I got hungry and came over here. It's full of people and I just feel so out of place."

"That's funny. I've never felt out of place anywhere in Maybon Tir," Susan said. "Even when I first moved here."

"Well, you're better with people than I am. Always were."

She hung her purse over the back of the chair, clearly not going anywhere. Mel was not amused, but Susan seemed okay with her being there, so she didn't say anything. She wasn't happy about having to share her time with Susan, though. Especially with Dorinda.

They ordered their dinners.

"A double cheeseburger?" Dorinda said to Susan after the waitress had left. "Are these burgers small or something?"

"No. They're huge," Mel said.

"Then how can you eat a double?" Dorinda asked Susan.

"Because I'm famished and because we have a bet."

"Okay. Suit yourself. I have to watch everything I eat anymore."

"I doubt that," Susan said.

Mel wondered what she meant. Did it mean she dug Dorinda's body? Did she want it or just think it was nice? Or was she just being polite? Mel was decidedly uncomfortable at the situation.

Their dinners arrived, and Mel just stared at hers. She knew it would take a herculean effort on her part to eat the big burger. Her appetite had shrunk since Dorinda had joined them. But one bite and she knew she could do it. It was juicy and delicious and fuck Dorinda. She was going to enjoy her dinner.

Susan started to slow down when she was about halfway through her burger.

"No reason to hurt yourself," Mel said. "If you can't finish it, it's no big deal."

"I'm going to finish." Susan laughed. "I want to win the bet."

"What did you guys bet?" Dorinda asked.

"It's personal." Mel said it a little more sharply than she intended. "I'm sorry, but it really is personal."

"No worries. Some things are best kept between couples."

"Indeed," Mel said.

Mel finished her burger and fries with no problem.

"Do you want some of my fries?" Dorinda said. "There's no way I'm going to be able to finish them."

Mel helped herself. She watched Susan as she ate.

"You gonna make it?" Mel asked.

"I got this."

It took her another fifteen minutes, but Susan finished every bite of the burger.

"I win." She grinned wickedly at Mel.

"Yes, you did. Which means I did, too, if you think about it."

"Okay, you two," Dorinda said. "You're both blushing so I can't help but guess what this is about. Don't forget I'm sitting here."

Uninvited, Mel thought to herself.

"Sorry," Susan said. "But you know how it is when you're really into someone."

"Yeah," Dorinda said flatly. "I do."

Mel threw a wad of cash on the table.

"That should cover our part. Now, if you'll excuse us, we're heading home."

"Oh. Okay. Well, have a good night."

"You, too," Susan said.

When they got to the car, Susan turned to Mel.

"Do you think we should have bought her dinner?"

"Why?"

"I just think it would have been nice."

"I don't know. She invited herself to join us. I didn't appreciate the interruption. I was looking forward to a quiet dinner with my girl. I didn't want her to think she should get used to doing that."

"I guess I understand that. I just think she was happy to see familiar faces. I don't think she really thought of it as interrupting."

"Maybe she didn't, but it was. And I didn't appreciate it."

"But, Mel, she doesn't know anybody else."

"I get that. But you're her ex. Not her best buddy."

Susan grew silent.

"Am I right? Or what?" Mel said.

"You're right," Susan said quietly.

"Okay. Now let's get home and get you taken care of. Your place or mine, baby?"

"Yours. It's the one with all the toys."

Mel laughed.

"You know, it might be fun to go toy shopping together. There's this store in Somerset that's like a flippin' grocery store sized toy store."

"That would be fun. Maybe next weekend?"

"Sure. Let's plan on it.

They went back to Mel's house, and as soon as the door was closed, Susan was in her arms. She kissed Mel and ran her hands down her chest.

"You're so fucking hot," she said.

Mel eased herself away from the door and took Susan's wrap off. She tossed it on the couch.

"Let's go shower. We need to get the salt and sand off of us."

They stood in the shower and stripped out of their suits. Then, Mel turned the water on and watched Susan's breasts rise and fall as Susan washed her long, dark hair. When she couldn't take it anymore, she bent over and kissed them. First one, then the other, she lovingly kissed up and down on them before finally taking a nipple in her mouth.

"No fair," Susan said.

"All we said was that you would come first. We didn't say where or how."

"Oh, God." She leaned against the wall of the shower and held Mel's head in place. Mel kissed down her stomach until she knelt between her legs. She darted her tongue out to taste the saltiness of Susan's pussy. She tasted delicious, her normal flavor mixed with the salt of the sea.

"Oh, shit," Susan said. "You're going to make me come."

Mel didn't respond, rather kept doing what she was doing until she felt Susan's fingers dig into her shoulders as she came.

Chapter Seventeen

Susan stood holding on to Mel until her legs quit quivering. When she felt Mel's tongue again, she mewled in delight. Mel certainly knew what to do to get her off, and it wasn't long before Susan's world was shattered again. When the pieces all came back together, she finally found her voice.

"Let's get to bed where it's safer," she said.

They dried off and hurried to the bedroom. Susan climbed on top of Mel and rubbed her wet pussy all over her.

"Oh, Jesus," Mel said. "You're driving me fucking crazy."

"Yeah? Good."

Susan licked up her own trail as she slid down Mel's body. She put Mel's knees on her shoulders and went about her business between Mel's legs. Soon Mel was holding her face to her and grinding her hips against her.

"You feel so good," Mel said.

Susan couldn't speak. She could barely breathe. But it was worth it. She wanted Mel to feel everything she made her feel. And soon she did. Mel arched off the bed and froze, and Susan knew she'd done well. She smiled to herself as Mel relaxed back onto the bed and eased her grip on Susan.

Susan kissed back up Mel's body and snuggled into her arms where she fell fast asleep.

When she woke up in the morning, Mel was already out of bed. She found her again at the kitchen table. Susan poured herself a cup of coffee and sat with her.

"Aren't you putting any clothes on?" Mel asked.

"Do I need to?"

"No way. I like what I'm seeing."

"Good."

"So, what's today look like for you?" Susan said.

"Surfing with Joey then hangin' with you at the bar. If that's okay."

"That's fine. I hope it won't be totally dead."

"I know. You need the tips."

"I really do. Although I've got to say, the women in this town are great tippers, so even when it's not super crowded, I do okay."

"Great. That makes me happy."

"You're so sweet," Susan said.

"Yeah?"

"Yeah."

She stood up and kissed Mel.

"Any chance I can talk you into coming back to bed?"

"Wish I could. But I've got to meet Joey. I'll see you this afternoon."

She kissed Susan good-bye and was out the door.

Susan was left to her own devices. She wandered back to the bedroom and lay down. She started thinking of Mel and the previous night and her hand automatically drifted between her legs. She played over her swollen clit to her wet center, still coated with the juices of her orgasms. She closed her eyes and placed her other hand on her breast. She pinched her nipple while her fingers rubbed herself. She got closer and closer as she thought of Mel and all the fun they'd had.

Just before she reached her peak, a picture of Dorinda flashed through her mind. She stopped what she was doing.

"What the fuck?" she said.

Still, she was too close not to finish. She pushed all thoughts of Dorinda away and took herself to a mind-blowing orgasm. She showered, put on her swimsuit and wrap, and cut through the neighborhoods to her house.

She sat on the patio eating breakfast, thinking of how much she was enjoying her life now that Mel was in it. Mel was a special person. So different from women she'd dated in the past. She didn't seem to have an agenda or seek to control Susan. She just wanted to have fun and wanted Susan to have fun. It was so refreshing.

She changed into her shorts and shirt and drove to the bar. She got there just before one. The parking lot was practically empty. She couldn't wait until fall got there. Fall meant football, and football meant crowds, and crowds meant money. But she still had a month to go before preseason started.

Susan pulled into her parking place and let herself in the back door.

"Hello," she said to Joanne.

"Hey there. How you doin' today?"

"Not bad. I can't believe how dead it is in here."

"No kidding. I'm thinking about retiring. I could work this hard at home."

Susan laughed, though it really wasn't funny. It was hard to remain upbeat when the bar was as empty as it was. There were two people at the bar and another two people in a booth. That was it. Susan put her apron on and went over to the people in the booth. She saw their drinks were empty.

"Can I get you some refills?" Susan said.

"No, thanks. We were just leaving."

Susan forced herself to keep smiling as she cleared the table. She got back to the bar and started polishing glasses. At least it was something to do.

"Those already sparkle," Joanne said. "How do you think I keep my sanity before you get here?"

"Great," Susan said. She sat on a stool behind the bar and visited with Joanne for a while.

"Oh, heaven help us. There's new blood in town," Joanne said.

Susan followed her gaze to the door and saw Dorinda walk in wearing the same short-shorts she'd had on the other day. But instead of the halter top, she was wearing a T-shirt.

"Hey, Susan," she said.

"Hey, Dorinda. What are you doing here?"

"I came to see where you work. You love it here so much, I wanted to check it out. Not very busy, is it?"

"It has its moments," Susan said.

Just then, Joanne cleared her throat.

"Oh, Joanne, this is Dorinda. Dorinda, Joanne."

Joanne extended her hand.

"Nice to meet you," she said.

"Nice to meet you, too."

"Any friend of Susan's is a friend of mine."

Susan had to turn away so her smile didn't show. Joanne was old enough to be Dorinda's mother, but she was going to give it her best shot to hit on her. Susan bit her lip so she wouldn't laugh.

"Can we get you something to drink?" Joanne said.

"I'd love a Bloody Mary."

"You want to make that, hon?" Joanne called over her shoulder.

"Sure. I'm on it," Susan said.

"Since when do you tend bar?" Dorinda said.

"Since it's slow. There's no waitressing to do, so I've been learning how to mix drinks."

"Well, that's good. Another trick of the trade. Might come in handy someday."

"It comes in handy now," Susan said.

She handed Dorinda her Bloody Mary, and she and Joanne waited as Dorinda tasted it.

"This is really good," Dorinda said. "I wish you'd had this skill before. Remember all the brunches we used to throw? I was the one who had to make all the Bloody Marys."

"Wait a minute," Joanne said. She looked from one to the other. "You two were an item?"

"Yes, ma'am," Dorinda said. "For quite a while."

"Oh, I didn't mean to step on any toes." Joanne looked at Susan.

"No worries," Susan said. She didn't have the heart to tell Joanne she wasn't threatened by her. Not that she had anything to be threatened about. She was thinking too much and starting to confuse herself. She moved to the other end of the bar and started polishing glasses again. Dorinda took her drink and moved down there.

"Hey. I came here to see you. Why'd you come down here?"

"I like to keep busy."

"I don't blame you. But you can keep busy talking to me."

"How's Lucinda today?" Susan searched for some safe terrain. She didn't know why she was feeling so nervous around Dorinda suddenly.

"She's doing well. She had a rough night last night, but seems to be in good spirits today. Although I suspect she'll sleep a lot today."

"That's probably good for her," Susan said.

"Yeah. She wants to stay awake more, but I think it helps her conserve her energy to sleep."

"You ready for a refill? Or do you have to get going?" Susan said.

"I'll take another one. I have nowhere to go and nothing to do today. My only goal today is catching up with you."

Susan's stomach fluttered. What was going on with her? Why did she care if Dorinda wanted to play catch up? She had nothing to hide.

❖

Mel and Joey agreed to meet at Kindred Spirits for some beer and pool before Joey had to go home.

"One pitcher," Joey said. "I need some time with my wife and boy."

"I get that," Mel said. "I get time with my woman at the bar."

"That you do. I don't. And I miss them."

"Fair enough. One pitcher."

When they walked in the bar, Mel was bummed to see how dead it was. But she saw Susan at the bar, leaning over it, chatting amicably with a customer. Good for her, Mel thought. Susan saw Mel walk in and stood up straight. She smiled, but it didn't seem to go to her eyes. Mel walked up next to the patron and saw it was Dorinda.

"Well, hello, Mel," Dorinda said.

"Dorinda."

Joey sat next to Mel.

"We haven't met," she said. "I'm Joey."

"Hello, Joey. How do you fit into things?"

"I'm Mel's best friend."

Mel was annoyed. She didn't like the fact that every time she turned around, Dorinda was there. She wanted her out of town like yesterday.

"Oh," Dorinda said. "It's nice to meet you then."

"You two want a pitcher?" Susan said.

"Yes, please," Joey said. She reached for her wallet.

"Wait," Mel said. "We'll play pool for it. Loser buys."

Susan laughed.

"It's all about pool with you two, isn't it?"

"You bet, babe," Mel said. She poured two glasses of beer and walked over to the nearest table. She and Joey lagged for first shot. Mel won and sipped her beer while Joey racked the balls. The game was over in no time with Joey cleaning the table with Mel.

Mel paid for the beer.

"Bummer," Susan and Dorinda said at the same time. Then they laughed. Mel smiled, but didn't think there was anything cute about Susan and Dorinda. She didn't like Dorinda anywhere near Susan. The idea they were getting chummy really rubbed her the wrong way.

"Another game?" Joey said.

"Sure."

"Rack 'em."

Mel racked the balls and watched as Joey almost ran the table. Mel took her turn and only knocked in two balls. That was so unlike her. She wondered what was up. Then blamed it on Dorinda. She needed to leave.

Joey won on her next turn.

"Okay. That's it for me. I'm outta here," Joey said. "Dorinda, nice meeting you. Susan, good to see you, and, Mel, I'll see you tomorrow."

Mel watched Joey walk out then turned to lean against the bar and talk to Susan.

"You can grab a stool," Dorinda said. "I don't bite."

Fuck you, Mel thought. I can stand if I want or sit if I want. Dorinda had really gotten under her skin.

"I'll play a game of pool with you," Dorinda said.

"No, thanks. I'd rather chill and talk to my girl."

She reached her hand out, but Susan didn't take it. She thought that odd, but didn't say anything. She was definitely going to have a chat with Susan that evening.

The shift seemed to last forever, and Mel often sat silently as Dorinda and Susan talked about the good ol' days. There was lots of laughter, which confused Mel, as Susan had made it sound like there were more tears than laughter when they were together. How quickly she seemed to have forgotten.

When her shift ended, Dorinda stood to leave.

"Are you okay to drive?" Susan said. "I'll be happy to give you a ride."

"No. I'm fine," Dorinda said.

Mel said a silent prayer that she'd get pulled over.

"You ready to head home?" Mel stood.

"Sure."

"Your place or mine?"

"Let's go to my place tonight," Susan said.

"No problem. I'll see you there."

Mel got to Susan's house and waited out front for twenty minutes before Susan finally got home.

"Thank God," Mel said. "I was starting to get worried."

"Sorry. We just started chatting in the parking lot. Time got away from me."

Mel was completely unamused. She fought to keep from barking at Susan.

"Well, you're home now anyway," she said.

"Yep. Let's get inside. We'll order a pizza. How does that sound?"

"Sounds great."

As they waited for the pizza, Mel broached the subject of Dorinda.

"So, what's with Dorinda?" she said.

"What do you mean?"

"Like, why is she always around now?"

"She's living here until Lucinda passes," Susan said. "You knew that."

"I know why she's in town. I just don't know why she's always around us."

She didn't want to point out she was always around Susan. But she was.

"I think it's all coincidental," Susan said. "This is a small town, lover."

"I don't. Maybe The Shack was. But she had to know you worked at Kindred Spirits."

"True. She did come to check out where I worked," Susan said.

"I'm wondering if she wants you back." There. She'd said it.

"What? That's preposterous."

At that moment, the doorbell rang. Mel got it and paid for the pizza. She set it on the dining room table.

"Let's eat," she said.

"You know you're crazy," Susan said.

"Prove that to me," Mel said. "You two were awfully chummy this afternoon. Prove to me she doesn't want you."

"I can't. But she knows I don't want her."

"Are you sure?"

"Yes. I'm with you."

Mel didn't mention that she'd barely spoken to her at the bar that day. That she and Dorinda had been chatting like old sorority sisters.

"I'm just not so sure I want you working with her anymore."

"Mel, I'm doing this for the family. For Lucinda. Not for Dorinda."

"So you say."

"What's that supposed to mean?"

"It's supposed to mean that maybe they might think something else. Maybe Dorinda thinks you're doing it for her. Maybe she's looking at it as a chance to get you back."

"You're just being paranoid," Susan said. "Dorinda knows I've moved on. This group of people were like family to me when I was with Dorinda. I'm simply helping the family out now."

"You just keep telling yourself that," Mel said.

"Maybe you should go home," Susan said.

"What? Ah, come on. So we disagree. That's no reason to kick me out."

"I think I'd like to be alone tonight."

Mel didn't understand. She was more confused than ever.

"Will I see you tomorrow night?"

"Leave your door open. I'll come over after my shift," Susan said.

"Fair enough."

She kissed her on the cheek and left.

CHAPTER EIGHTEEN

Susan tossed and turned in bed that night. Sure, she'd had a great time with Dorinda that day, but it was just fun and games, right? She was falling in love with Mel, wasn't she? She thought she was. She wasn't ready to say anything like that to Mel. It might scare her off, but she sure thought she was feeling that. So why the heart flutters with Dorinda? She tried to tell herself it was stomach flutters from nerves. Dorinda hadn't been nice to her when they were together, and now she wasn't sure which Dorinda would show up, so she was nervous when she saw her. That had to be it. She fell into a restless sleep where Mel and Dorinda did battle in her dreams.

She dragged herself out of bed the next day, took a shower, and went to work. It was a slightly busy Monday afternoon. At least compared to the day before. So she waitressed and had fun talking to all the customers and made good tips. She had a great day. Until it was seven o'clock and it was time to go to Dorinda's. Lucinda's, she corrected herself. She was going to Lucinda's.

Susan arrived promptly and found Dorinda lying on the couch.

"What are you doing?" Susan asked. She tried hard not to look appreciatively at Dorinda's long legs and perfectly pedicured feet resting on the arm of the sofa.

"I'm relaxing. I put in a hard day."

"Oh, no." Susan suddenly remembered why she was there. "How's Lucinda?"

"Sleeping now. But she's been in a lot of pain today."

"I'm so sorry. That's so hard to see."

"Yeah, it is. You've seen it firsthand," Dorinda said.

"Yeah. It was almost too much. So if she's sleeping, I guess I don't really need to be here, do I?"

"What if she wakes up?" Dorinda said. "She'd be so sad if she didn't get to see you."

"That's true. And I'd be bummed if I missed any moment I might get to share with her."

"So I figured we'd order Chinese and play Trivial Pursuit. How does that sound?"

Dorinda had really turned into a thoughtful person. Those were two of Susan's favorite things. It was so sweet of Dorinda to think of that. They set up the game after they'd called in their order. By the time the food got there, neither of them had a pie yet. They were missing all sorts of questions and were cracking each other up. Susan couldn't remember the last time she'd laughed that hard. Her stomach actually hurt from laughing.

"Okay, okay," Dorinda said after they'd served up their food. "It's time to get serious."

"Oh yeah? This mean you're going to start kicking my ass?"

"You'd better believe it."

They laughed some more and got back to the game. The game lasted forever, with Susan finally coming out victorious. As they were putting everything away, she glanced at her watch. It was eleven fifteen.

"Oh, shit. I need to get going," she said.

"Oh, wow. That was a long game," Dorinda said. "I'll walk you to your car."

She walked out with Susan and they chatted a little bit more.

"I really need to go," Susan said.

"Oh, yeah. Okay. Tell Mel hi for me."

Susan drove to Mel's house. The door was open and Mel was asleep on the couch. She crossed the room to her and kissed her on the cheek.

"Hey you. Come on. Let's get you to bed."

Mel sat up.

"I tried to wait up for you," she said groggily.

"It's okay. You work hard. I'm sure you were tired."

"What time is it?" She looked at her watch. "Eleven thirty? What took you so long to get home?"

"We got to talking."

"You and Lucinda?"

"No. Me and Dorinda. Lucinda was asleep the whole time I was there."

"Then why'd you stay?" Mel said.

"In case she woke up. I wanted to be there for her."

"Fair enough."

She got off the couch and took Susan's hand. They walked down the hall to the bedroom.

"I'm sorry I'm so beat," Mel said.

"That's okay," Susan said. She didn't want to let Mel know how disappointed she was. She really needed Mel right then. She wanted Mel to take her like she'd never taken her before. But clearly that wasn't going to happen.

Mel stripped and climbed into bed. She propped herself on an elbow and watched Susan get undressed.

"Suddenly, I'm more awake," Mel said.

"Yeah?"

"Yeah. Get over here."

Susan crossed to the bed. She straddled Mel, and Mel ran her hands up and down her sides. She teased her breasts and tweaked her nipples. When Susan could stand no more, she walked on her knees up to straddle Mel's face. She held on to Mel's headboard as Mel's tongue worked its magic on her. She bobbed up and down and ground into her, meeting every lick.

"Holy fuck, Mel. You make me feel so good."

She ground down and cried out as she rode the wave of the orgasm.

She climbed off Mel's face and moved between her legs. She sucked and licked her lips before moving to her clit. She slid three fingers inside her, and soon Mel was moaning her usual moan, and Susan knew she was satisfied. She moved next to her on the bed.

"I'm crazy about you, Mel."

"I'm crazy about you, too."

Susan drifted off to sleep with a smile on her face. She woke the next morning when she heard Mel get out of bed.

"Do you have to go now?" she purred. "Can't we have a repeat of last night?"

Mel looked down at her. Susan kicked the sheet off and spread her legs.

"Pretty please?"

"Oh, shit," Mel said. "I'm going to be late."

"But won't it be worth it?"

Mel climbed back into bed and kissed Susan's neck while she ran her hand down her body.

"I love the way you touch me," Susan said.

"I love your body."

Mel slid her fingers inside Susan and stroked her until she came.

"Mm. That was just what I needed," Susan said. She stretched and climbed back under the sheets.

"I need to get going." Mel dressed quickly and kissed her. "I'll see you at the bar this afternoon."

"I can't wait."

❖

"I think you're paranoid," Joey said.

"I don't know. You saw them together at the bar the other day."

"Yeah. So?"

"And then she was a half hour late getting home last night. What the hell were they doing until eleven thirty? Huh?"

"Maybe they were talking and lost track of time," Joey said.

"I don't know. When this all started, Susan would have gotten out of that house and away from Dorinda as fast as she could. And now she's staying late and coming home at that ungodly hour? It doesn't make sense. I don't trust Dorinda," Mel said.

"But you trust Susan, right?"

"I don't know. I'm starting to wonder if I do. Joey, if she dumps me and goes back to Dorinda, I don't know what I'll do."

"I think you're getting a little ahead of yourself there. Way ahead of yourself, actually."

"I don't know about that," Mel said. "It's like Dorinda knows her so well and they have all these memories they share."

"You're new. You're just getting to know each other and make your own memories."

"Maybe."

"No maybes about it. Now come on. We need to get to work."

Mel worked hard that day, but Susan and Dorinda were always in the back of her mind. She felt like she was losing Susan and hoped she'd be able to figure out a way to stop that from happening.

At lunch, Joey broached the subject again.

"Man, it's all you can think about, isn't it? I don't think you've said a word all day. You're totally lost in thought."

"I really feel like I'm losing her."

"Look, whose bed is she in at night?"

"Mine. Usually. Though she slept alone the other night. She kicked me out."

"Seriously?"

"Seriously."

"Hm."

"Hm what? What's that supposed to mean?" Mel said.

"Nothing. I'm sure it's nothing."

"You've got to admit it's odd."

"Yeah. I'll give you that."

They went back to work, and Mel pushed herself as hard as she could. She was exhausted when the day was through.

"You want to go to the bar with me?" Mel said.

"No, thanks. I'm going to go pick up DJ and have some quality one-on-one time with him."

"Right on. Give the little guy a hug from me."

"Will do."

Mel took a quick shower and headed for Kindred Spirits. It wasn't very busy, but a few of the booths were taken so Susan was waitressing. She found a booth and waited. Susan showed up shortly thereafter.

"Hey, gorgeous," Mel said.

"You want the usual?" Susan said.

"Please."

"Coming right up."

That was odd, Mel thought. No "hello," no "go to hell," no nothing.

Susan brought her beer.

"Everything okay?" Mel asked.

"Sure. Why?"

"You just didn't seem very glad to see me."

"Sorry."

That was it? No explanation? Mel was scared.

"Hey, I was thinkin' of goin' out for steaks tonight after work. What do you say?"

"Sounds good. I'd better get back to work."

Mel watched her walk back to the bar and sit there while she waited to do another round. Why wasn't she sitting with Mel?

Mel took her half pitcher and sat at the bar next to Susan.

"Is it okay if I sit here?"

"Sure," Susan said. "That would be great. How was your day?"

That was more like it. Maybe Joey was right. Maybe she was just being paranoid.

"It was good. Hard. I pushed myself like a big dog."

"Why?"

"I don't know," Mel said. "Just felt like it."

"I don't get it, but it's your body, so okay."

Susan's shift finally ended, and Mel walked her out to her car. She kissed her and pressed against her, but the kiss she got back was lukewarm at best.

"What's up?" she said.

"Nothing. I'm just tired," Susan said.

"Okay. If you're sure that's it."

They separated then and agreed to meet at the restaurant. At least, Mel thought, Dorinda had Lucinda duty that night so they wouldn't end up bumping into her. Mel parked, and a moment later, Susan was pulling into the lot. Mel just wanted a nice, relaxing dinner. She was starving and wanted to be able to eat a steak in peace.

She took Susan's hand as they walked inside.

"Wow," the hostess said. "Mel O'Brien has a girlfriend. I'd heard it, but didn't believe it."

Mel blushed and Susan squeezed her hand. They were seated at a table near a window.

"It's so cute how everyone is shocked that you have a girlfriend," Susan said.

"I tell ya, I tried, but couldn't find Ms. Right."

"And now you think you have?"

"I think I'm on a journey to find out."

"Well said. I'm glad we're taking it slow as far as that goes," Susan said. "Some lesbians would have done the whole 'I love you' thing and moved in together. I'm glad you're not like that."

"Nope. We need to both be sure before we do that."

Susan fell silent. She picked up her menu.

"Was it something I said?" Mel said.

"What? No. I just need to find something to eat. I'm famished."

Mel picked up her menu, too. She didn't really need to. She knew what she was getting, but she wanted to hide the fear on her face.

After dinner, Mel asked if Susan wanted her to come over or if she wanted to come over to her place.

"I think I'd like to just be alone tonight," Susan said.

"Okay," Mel said when they were in the parking lot. "Are you going to tell me what's going on?"

"What do you mean?"

"This is twice in the last few days that you don't want to sleep with me. Pardon me for questioning it."

"It's nothing. I just want some alone time. What's wrong with that?"

"Nothing. I just noticed it didn't start happening until you started hanging out with Dorinda."

"Look. I get that you don't like her. But she's changed. She's not the horrible woman I lived with."

"Great. So, what? You want to get back together with her?"

"That's not what I'm saying at all. I'm just asking you to back off and quit blaming everything on her."

"That's easier said than done. Last night you were a half hour late getting home. Why? Dorinda. I worry about you when you're not home on time, babe."

"You were *sleeping*," Susan said.

"Look, I don't want to fight."

"Neither do I. But I don't like all this jealousy."

"I can't help it. I'm sorry. I'll try to do better."

"Please do. And we were just talking about how other people rush into living together. We haven't done that. And one of the advantages of that is being able to have a night alone once in a while. Don't take offense to it. It's just something I need."

Mel still thought it odd that she hadn't needed a night alone until Dorinda showed up, but she kept her mouth shut. She kissed Susan on the cheek and drove home.

CHAPTER NINETEEN

Susan chose her clothes carefully for her trip to Dorinda's house. She wore cut-off blue jean shorts and a tight green T-shirt. She knew the shirt showed off her figure and her eyes. She looked good and she knew it. She wasn't sure why it was important that she looked good for Dorinda, but she did. Actually, she told herself she wanted to look nice for Lucinda. Dorinda didn't matter. But she didn't believe it.

She let herself in to the house, and Dorinda was nowhere to be found. She was disappointed. Then she saw Lucinda sitting up in her bed and crossed the room to see her.

"Don't you look lovely today, Susan?" she said.

"Thanks. You're looking awfully good, too."

"Thanks. I'm having a good day."

"Great. So what shall we do today?" Susan said.

"I think Dorinda is going to go run errands," she said. Susan felt a lump in the pit of her stomach. Why? What did she care what Dorinda did? "So we can visit and watch soap operas."

"That sounds great," Susan said.

Just then Dorinda came out of the back of the house. She looked gorgeous in her short-shorts and tight red T-shirt. The sight took Susan's breath away.

"I'm off to run errands," she announced. "You two have fun and don't get into any trouble."

She bent to kiss Lucinda's forehead. When she straightened, she was inches from Susan. She looked Susan in the eyes, and Susan felt her insides melt. Dorinda moved closer. Susan felt like her feet were glued to the floor. She couldn't move. And then she felt them. Dorinda's lips on hers. It was brief, but the shocks it sent through her system were very real.

"Okay," Dorinda said as if nothing had happened. "I'll see you two in a while."

Susan dropped into the chair by Lucinda's bed. She felt Lucinda looking at her. She looked over.

"I thought you loved this Mel person," Lucinda said.

"I do. I might. I mean, I'm falling in love with her. I think."

"Well, then what are you doin' kissin' on Dorinda?"

"She kissed me. I didn't kiss her."

"I think you kissed her back. But that's just the way it looked to me."

Susan sat back hard.

"Ugh."

"Look," Lucinda said. "It's none of my business, but didn't you leave her once? And didn't you have a good reason to do that?"

"Yeah. But she's changed. She's not the same person."

"Or she's putting on a great show for you."

"Oh, Lucinda, what am I going to do?"

"How do you feel about Mel?"

"I'm crazy about her," Susan said.

"And how do you feel about Dorinda?"

"I don't know. And it makes me feel horrible because Mel is so jealous of her, and I told her there's nothing to be jealous about and then this happens…"

"I'm sorry, sweetie," Lucinda said. "I wish I had an answer for you. Maybe date them both? Just to see which one truly owns your heart?"

"That would crush Mel."

"But if she really cares about you, she'd have to go along with it, right? But you've got to be honest with her. No sneaking around behind her back. Tell her you're dating them both."

"It all just sounds like easier said than done," Susan said.

"I don't think so. Or tell one of them to take a hike."

"I don't want to do that."

"Then date them both for a while. Besides, you don't know how long Dorinda will be here anyway."

The full meaning of that statement caught Susan off guard. She didn't know how to respond.

"Only six months anyway," Lucinda went on.

Susan took Lucinda's hand.

"Let's talk about something else."

Lucinda squeezed her hand.

"Let's talk about pain pills. Oh, my God."

"Okay. Okay. Your usual dose or a bolus?"

"A bolus. Hurry. Please."

Susan got a pill and placed it under Lucinda's tongue. She held her hand until she felt it relax in her own. She sat with her until Dorinda came in.

"Hey," she said.

"Hey," Susan said.

"How's Lucinda?"

"Sleeping. She had some pain so I gave her a bolus."

"Ah. Good. Thanks."

"I hate to see her like that," Susan said. She was fighting tears.

Dorinda took her in her arms.

"It's okay. It's not easy. I know this."

She stroked Susan's hair, and Susan felt her whole body go warm at her touch. Dorinda stepped back.

"Do you think we should talk about it?"

"About what?" Susan assumed she meant Lucinda, but didn't know that she wanted to talk about her feelings. She'd just start crying again.

"The kiss," Dorinda said.

"Yeah. About that…"

"Look. I really like you. And I know I was a total douchebag when we were together. But I've changed. Surely you can see that? And I want to date you."

"But I'm with Mel."

"Dump her."

"I don't want to," Susan said. "Maybe I could date you both."

"I don't like to share," Dorinda said.

"Neither will she. But I think it's only fair. That way I can make an honest decision of who I want to be with."

"That's not totally fair, though," said Dorinda. "She has more time to spend with you."

"We can make it work."

"Fine. Tell me you'll go out with me Saturday night."

"Okay. I'll talk to Mel tonight."

"Great. Now, I'll see you Friday?"

"I'll be here."

Dorinda kissed Susan again and Susan was lightheaded as she let herself out of the house. She drove to Mel's house where they'd agreed to meet and found Mel on the couch drinking a beer.

"Hey, babe." Mel got up and kissed Susan on the cheek. "How'd it go today?"

"Mel, we need to talk."

Mel felt sick. These were the words she'd been dreading hearing. She was about to lose the one woman she really thought was in it for the long haul.

"Yeah?" she said. "What about?"

"Dorinda and I had a talk today."

"I hardly see why that would be any concern to me."

"Mel, please," Susan said. "This is hard enough. Please let me say this."

"Go ahead." Mel leaned back against the sofa in defeat. She knew what was coming and she just wanted to get it over with.

"I've decided I'd like to start seeing Dorinda again—"

"Just like that, huh? Never mind you just told me you're crazy about me just the other night."

"Would you let me finish, for Christ's sake?"

"What else do you need to say?" Mel shot back.

"I want to continue seeing you, too."

"What?" Mel was stunned. So she wanted to keep one foot grounded in security while she tested the waters with the other? How fair was that to Mel? "I don't know about that."

"Why not? Mel, I'm crazy about you."

"Then go tell Dorinda to fuck herself."

"It's not that simple."

"I think it is," Mel said.

"I can't choose between the two of you," Susan said. "Not yet."

"You can't make up your mind between someone who hurt you physically and emotionally versus someone who's only treated you with kindness and respect? That seems odd."

"She's changed."

"Sure she has."

"Mel, please. I don't want to lose you."

"I think you already have."

Mel felt the urge to cry, something she hadn't done in so long she couldn't remember the last time she had. She wasn't going to, though. If Susan didn't want her, she wasn't worth a tear.

"I'm serious, Mel," Susan said. "I want to date you both. I want to make up my mind over who I want to be with."

"You need to leave."

"No. Not until this is resolved."

"This is my house, and I'm asking you nicely to leave. Now, please do so."

"When will I see you again?" Susan said.

"I don't know."

"Mel, please—"

"Get out of here, Susan. I've tried being polite, but I'm not feeling it. Get the fuck out of here, okay?"

She saw the tears flow down Susan's cheeks and fought to remain cold. She wanted to take Susan in her arms and hold her until the tears stopped. But Susan had made her choice. She had to go while Mel thought things over.

With Susan gone, Mel popped open another beer and sat on the couch. She texted Joey to see if she could come over. Joey said sure and she was out the door.

Mel knocked on the door and Samantha opened it.

"Where's Susan?" she said.

"She's not here," Mel said.

"Okay. Is everything all right?"

"No. Nothing is," Mel said.

"Oh. Well, Joey's in the playroom with DJ. I'll get you a beer."

Mel found Joey building blocks with DJ. She looked up when Mel walked in.

"Hey," she said. "Where's Susan?"

"I neither know nor care."

"Uh-oh. What happened?"

"She wants to start dating Dorinda, Joey."

"Oh, man. I'm sorry, Mel." She patted DJ on his head and stood. "You want to talk about it?"

"Yeah. Yeah, I do. I'm so confused."

Samantha was back with a beer for each of them and a glass of wine for herself.

"Would you two rather be alone?" she said.

"No," Mel said. "I'd love to have you here. Maybe you can make some sense out of everything."

"What's going on?" Samantha said.

Mel wondered how she could always sound so calm and pleasant. She wondered if she managed to maintain that composure working with the kids all day.

"Susan wants to start seeing Dorinda," Mel said. "But she also wants to keep seeing me."

"Oh, wow," Samantha said. "That is a predicament. How do you feel?"

"I'm pissed," Mel said, then remembered DJ. "I mean I'm mad. I'm really mad. How dare she? One minute she's telling me she's crazy about me and the next she wants to mess around with someone else. And she still says she's crazy about me. I don't get it."

"Clearly, she's confused," Samantha said.

"Confused, sure," Joey said. "But she's got a lot of damned nerve wanting to date both of them."

"Watch the language, hon," Samantha said. "And you're right. But the poor girl is flustered. Here is this wonderful woman who's crazy about her and they go out for a while and everything is perfect. Then along comes the evil ex, who's not so evil anymore and who wants to woo her back. She's in a tough spot, Mel."

"Screw her," Mel said. "Having two women to mess around with. How is that tough?"

"You're not listening," Samantha said gently.

"I am. I hear you. But what about me? What about what's fair to me?"

"Yeah," Joey said. "What about Mel's wants and needs? And pride, for that matter?"

"Well, you need to decide what's more important to you, Mel. Susan or your pride?"

"I've given my heart to her."

"Does she know that?" Samantha said.

"Isn't it obvious?" Joey said.

Samantha laughed softly.

"Oh, my poor bois. You assume things are obvious to your femmes that aren't. Unless you tell her, she's going to be insecure."

"But I told her I was crazy about her," Mel said.

"Did you? Out loud and everything?"

"Yes."

"See?" Joey said. "She knew how Mel felt and still she's playing these games. Who agrees to start dating someone else when they already have a girlfriend? A hell of a girlfriend, at that?"

"Look, Mel," Samantha said. "You need to consider this. She's not leaving you for Dorinda. She's giving you an equal shot. She wants to keep seeing you, as well. You need to take advantage of that and really turn on the charm."

Mel exhaled loudly.

"I don't know. I don't like the idea of sharing."

"I might not know this Dorinda woman," Samantha said. "But I know that outside of my Joey, there's only one woman who can truly melt a woman's heart. You just need to work your mojo."

"I don't feel like she's deserving of my mojo."

"She is if you truly love her. Now, come on. Dinner's ready."

"I'm not hungry," Mel said.

"You need to eat," Samantha said. "Joey, will you put DJ in his high chair please?"

They sat to dinner and Mel ate most of the casserole on her plate. She had a great time feeding DJ and soon felt better about life. Not great, but better. Maybe Samantha was right. Maybe she just needed to really turn on the charm and she'd win her over.

Mel said good night and drove off in search of Susan. She drove to her house, but she wasn't there. Begrudgingly, she drove by Dorinda's house. No sign of her car there, either. She wondered where she could be. Surely she wouldn't be at Kindred Spirits. Not on her day off. But she drove by and her car was in the parking lot. She pulled in and went inside.

She saw Susan at the bar with her lemon drop in front of her. She crossed the quiet bar to sit next to her.

"I'd have thought a hot woman like you would be with one of the women she was dating. I didn't expect to find you alone at the bar."

She signaled to the bartender for a half pitcher.

"Very funny," Susan said. "I hurt someone I care very much about today. I just wanted to be alone."

"You know, you don't have to hurt me," Mel said.

"I can't rehash it, Mel."

"I get it. Do you want to come home now? It's been a long day."

"I think I need to be alone."

"Okay. I'll take off. Maybe tomorrow or sometime we can discuss the ground rules."

"The ground rules?" Susan said.

"Well, yeah. Like sex, for example. Will you be just dating us or will you be sleeping with us, as well? And what about us? Are we only allowed to date you or can we date other people, too? There's lots to be worked out."

"Oh, man. I hadn't considered any of that."

Mel wanted to scream at her. To say of course she hadn't. She just thought she could have it both ways and that would be the end of it. Well, Mel planned to charm her pants off her, even as she made her feel like a fool. It was a talent few had, but she was going to use her talents to their fullest.

"Yeah. I've gotten used to sharing my bed with you." She lowered her voice. "My toys with you. I need to know what's allowed and what's not."

"I don't know. I suppose I'll have to think about it."

"Because if you really want to sleep with her, then how can I believe you still have feelings for me?"

"I'm so confused, Mel. I don't know what I want."

"So figure it out and let me know, okay?"

"I know I want to keep seeing you."

Mel wished she hadn't ordered her beer now. All she wanted to do was get out of there. She'd said her piece. She didn't need to hear Susan try to make it like she was the poor, pitiful one.

"Okay, but just dating. No sex, right?"

"Mel, I can't imagine not having sex with you."

"Well, you can't sleep with either of us, I don't think. I think that's asking too much for us to sit back and let another woman have her way with you. I think I draw the line at sleeping with us."

"I guess that makes sense. But it's going to be so hard."

"It's not going to be easy on Dorinda and me either, Susan. None of this is."

"I get that. I just want to make sure I'm with the right woman."

"And I think you already were, but if this is what you need to do to prove it to yourself, then so be it. I'll see you tomorrow after work," she said and left the bar.

CHAPTER TWENTY

"So what did you do after you left last night?" Joey asked Mel as they got their tool belts on and got ready for work.

"I went looking for Susan. Found her at the bar."

"Yeah? And? How'd it go?"

"I simply pointed out to her that there needed to be some ground rules," Mel said. "She tried to make it out like she was the one suffering because she couldn't choose, but I didn't let her get to me."

"Did you hold your temper?"

"I was sweet as sugar," Mel said. "One thing I told her is that she can't have sex with either of us."

"Ouch. You gonna be able to live by that?"

"I'm going to have to. The way I look at it, she won't last. She'll cave and choose me quicker if she's not getting any from either of us."

"And do you trust her?" Joey said. "Or more importantly, do you trust Dorinda not to have sex with her?"

"I have to, Joey. I have to trust Susan. Dorinda? I don't trust as far as I can throw, but I need to trust Susan. Now more than ever."

They got through the workday and Mel went home and showered. She put on her khaki shorts and Kelly green shirt. The one she knew showed off her eyes. She wasn't going down without a fight. That was for sure.

She walked into Kindred Spirits at five o'clock. The place was busier than usual, but Mel found a booth and sat to wait for Susan. She was there in just a few minutes.

"Wow, Mel. You look hot."

"Thanks. So do you."

"Can I get you the usual?"

"Please."

"What are we doing after I get off?" Susan said.

"We're going to The Shack and then for a walk along the beach. It should be the perfect night for it."

"Oh, wow. That sounds romantic. I can't wait."

She brought Mel her beer.

"I wish I could sit down and talk to you," she said. "But I'm awfully busy."

"That's okay," Mel said. "I'll have you to myself in a couple of hours."

"Yeah, you will." She smiled.

Mel's heart skipped a beat. Damn, it was going to be hard to spend time with Susan and not bed her. She was so fine and Mel wanted her in the worst sort of way. Probably because she couldn't have her. Wasn't that always the case? You always wanted what you couldn't have. Just look at Joey and Samantha. But Joey had eventually won out, and Mel hoped she would, too.

She was still working on her third half pitcher when Susan got off work. Susan grabbed a lemon drop and joined her.

"So, you had a good day, then, with all these people, huh?" Mel said.

"I did. I made bank today. And everyone was in such a great mood. It was a lot of fun."

"That's awesome."

"Yep."

They sat in awkward silence.

"So, I'm guessing I won't see you tomorrow night, right?" Mel finally said.

"No. I won't come over after Dorinda's. There's no point, right?"

"I suppose not. I might come down here after work, though."

"That would be great."

"Okay, good. Oh, and what about Saturday?" Mel said.

"Dorinda asked me out for that night."

"Ah. Okay. I guess."

"I'm sorry. I guess. I mean… Oh. I don't know."

"It's all good," Mel said. She didn't feel it, but knew she had to keep up the laid-back front.

"I'd like to see you sometime Saturday. Surf lessons, maybe? We were supposed to go to that super-sized toy store I was telling you about, but I don't think that would be very appropriate now."

Susan pouted.

"You sure?"

"Positive. We'll surf."

"Okay. I'll come over as soon as I wake up."

"Great."

They finished their drinks and Susan followed Mel to The Shack. The place was fairly crowded and the jukebox was blaring. They took the last empty table. Mel looked around the place and recognized Tiffany over by the jukebox with a group of friends. She walked over.

"Hey, Mel."

Mel stood and hugged her. The feel of those young, firm breasts caused her boxers to dampen. She turned to face Susan.

"Susan, you remember Tiffany, don't you?"

"Of course." Susan held out her hand. Tiffany took it, and Mel's mind flashed briefly to how much fun it would be to have both women in her bed. She shook the image from her mind and sat down.

"It was good to see you again," she said.

"Always good to see you, Mel." She walked off.

After they'd ordered, Mel decided it was time to talk rules again.

"So, what about dating other people?" she said.

"What do you mean?"

"Well, you're dating someone else, so can I?"

"Mel, if you're thinking of dating Tiffany, I can't help but point out how young she is again."

"Not her necessarily," Mel said. "Just in general. If you can date other people, so can I, right?"

"I guess…but no sex."

"Ah, yes. The no sex clause."

"If I can't have sex with either of you, then you can't have sex with anyone either," Susan said.

"Really, then what's the point of dating anyone?" Mel laughed.

Susan apparently didn't see the humor.

"I am perfectly capable of dating without sex."

"Good for you."

They ate their dinners, then Mel took Susan's hand as they walked along to beach. The fog had stayed away that evening and the night was still warm. The surf broke next to them peacefully. It was almost like romantic music made just for lovers. But Mel couldn't think that way. Susan was no longer her lover. They were simply dating.

When they got to the pier, Susan turned and ran her hands over Mel's chest.

"What's up?" Mel said. Her whole body was alive at Susan's touch. Every nerve ending was on alert.

"Nothing. I don't think it's anywhere in the rules that we can't kiss."

"No. I don't think it is."

"So." Susan slinked her arms around Mel's neck. "Why don't you kiss me, Mel?"

Mel looked at her, saw the moonlight in her eyes and the need in them as well. She lowered her mouth and brushed Susan's lips with her own.

"I meant a real kiss," Susan said. She pulled Mel to her and kissed her hard. She opened her mouth and urged Mel to enter.

Mel gave in with a groan. She needed Susan so desperately. She wanted her with every ounce of her being. She pulled away.

"What?" Susan said.

"You're not doing anything to help me with that no sex business."

"I know. I want you so bad. I'm so wet right now." She took Mel's hand and went to put it between her legs.

"No way." Mel pulled away. "You're not going to do that to me. No sex means no sex. Now, let's get you home."

Susan thought it was awfully chivalrous for Mel to follow her home. She walked down to Mel's car and invited her in.

"No," Mel said. "I'd better get going. I'll see you tomorrow at the bar."

"Okay." Susan leaned in for a kiss, which Mel returned, slightly. "Aw, Mel. Come on."

"No way," Mel said. "You're not going to get me all amped and then leave me like that. Now get inside and I'll take off."

"Fine." Susan was disappointed. She liked kissing Mel. She was the best kisser she'd ever met. She didn't want to go in alone, but she did. She waved to Mel from the porch, then entered her house and closed her door behind her.

She was a horny wreck. Mel always did that to her. She didn't know if she'd be able to keep up the no sex part of the deal. Surely, Mel would acquiesce, right? Surely, she wanted Susan as desperately as Susan wanted her?

Susan stripped off her clothes and put them in the laundry hamper. She walked, naked, to her bedroom, aware of every breath of air touching every inch of her body. Her body was one giant erogenous zone and she needed someone to take care of it. But there was no one. Not for now, anyway.

She lay on her bed, bent her knees, and let her legs fall open. She moved her hand down between her legs. She was so wet thanks to Mel. She closed her eyes and imagined it was Mel's fingers playing over her slick clit. She imagined it was Mel stroking her deep inside.

Her breathing got heavy, and she wished she had one of Mel's toys to play with. She wished Mel was watching her pussy swallow her monster dong. Her fingers weren't doing the trick.

She got out of bed and grabbed the toy she'd used on Mel. She turned it on and slipped it inside.

"Oh, fuck," she said. The toy felt so good moving around inside her. She turned on the clit stimulator and that was all it took. Her world split into a million pieces as she climaxed over and over again.

She was panting when she was through coming. She'd needed that. She lay back, exhausted, closed her eyes, and fell into a deep sleep.

She woke up the next day at noon and hurried to shower and shave and get dressed for work. She showed up right at one, with no time to spare.

"You okay?" the bartender asked.

"Yeah, I just thought I was going to be late."

"Oh, well, you just made it."

"Yeah, I know."

The place was jumping, and Susan waitressed all day. Everyone was in a good mood. Must have been because it was Friday, she reasoned. She'd only been working a couple of hours when Joey and Mel walked in.

"Hey, you two," Susan said. "You're awfully early."

"Brenda let us go early," Joey said.

"That was nice of her."

"No doubt. Can we get a pitcher?" Mel said.

"Coming right up."

When Susan came back with the pitcher, Mel couldn't help but notice a radiance about her.

"You look really good today," she said.

"Thanks. It's a good day. Nice and busy. Speaking of which, I'd better get back to it."

"Right on. Don't work too hard."

Susan smiled at her before she walked off.

She came back as often as she could to check on them. Mel looked so good that afternoon, and Susan was drawn to her.

"I don't want to work," she said. "I want to sit here with you two."

"Well, you're welcome to join us once you're off work," Joey said.

"I can't," Susan said with a pout. "I need to take care of Lucinda."

"So, what happens if you're a little late?"

"I'm not that way."

"Fair enough," Joey said.

Susan looked over at Mel who was focused on her beer glass. She clearly didn't care if Susan joined them or not, so she felt better when seven o'clock rolled around and she could leave.

She walked over to their booth.

"I'm gonna get going," she said.

"We were just leaving, too," Joey said.

"Let me walk you out to your car," Mel said.

"Sure. That would be great."

She took Mel's hand and went out the back door. They got to her car and she turned to find Mel inches from her.

"Good luck with Lucinda tonight," Mel said.

"Thanks," Susan said. Though, as much as she hated to admit it, her mind was more on Dorinda than Lucinda.

"I hope she has a pain free night."

"Me, too. I hate to see her in pain."

"Well, I guess I should let you go now," Mel said.

"Yeah, I should get going."

Mel leaned in and kissed her. It was soft and tender and Susan felt it to her core.

"I'll see you tomorrow?"

"Yeah."

"Come over when you wake up. I'll be waiting."

"Okay. I'll see you then."

She was trembling when she got in her car. She took a deep breath before she started it. She was crazy about Mel. She made her feel things no one had made her feel before. But Dorinda had changed and deserved a shot. She drove to Lucinda's house with butterflies in her stomach. She wanted to kiss Dorinda again now that she was here. But her first priority was to Lucinda, she reminded herself. That was the reason this whole thing had started.

Susan let herself in and crossed the room to Lucinda. She was lying there staring into space.

"Susan? Is that you?" Dorinda called.

"Yeah. It's me." She couldn't stop staring at Lucinda. She watched her chest. It rose and fell so she knew she was breathing. But she looked completely out of it.

Dorinda walked up behind Susan and wrapped her arms around her.

"How you doin'?" she said.

"More importantly, how's Lucinda?" Susan said. "She looks out of it."

"Oh, she was in a lot of pain a little while ago. I gave her a pill. I figure she's stoned out of her gourd now and will be fast asleep soon."

"Dorinda, you're careful not to overmedicate her, aren't you?"

"Of course." Dorinda let go of Susan. "What kind of question is that?"

"I don't know. I guess I just hate to see her like this."

"Would you rather see her in pain?"

"No. But I'd rather have her lucid. So I can interact with her."

"Well, I'm lucid." Dorinda grinned.

"Yeah, but you're not going to die in the next six months," Susan whispered.

"You never know."

"Don't be morbid."

Dorinda put her arms around Susan's waist and pulled her close.

"So, we have nothing to do now until she comes to. What do you say we make good use of our time?"

"That sounds like a good idea."

"Why don't we go down the hall to my room? I'd love to have my way with you."

"No sex," Susan said rather abruptly.

"Huh?"

"That's one of the rules. I can date you both but can't have sex with either of you."

"That's hardly fair," Dorinda said. "We can have sex and just tell her we're not."

Susan pulled away.

"No," she said. "She took it really well overall, this business of sharing. All she asked was that I not have sex with either of you."

"You really expect me to believe she's not doing you?"

"*Doing* me?" Susan said. "We are not having sex, if that's what you're so crudely implying. There have to be rules. That's one of them."

"What are the others?" Dorinda plopped herself down on the love seat.

"The only other big one is that since I'm seeing other people, you can see other people, too."

"Well, there you go. I don't want to see other people. I only want to see you. Clearly, if she wants to see others it should make you think twice about her."

"Please, Dorinda. When I'm with her, we don't talk about you. When I'm with you, I'd rather not talk about her."

"Fair enough." She patted the love seat next to her. "Come on. Sit."

Susan sat next to Dorinda. She smelled clean and spicy. It was a good smell.

"Are you wearing a new perfume?" Susan said.

"I am."

"It smells good."

"Thanks. Are you wearing perfume?" Dorinda said.

"No. I forgot to put it on this morning."

Dorinda nuzzled Susan's neck.

"You still smell good," she said.

She kissed up her neck to her cheek and finally stopped with her lips just millimeters from Susan's.

Susan felt the butterflies fluttering fast and hard in her stomach. Her heart was thumping. She wanted Dorinda to kiss her and she wanted it bad. Dorinda finally lowered her lips and claimed Susan's in a tender kiss. Susan wanted more. Dorinda seemed happy to provide it.

Dorinda pressed hard into Susan's lips then and ran her tongue over them. Susan opened her mouth to let Dorinda in. Their tongues frolicked together, and Susan felt herself grow wet.

They kissed like that forever. Dorinda eased Susan back on the love seat and climbed on top of her. Their kissing intensified. Soon, Susan thought she would explode. She tried to push Dorinda off of her.

"Huh?" Dorinda said, as if coming out of a trance. "What gives?"

"You should get off of me," Susan said. "Please."

"No way, Sus. I'm enjoying myself too much."

Dorinda kissed Susan so hard on the mouth, Susan was afraid she'd bruised her lips. She squirmed under her, trying to get out. She was hot and bothered and needed to stop before she broke her promise to Mel.

Dorinda slid her hand between their bodies and cupped Susan's breast. She let out a moan in Susan's mouth. Susan found strength somewhere and was able to push Dorinda off.

"What? Come on. We're just getting warmed up."

"I think I should go," Susan said and stood.

"Aw, come on. I'm sorry I got carried away. It's just that you're so beautiful and I've missed you so much."

"I get it, Dorinda. You are driving me crazy. So crazy I was practically ready to break the rules. But I can't. I owe that to both of you."

"I still don't get it. Sex is part of dating."

"How do you feel about me sleeping with her?"

"That thought makes me want to hurt something," Dorinda said.

"See?"

"So don't sleep with her. Sleep with me."

"That's cheating and I won't do that. Please, don't ask me to again."

"Okay. I won't."

"Thanks. Now I think it's time for me to leave."

"Can I walk you to your car?"

"No. You stay here in case Lucinda needs you. I'll see you tomorrow night."

Susan didn't know what to feel as she drove home. She wondered if she had what it took to date two women. But she was bound and determined to try. She needed to see who she truly wanted to be with, and this was the only way to find out.

CHAPTER TWENTY-ONE

Mel woke early Saturday morning. She was excited about her day with Susan. She planned to have her surfing on her knees by day's end. She also planned to leave her absolutely exhausted for her date with Dorinda that night. Mel smiled to herself over her coffee. Maybe she wasn't playing completely fair, but she wanted Susan for her own. End of story.

At ten thirty there was a knock on her door.

"Come in," Mel called.

Susan came walking in wearing her swimsuit and wrap. She looked stunning, even though she looked like she'd just woken up. How could someone look that good when they just woke up?

Mel stood and kissed her on the cheek.

"Want some coffee?" she said.

"Please."

"What are you doing up so early?" Mel said.

"I don't know. I woke up and decided I may as well head over rather than try to sleep some more. I want to learn to surf on my knees today. You promised."

"I did. And I will teach you. It's gonna be a little trickier than just lying down."

"I figured."

"So, plan to wipe out quite a bit today."

"Oh, ye of little faith." Susan laughed. "I plan to nail it the first time."

Mel laughed with her. It was nice and easy to be with Susan. It was hard to remember she wasn't hers anymore.

"We'll see," she said.

They each had another cup of coffee.

"How was your night?" Mel said.

"Huh? What? Why?"

"Huh? You know. How was Lucinda?"

"Oh, she was out of it. She'd had a bad day and Dorinda had just given her her meds when I got there. She was basically stoned."

"Ah." Mel wanted to ask how things had gone with Dorinda, but she knew, as curious as she was, that she really didn't want to know.

"Okay." She gathered their coffee cups and put them in the sink. "You ready?"

"Heck yeah."

"I love how excited you are."

"I want to learn to surf. You're the best teacher, I'm sure."

"I don't know," Mel said. "Joey might be the best, but I'd rather teach you."

"I'd rather you teach me, too."

They parked at The Shack and Mel carried the board as they crossed the beach to the water. There was a lone figure out bobbing in it.

"Hey," Mel said. "I wonder if that's Joey."

"Did you see her truck?"

"I wasn't looking for it," Mel said. She didn't pay any attention to anything but Susan when she was with her. "Let's paddle out and see if it's her."

They got in the water and Mel helped Susan lie on the board. They made their way out to the figure, and sure enough, it was Joey.

"How are the waves today?" Mel asked.

"So far, so good."

"Right on. We're going to teach Susan how to surf on her knees today."

"Excellent. She'll be needing her own surfboard soon."

They all laughed.

"I hope so," Susan said. "So far, I love surfing."

"Don't we all?" Joey said. "Hey, it was good seeing you two, but I've got to get home. DJ has a birthday party I need to take him to. You two have fun."

They watched as she paddled in to shore.

"Okay," Mel said. "First thing we need to do is get you on your knees."

"Sounds dirty," Susan said.

"Funny," Mel said. "Now, come on. I'll hold the board. You just pull your knees under yourself."

Susan struggled to maintain her balance and fell over into the water. She surfaced and spit out water.

"This is not as easy as it seems. Either that or I'm really lame."

"That's why you're not standing yet. It's not that easy. Now, come on. Let's try again."

Mel held the board and Susan climbed on it.

"Now, easy, easy. One knee at a time under you."

Susan was shaking as she tried to maintain her balance. Mel held as tightly as she could, but once again, Susan fell over.

They repeated this routine five more times until Susan managed to get her knees under herself and maintain her balance.

"Now," Mel said. "You're going to have to lean forward and put your hands in to paddle. Can you do that? Just practice. I'm holding the board."

Susan leaned forward and dipped her hands in the water. When Mel felt confident she could do it and stay on the board, she steered them deeper to where the waves were forming.

"Are you ready?" Mel said.

"As ready as I'll ever be."

"Okay. Here comes a wave." Mel gently pushed the board and yelled, "Paddle."

Susan was off. She was paddling and she looked like she was going to catch the wave when suddenly, she seemed to lose all hope and wiped out. She surfaced and Mel swam over to her.

"Are you okay?"

"Yep. That was my first try. I'll get this down."

Mel knew there would be more wipeouts before there was a perfect ride, but she didn't mind. It worked well for her plans to wear Susan out for the night.

Susan was wearing out after about an hour.

"You want to call it quits?" Mel said.

"Heck no. I've got this. Trust me."

"Okay. But we can always take a break."

"But I'm so close, Mel. So very close. I can feel it."

"Okay. We'll give it another shot."

They assumed their positions and along came a perfect wave. Mel gave Susan a slight shove.

"Paddle," she called after her.

Susan paddled and Mel watched as Susan gripped the sides of the board and rode the wave in like a pro. She dragged the board back out to where Mel was waiting. She wrapped her arms around Mel's neck.

"That was so much fun!" she said.

"I'm glad." Mel gave her a salty kiss. "That was an excellent ride."

"Oh, my God. I want to do it again."

"Okay then. Let's do it again."

Susan wiped out a few more times, but she had more successful rides than wipeouts, so they considered it a successful day.

It was one thirty when Mel finally claimed starvation.

"You ready to call it a day?"

"Oh, man. Do I have to?"

"I'm starving. You've got to be hungry, too, with all the work you're doing."

"Wow. I guess I am. I hadn't even noticed."

"So, let's go grab some food."

A hard day on the board and a big lunch should really wipe her out, Mel thought. She's going to be too tired to be very good company tonight. The thought made her smile.

"What?" Susan said.

"What what?"

"You've got a shit-eating grin on your face. What's that about?"

"Nothing. I've just really enjoyed today."

"Yeah. It's been fun."

They got to The Shack and each ordered a double cheeseburger.

"Seriously? How do you keep your figure?" Mel said.

"I'm lucky. I have a great metabolism."

"Well, I'm glad you can eat what you like. That's great."

They ate and laughed about their day.

"You really are a natural at surfing, babe," Mel said.

"Thanks. It's a lot of fun. When do you think I'll be able to stand?"

"A couple more lessons, that's for sure."

"Okay. If you insist."

"I do."

They finished lunch and walked back out to Mel's van. Mel pressed Susan against it and kissed her.

"You taste like cheeseburger and salt," she said.

"And you taste like beer."

"Sorry."

"It's okay," Susan said. "I like it. You taste like you."

"So, what now?" Mel said as she nuzzled Susan's neck.

Susan gently pushed her away.

"I think it's time for me to get ready for my night."

"Oh, yeah. That's right." Mel acted like she'd forgotten. "Okay. Come on. I'll get you home."

❖

Susan was sad to say good-bye to Mel. She'd had so much fun with her. But she had to believe she was going to have fun with Dorinda that night. Except she was so tired. She wished she had time for a nap. Maybe a quick nap in the tub, she thought.

She ran a bath and sank into it. It felt so good. She was surprised how sore her muscles were from holding onto the surfboard. She relaxed in the warm water, and the next thing she knew, her phone was buzzing.

She checked and it was Dorinda calling. It was time for their date. Shit!

"Hello?"

"Hey, you. I've been knocking on the door and there's no answer. Are you home?"

"Yeah. Sorry. I fell asleep in the tub. Let me get dressed and I'll be right out."

"Can I come in?"

"Sure. Give me a sec."

She grabbed a robe and put it on then went to the front door.

"You didn't have to put a robe on," Dorinda said. "Not on my account."

"Very funny. Wait here and I'll go get dressed."

She slipped into a skirt and blouse and walked out to meet Dorinda.

"You look great," Dorinda said. She pulled Susan to her and kissed her lips. "I almost don't want to go out. Staying in sounds like a lot more fun."

"Come on. Let's get out of here before you do something you'll regret."

"I won't regret anything, baby. Trust me on that."

"Seriously. Let's go."

Dorinda released her grip on Susan and pouted as they left the house.

"So, what do you have planned for our night out?" Susan said.

"Dinner and a movie."

"Sounds romantic," Susan said, though she was still stuffed from lunch. She'd do her best to eat something light for dinner.

"I hope so," Dorinda said. "And then back to your place for a nightcap."

"Dorinda. You know the rules."

"I also know she won't know if we break them."

"But I will."

"We'll see how the night goes," Dorinda said.

Susan was pissed. She felt like Dorinda wasn't going to give up, and that really set her off. Rules were rules. And if she wasn't going to sleep with Mel, she certainly wasn't going to sleep with Dorinda. She bit her tongue though, as she got in Dorinda's car.

"So, what's for dinner?"

"A steak. I know how you love them. There's a steak house here in town. Have you tried it?"

"I've been a couple of times. Their food is really good. Wait a minute. What happened to being a vegetarian?"

"Oh, I'm so over that. I've been craving a thick steak."

"Well, you won't be disappointed."

Dinner went well, but Susan could barely eat any of her steak. She was simply too full from lunch with Mel.

"What's wrong? Don't you feel well?" Dorinda said. "I've seen you eat a half a cow before."

"I just had a big lunch," Susan said.

"I don't believe you. I think you're nervous about later on tonight." Dorinda took Susan's hands and looked her in the eye. "Don't worry. It's just like riding a bike."

Susan gently took her hands back. She didn't say a word.

Dorinda drove Susan to a movie theater in Somerset for a romantic comedy. Susan tried to relax and enjoy the movie, but all she was aware of was Dorinda's arm wrapped possessively around her.

They left the theater, and Susan's stomach was in knots. She was hoping she wouldn't have to fight with Dorinda. It had been such a pleasant night. She hoped Dorinda would just leave it at that. But when they got to Susan's house, Dorinda turned the car off.

"Thanks for a great night," Susan said.

Dorinda had one hand lazily draped over the steering wheel and her other arm on Susan's seat. She leaned forward, and Susan sat still, ready for her good night kiss. Instead, Dorinda pushed her against her door and kissed her hard. She ran a hand over Susan's breast and clamped down on it, hard.

"Ouch," Susan said. "You're hurting me."

"Hurts so good, don't it, baby?"

"No," Susan said. "Let me up."

Dorinda sat up. She opened her door and went around the car to open Susan's.

Susan didn't like her being out of her car. She wanted a kiss good night and to be left alone.

"Thanks," Susan said as she got out of the car.

Dorinda took Susan's hand and led her to the front door. She kissed her again. It was a powerful, almost painful kiss.

Susan did not have her usual response to a kiss. She was afraid, not aroused. And that wasn't a good thing. She fought to push Dorinda off, but Dorinda was strong. She finally bit her lip.

"What the fuck?" Dorinda said.

"I wanted you to stop."

"No, you didn't. Now open the door and let's get down to business."

"No," Susan said. "No sex. What part of that do you not understand?"

"Come on. You know you want it."

"No." Susan wondered how she would get out of the situation she was in. She needed to get rid of Dorinda, who clearly wasn't taking no for an answer.

"Look," Dorinda said. "The only reason she wants that as a rule is because she knows she's not as good as I am. She's intimidated. She doesn't want you to remember what real sex is like."

"That's not true," Susan said. "The rules are there for everyone. No sex means no sex. Not with you, not with her, not with anyone. Now, if you'll excuse me—"

"No I won't. I'm coming in. You're not going to stop me."

"What are you doing, Dorinda? Do you really think this behavior is going to charm me into taking you back?"

"Please, Susan." Her tone softened. "Please, I need you."

Her hand was on Susan's breast again.

Susan brushed it away.

"Stop it!"

Dorinda seemed to come to her senses.

"I'm sorry. I'm so sorry. It's just that I need you so bad, Sus."

"Well, you're not going to have me. Now go to your car. You can see me get inside safely from there."

"I'll wait here."

"No, you won't. You need to leave. Now."

"Okay, okay. I'm leaving. I'll see you Monday?"

"I'll be there," Susan said.

"Maybe I'll stop by Kindred Spirits to see you tomorrow."

"That would be fine."

Susan watched until Dorinda was in her car before letting herself into her house. She turned on the light and sat at the kitchen table. What was Dorinda's problem? Why wouldn't she take no for an answer? Susan buried her face in her hands and cried. She didn't want to battle like this. She wanted to be able to have a nice, easygoing time with each of them. Dorinda didn't want to play fair and that wasn't right. She was also mean-spirited when she didn't get her way. It brought back memories of when they were together. It had her questioning whether or not she really wanted to be involved with her.

CHAPTER TWENTY-TWO

M el woke up alone in her bed, and at once wondered how Susan's date with Dorinda had gone. She hoped it hadn't gone well at all, of course. She wanted this business with Dorinda over sooner rather than later. She really didn't think Susan would go back to Dorinda, but she had to admit, there was a little niggle of fear inside her that it just might happen.

She got out of bed and poured herself a cup of coffee. She texted Joey to see what her plans were for the day. She was taking DJ to the playground, did Mel want to come along? Mel said sure. She'd meet them there in an hour.

She took a shower and put on some nice shorts and shirt, since she planned on going by the bar to see Susan after playing with DJ. It wouldn't matter if she got a little dirty. She was sure Susan would understand. Susan thought DJ was adorable. She wouldn't mind a little sand on Mel if it meant she'd been playing with DJ.

Joey and DJ were already playing when Mel showed up.

"How you doin' today?" Joey said.

"Okay."

"Just okay? What's up with that?"

"Susan had a date with Dorinda last night."

"Ah. How did it go?" Joey said.

"I don't know. I won't know until I see her at the bar."

"And you're worried?"

"I don't know."

"Look," Joey said. "I've seen her with you. She's crazy about you. I don't know what she sees in a crazy ex like Dorinda, but I know she's going to choose you. She'd be a fool not to."

"You're my best friend. You're supposed to say that."

"It's the truth, Mel. Trust me on this."

Mel played with DJ, chasing him around the play structure and climbing through tunnels. She lifted him up so he could go down the slide. They played hard and finally DJ started getting whiny.

"I'd better get him home for a nap," Joey said.

"Yeah. I'm going to head over to the bar."

"Good luck. I'll see you tomorrow."

"See ya."

Mel knew Susan still had four hours left on her shift, but she didn't care. She wanted to see her and would gladly be a barfly for that long. She hoped to take her out after her shift, as well. She'd love to take her home, but knew the rules. Damned rules. She laughed. She'd made the stupid things up. And she didn't want Susan sleeping with Dorinda, so it was worth it. Pretty much.

She walked into the bar and her heart sank. There sat Dorinda, chatting amicably with Susan. Susan looked over and saw Mel. She came out from behind the bar to give her a hug. Mel hugged her tight and wanted to say "neener, neener, neener," to Dorinda.

"What have you been doing today?" Susan said.

"Playing with DJ."

"Oh, how fun. I really want to spend some more time with him. He's such a little cutie."

"Yeah, he is."

Mel took a seat close enough to Dorinda so Susan could talk to both of them, without having to actually sit next to her. When Dorinda excused herself to use the restroom, Mel took advantage of her absence.

"So, has she asked you out for tonight?" Mel said.

"No."

"Would you like to go out with me tonight?"

"I'd love to."

"Great," Mel said. She felt immediate relief. She didn't know if she'd be able to get through another night of Dorinda alone with Susan. Yes, realistically she could, but she didn't like it.

Dorinda was back. The conversation was stiff among the three of them. Susan was clearly uncomfortable, but Mel wasn't going to leave. There was no way she was missing out on any time with Susan.

The bar got busy, and Susan had to waitress.

"You know she's going to choose me," Dorinda said. "You may as well give up."

"We'll see how tonight goes," Mel said.

"What do you mean?"

"I mean, we'll see how our date goes tonight."

"I'm taking her out tonight," Dorinda said.

"How do you figure?"

"I just assumed. It's one of my free nights. She'd rather go out with me."

"Well, I asked her and she said okay."

"She's confused. Clearly, she didn't realize I already had plans for us."

"Did you tell her that?"

"No, like I said, I assumed. She'll change her mind when she hears, though."

"I doubt it. She and I are going out."

The look Dorinda gave Mel chilled her to her bones. Not because she was afraid of her, but the depth of anger was unhealthy. And Mel knew it had been directed at Susan in the past. She'd kill Dorinda if she hurt Susan again.

Susan's shift finally ended. Susan took her apron off and joined the women on the other side of the bar.

"You ready?" Mel said.

"Sure."

"I actually made plans, so you're going to have to take a rain-check with Mel," Dorinda said.

"Mel asked me out. You didn't. I had no idea you had plans."

"Well, I'm telling you now. So, say good night to Mel and we can get going."

"And I'm telling you. I'm going out with Mel. Sorry, Dorinda. Next time, let me know and I won't make other plans."

"That's bullshit," Dorinda said. "You should have known I would want to take you out."

"How?" Susan said.

Mel stood watching the exchange. She didn't know what to do. It was really up to Susan to stand up for herself, but Mel wanted to step in and put Dorinda in her place.

"Because I sat here all day with you. You had to have known I wanted to take you out."

"Not if you didn't ask her," Mel said.

"Shut up. This is between me and her."

"Actually, I'm involved, too, because I'm taking her to dinner and I'm starving. So, say your good nights so we can get going."

Susan went to hug Dorinda, who instead kissed her hard on her mouth. Mel watched in disgust. But it was when Dorinda's hand closed over Susan's breast that she refused to stand around and watch. She walked over and broke them up. Dorinda's gaze bored into hers, while Susan pulled away fighting tears.

"Look what you did to her," Mel said.

"That's the thing about that one," Dorinda said. "She doesn't always know what's best for her."

"I think she does."

"You don't know her," Dorinda said. She turned to Susan. "I'll see you tomorrow night?"

"I'll be there," Susan said.

They watched as Dorinda left.

"Are you at all hungry? Or is your appetite gone?" Mel said.

"No, she's gone. I could eat. Can we have crepes?"

"We can have whatever you want."

"Thanks, Mel. I appreciate it."

Mel took her hand and walked her out to her car.

"I'll meet you there?" Mel said.

"Sure. And, Mel?"

"Yeah?"

Susan pulled her in for a kiss. It was gentle at first, but soon grew more passionate. Mel had to pull away.

"That was nice," Susan said.

"Yeah, it was. We should get going now."

"Okay. I'll meet you there."

❖

Susan was happy to be with Mel again. She was really not sure about seeing Dorinda anymore. She was showing signs of the woman Susan had left. She was scaring Susan. But Susan had made this decision to see both of them, and she would see it through until she was sure one woman owned her heart over the other.

She arrived at the restaurant, and Mel was already there. She opened Susan's door for her and took her hand with a questioning look in her eye. Susan smiled at her to let her know it was okay to hold her hand. In fact, she really liked it. It made her feel safe and secure.

They went into the restaurant and the hostess smiled at them in a knowing way. Mel blushed and Susan smiled. Mel was so cute when she blushed. They were seated at a table.

"What are you all smiles about?" Mel said.

"You blushed big time when the hostess smiled at us. And you're so damned cute when you blush."

Mel blushed deeper then, and Susan smiled wider.

"You're proving my point."

Mel grabbed her menu and hid behind it. Susan reached out and lowered it.

"I'm just teasing you, you know."

"Oh, I know. I'm okay with it."

"Oh, good. I'd hate to offend you."

"Nah. Don't worry about that. I'm pretty thick skinned."

"That's good to know."

They ordered dinner and talked pleasantly. Susan was careful to keep the subject off Dorinda, and Mel seemed to be fine avoiding her as well. They talked about DJ and Samantha and Joey, and soon dinner was there. They ate and talked and laughed, and Susan was sad when the meal came to an end. She really enjoyed her time with Mel and hated that it was over. Mel walked her out to her car.

"I had a great time tonight," Mel said.

"Me, too."

"I guess I should be going."

Susan's stomach was in knots. She knew what she wanted, but was she strong enough not to jump Mel's bones?

"Come over to my place?" she said.

"I don't know," Mel said. "Would that be wise?"

"Sure it would. We'll just have another drink and then you can go."

"Susan, I don't know…"

"Please? I don't want this night to end."

"Okay," Mel said. "I'll see you there."

Susan was excited as a girl on her first date. She was so happy to have the night continue. She really didn't want it to end. She pulled up in front of the house, and a few minutes later, Mel was there. Susan opened the door and walked in. Mel closed the door behind her and Susan was in her arms. She kissed her softly, tenderly, then passionately. Mel fought the urge to respond, but it was too strong. Without breaking the kiss, she walked Susan back to the couch. She sat down and pulled her next to her.

Susan seemed to float out of her body and stare down at the two of them. She came back to herself and slowly disengaged from Mel. Mel turned to face forward and grabbed her knees. She closed her eyes and tried to catch her breath.

"Would you like something to drink?" Susan's voice shook with desire. But rules were rules, right?

"Yes, please. I'd love a beer."

"Great."

She poured herself a glass of wine and brought the drinks to the living room.

"I'm really sorry," Mel said.

"No. You didn't do anything wrong."

"Yes, I did. Or I might have if you didn't stop me."

"But it wasn't wrong. I want it, too, Mel. I need you so badly, but I can't do it. We agreed to that."

"I know. And it's painful, but it's the way it is."

"So, let's just relax and drink our drinks. We can do that."

"I don't know, Susan. I'm pretty worked up. I think I'd better leave."

She stood. Susan reached up and took her hand. She gently pulled her back down to the couch.

"No, Mel. I don't want you to leave."

"But it would be better for both of us. Easier, anyway."

"No. I want you to stay the night. Tonight. And every night after. I love you, Mel. It's been you all along."

Mel took her in her arms and hugged her tight.

"Oh, thank God," Mel said. "Thank you, baby. I'm so happy. I don't know what I would have done if you'd chosen Dorinda."

"I don't know what I was thinking. I think I was just feeling sorry for her. You know, for losing Lucinda and all. I don't know. I think I confused those feelings for actual attraction. She's nothing compared to you."

"She has a bit of a temper, but we knew that. I wonder how she's going to take it when you tell her you chose me."

"She'll just have to take it. Too bad."

"I'll go to Lucinda's with you tomorrow night."

"Okay. That would be great."

"Yeah. That way I can meet Lucinda and be there for you when you tell Dorinda. I don't trust her not to try to hurt you."

"Thanks, lover. I appreciate that."

She took Mel's beer and set it on the coffee table with her wine. She leaned over and kissed Mel, forcing her onto her back on the couch. She climbed on top of her.

Mel moved her hands all over Susan's body, and for once Susan didn't have to worry about putting on the brakes. She allowed herself to feel, to get wet, to want. She sat up on top of Mel and took her shirt and bra off. She leaned over and allowed Mel to take one breast in her mouth. It felt amazing. Her tongue knew just what to do as it played around and over her nipple.

Susan was breathless. She stood and reached a hand down to Mel. They walked down the hall to the bedroom.

"Are you absolutely sure about this?" Mel said.

"I'm positive."

Susan finished undressing then lay on the bed while she watched Mel strip.

"You're so gorgeous," Susan said.

"You're not so bad yourself." Mel laughed.

Mel kissed Susan again and ran her hand all over her body.

"I love your body," she said. "I've missed it so much."

"It's all yours now. For as long as you want it."

"I'll take it forever," Mel said.

"I like that."

Mel let her hand drift between Susan's legs. Susan spread her legs wider. She felt Mel's fingers teasing her clit. She felt them move past and plunge deep inside her. She loved the feel of Mel stroking her walls. Mel moved back to her clit. Susan arched off the bed and moved her hips in time with Mel's touches. Soon everything was gone except Mel and her magical fingers. And then it happened. The climax hit and sent her soaring over the edge. When she came back to earth, Mel was holding her tight.

"Oh, no," Susan said. "It's not like that."

Mel grinned.

"Oh, no?"

"No. Your turn now."

Susan kissed down Mel's tight belly and climbed between her legs. She licked her from end to end before dipping her tongue inside her.

"Oh, shit," Mel said. "Oh, fuck that feels good."

Susan moved her tongue to Mel's clit, and Mel cried out almost immediately.

"Oh, wow, baby. I've missed you so much."

"I've missed you, too," Susan said.

"Thanks for choosing me."

"I really had no choice. My heart and my hormones both said you were the one. I had no burning desire to be with her. And she's just really not a nice person."

"No, she's not."

"I don't want to talk about her anymore," Susan said.

"Fair enough." Mel spooned against Susan and pulled her tight. "And, Susan?"

"Yeah?"

"I love you, too."

CHAPTER TWENTY-THREE

M el quietly slipped out of bed the next morning.
"Mm," Susan said.

"Sh. You sleep," Mel said. "I need to get to work."

"Don't go. Call in sick," Susan said.

"If only I could." Mel laughed. She kissed Susan's lips. "I'll see you at the bar this afternoon, baby."

"Okay."

She heard the quiet sounds of Susan's gentle breathing and knew she was asleep again. She hurried home to change and headed to work. When she got there, she was immediately busted by Joey.

"Someone's got a spring in her step this morning," Joey said.

"I had a great night."

"Yeah? So you went out with Susan and it went well? I'm glad to hear that."

"It went better than well," Mel said. "She chose me, Joey."

"No shit? That's great news, buddy."

"Yeah. I think so. I'm so fuckin' happy. When she asked me to call in sick today, I actually contemplated doing it."

"Yeah, well, I'm glad you didn't."

"No. I couldn't. But damn, I wanted to stay and spend the morning with her."

"I'm sure you did. So, what happens with Dorinda's aunt?"

"I don't know. That's up to Susan. We're going over there to-gether tonight. I can't imagine she's going to want to keep volun-teering since she really doesn't trust Dorinda, but it's totally up to her."

"But you'd be fine if she quit?" Joey laughed.

"Hell yeah. But it's not my place. I'd honestly rather she never see Dorinda again, but that puts her in a weird spot. She loves Lucinda and would like to get to spend whatever time she has left with her."

"True. Maybe if you go with her, she can keep volunteering."

"Yeah. That's what I'm thinking. I hope she'll see things that way, too."

They worked all day, with Mel unable to focus on much. She just went on autopilot most of the day. All she could think about was getting to see Susan again after work and spending the night with her that night. Life was so good for Mel right then. Susan loved her. She actually loved her. Mel hadn't mentioned that bit to Joey, though. She wanted to keep it between the two of them for now. It was too special to share.

The workday was over and they were packing up their equipment.

"You want to meet me at the bar in a while?" Mel said.

"No. I need to pick DJ up from daycare today. So, I've got to get home."

"Fair enough. I'll see you tomorrow."

"Good luck tonight," Joey said.

"Thanks."

Mel showered and dressed and headed to the bar. It was only four thirty, so she had plenty of time to just hang out before Susan got off work. She hoped it would be slow and Susan would be able to chat, but that wasn't the case. She got there to find the place jumping. She finally found an open booth and sat down.

Susan came over as soon as she emptied her tray. She kissed Mel.

"Hey, lover."

"Hey, baby. How's it goin'?"

"Crazy busy. You want some beer?"

"Yes, please."

"Okay," Susan said. "I'll be right back."

Susan made her rounds through the bar, picking up empties and getting orders for refills. Finally, she was back with Mel's beer.

"Are we still on for tonight?" Susan said.

"You bet."

"Good. Because I'm really afraid of Dorinda."

"Don't worry. She won't do anything while I'm there."

And with that, Susan was off again to make her rounds. It didn't really bother Mel that Susan couldn't sit with her. She knew she was making good money that day, and Mel was perfectly content to watch her work her way through the bar, knowing she was hers and hers alone.

Finally, it was seven o'clock. Susan took off her apron and came over to join Mel. She was holding a lemon drop.

"Aren't you supposed to go immediately after your shift?" Mel said.

"Yeah, but I figure, what the hell? I can have one drink."

"So, babe…about Lucinda."

"Yeah?"

"Are you going to keep volunteering to help out with her?"

"I don't know. I really want to, but don't see how I can. And that tears me up inside."

"You know, babe," Mel said. "I can always go over with you if you decide you want to keep doing that."

"I appreciate that, but it's not really fair to you to ask you to stay there until eleven at night when you get up at the crack ass of dawn."

"I can nap there. My point is, I don't think Dorinda would stick around if I was there."

"Maybe not," Susan said. "We'll just have to see how tonight goes."

"Okay. Speaking of that, we really should get going."

"Yep. It's time."

Mel followed Susan to her car. She took her in her arms and held her.

"I know tonight's not going to be easy for you," she said.

"No, it won't. But I'm so glad you're going with me. Thank you."

"My pleasure, babe."

Mel followed Susan to Lucinda's house and took a deep breath as she exited her car. She walked over and took Susan's hand and they headed for the front door.

❖

Susan felt instant comfort when Mel took her hand. She'd been terrified all day of breaking up with Dorinda, but with Mel there, she could do anything. She almost felt like it was cheating bringing Mel with her, but she was scared and felt she needed her to insure her safety.

They walked up to the door.

"You ready to do this?" Mel said.

"Ready as I'll ever be. Let's go inside."

They let themselves in and found Dorinda lying on the couch in just a robe.

"We must have interrupted your shower," Mel said. "Go ahead and get dressed. We'll keep an eye on Lucinda."

Susan looked over at Mel and saw a look on her face that dared Dorinda to argue.

"Actually, this is my home and I'm comfortable in just a robe, thank you very much."

But she pulled her robe closer around her and looked anything but comfortable.

Dorinda reached out and pulled Susan to her.

"What's she doing here?"

"I'm sorry, Dorinda." Susan tried to disengage her arm, but Dorinda held tight. "But I chose Mel."

"I'm not giving up so easily," Dorinda said.

"It's over. Leave her alone," Mel said.

"You stay out of this," Dorinda said.

Mel crossed the room and removed Susan's arm from Dorinda's death grip.

"Come on, Susan. Introduce me to Lucinda."

"It's not over," Dorinda said from behind them.

Neither Mel nor Susan said a word. Susan simply led Mel to Lucinda, who was sitting up in bed, but looked a little out of it.

"How are you tonight?" Susan said.

"I'm okay. In a little pain, but not enough for meds yet."

"Are you sure?" Susan didn't want Lucinda to be in any pain. Ever.

"Oh, honey," Lucinda said. "I don't want to spend the last few months of my life stoned or sleeping. I can take a little pain."

"Okay. If you say so."

"I do." She moved her focus to Mel. "So, you're Mel, huh?"

"I am. It's a pleasure to meet you."

She moved to shake Lucinda's hand, but Lucinda pulled her in for a hard hug. When Mel was standing, Lucinda looked past them. She must have seen that Dorinda had left the room.

"You made the right choice, sweetie," Lucinda said. "She was never for you. It ended before for a reason."

"I know," Susan said. "She was just being so sweet to me."

"A wolf in sheep's clothing."

"Indeed."

"I'm going out now," Dorinda said from behind them. "I'll be back by eleven."

"Okay," Susan said.

Mel grabbed a chair from the dining room and joined Susan in sitting by Lucinda.

"What do you want to do?" Susan said.

"Let's just visit," Lucinda said. "It's been a while since we've done that since you've been into Dorinda when you came over."

Susan felt horrible.

"I'm so sorry," she said.

"It's okay," Lucinda said. "Matters of the heart are hard to control."

"Yeah, but I was here for you. Not her."

"True, but when you started having feelings for her and I was fine, I didn't blame you one bit for paying attention to her. Just like I'm not going to blame you one bit for not coming over again."

"I haven't decided that yet, Lucinda. Mel can come over with me and we could sit with you at night."

"And as much as I'd like that, hon, I think the tension between you and Dorinda would be too much. I know how sensitive you are."

Susan fought the tears in her eyes. At once, Mel was standing, holding her against her.

"It's okay, baby," Mel said.

Susan nodded against her.

"I'll miss you, Susan, but I won't be around much longer anyway. I can tell. I can feel it. And it will be a welcome relief to be gone."

Susan cried openly then.

"I can't even think about it," she said.

"Is there some tissue around here?" Mel said.

Lucinda handed her a box that had been next to her bed. Mel took a tissue and wiped Susan's eyes, then let her take one to blow her nose.

"I'm going to miss you so much, Lucinda."

"Oh, hon. I'll be with you forever. You've got to believe that. I'm not ever going to leave you."

"Do you believe that?" Susan said. "What do you believe about death?"

"Well, you know, I've always believed in reincarnation, but I think that until you come back as someone else, you can hang around with those you loved on earth."

"That would make me happy." Susan sniffed. "I like that idea."

"And you've always been so good to me, Susan. You're such a special person in my life." She looked at Mel. "So, you'd better treat her like the good woman she is or I'll be haunting you."

Mel laughed.

"Sorry. I was just thinking of having my own personal ghost to haunt me. But seriously, I'll take care of her forever, Lucinda. I give you my word."

"Thank you. Now, I'm getting tired. Will you give me my pain pill, hon? I'm due for my usual dosage. Then I'll drift off to sleep. Thank you both for what you've done. Susan for me and Mel for Susan. I really appreciate it. I'll miss you, Susan, but like I said, the battle is almost over."

Susan went to the table and got Lucinda's pain pill. She gave it to her with a glass of water.

"It won't be long till I'm asleep now," Lucinda said.

"Good-bye, Lucinda," Susan said, now openly weeping again. "I love you."

"I love you, too." She closed her eyes and drifted off to sleep.

Mel took Susan to the love seat and held her until she settled down.

"I can't believe I'm never going to see her again," Susan said.

"She's okay with that, babe. So you need to forgive yourself."

"I know, but I'm going to miss her so."

"Yeah. I get that."

Dorinda came home then and saw Susan crying. She crossed the room and took her in her arms.

"What did you do to her?" she asked Mel.

Susan sat up and tried to push away from Dorinda, but Dorinda wouldn't let go.

"I didn't do anything," Mel said. "She just said good-bye to Lucinda so she's a little emotional."

Dorinda loosened her grip on Susan.

"What do you mean you said good-bye?"

Mel stood.

"She's not going to be coming over anymore."

"What? Why not?"

"I think it would be too awkward," Susan said. "And Lucinda understood. We made our peace and said our good-byes. Now I'll tell you good-bye, and Mel and I will be out of here."

"But what about me?" Dorinda said. "Who's going to come by and give me a break?"

"I think she sleeps most evenings, so you should be okay," Susan said.

"I don't think you're being fair. About anything."

"I'm sorry you feel that way," Mel said. "But that's the way it is. Now, if you'll excuse us."

Dorinda pulled Susan to her for a hug. Susan allowed the hug to happen. What harm was there in it? Then, Dorinda pulled back slightly and kissed her on the mouth. It was a hard kiss, and Susan felt her tongue tracing her lips, trying to pry them open.

The next thing she knew, Dorinda was torn away from her. She saw Dorinda lying on the love seat with Mel standing over her.

"Don't you ever touch her again," Mel said.

"Fine. Get out of here," Dorinda said.

Susan took Mel's hand and happily left.

When they got to Susan's car, Mel stood inches away from her.

"So," she said. "You've had a pretty rough night."

"Yeah. It's been emotionally draining."

"Would you like to be alone tonight?"

"No way," Susan said. There was nothing she wanted more than to feel Mel's arms around her. "I want you to come home with me."

"Are you sure?"

"I'm positive."

Susan checked her rearview mirror several times to make sure Mel was really behind her. The past two days had seemed like part dream, part nightmare. Mel had told her the night before that she loved her, though, and that made everything else tolerable.

They got home and Susan let Mel in. Once inside, she handed her a key.

"What's this?" Mel said.

"It's a key to my place. So you can let yourself in whenever you want."

"Wow. Thanks, babe."

Mel put it on her keychain.

"I'll get you one of mine tomorrow."

"Sounds good," Susan said. She took Mel's hand. "Now, I think we have some business to take care of."

"We do? Are you sure you're up for it? I mean, you just had a gut-wrenching time of it over there."

"Which is why I need you. I need you to show me I'm loved the way only you can."

"You certainly don't have to ask me twice," Mel said.

They stripped their clothes off as they made their way back to the bedroom. Once they got there, Susan lay back on the bed and Mel climbed on top of her. Mel kissed her gently, first on her lips then on her cheek and neck. Susan shivered at the sensations Mel was creating. She felt her nipple tighten and knew there were goose bumps around her areola.

As Mel moved lower, she continued to deposit tiny gentle kisses along her path. She took Susan's nipple in her mouth. Susan felt her clit swell. She needed Mel and couldn't wait until Mel took her completely.

Mel continued kissing down Susan's body and Susan felt every nerve ending tense up. She was more than ready for Mel. When Mel finally climbed between her legs, Susan knew it wouldn't take much. She felt Mel's tongue inside her.

"That's it, baby. Make love to me."

And that's what Mel was doing. They weren't just having sex or messing around. They were making love. That was the last coherent thought Susan had as the orgasms then racked her body. She rode wave after wave before finally settling back on the bed with Mel.

"That was amazing," Susan said. "You sure know how to love me."

"I'm glad you enjoy it since I plan on doing it for years to come."

"I do like the sound of that," Susan said. She moved to slip between Mel's legs, but Mel stopped her.

"How about I just hold you for now? It's getting late and we have forever for lovemaking."

"Will you really promise me forever, Mel O'Brien?"

"Forever and then some, Susan. Forever and then some."

About the Author

MJ Williamz was raised on California's central coast, which she left at age seventeen to pursue an education. She graduated from Chico State, and it was in Chico that she rediscovered her love of writing. It wasn't until she moved to Portland, however, that her writing really took off, with the publication of her first short story in 2003.

MJ is the author of eleven books, including three Goldie Award winners. She has also had over thirty short stories published, most of them erotica with a few romances and a few horrors thrown in for good measure. You can reach her at mjwilliamz@aol.com.

Books Available from Bold Strokes Books

Complications by MJ Williamz. Two women battle for the heart of one. (978-1-62639-769-9)

Crossing the Wide Forever by Missouri Vaun. As Cody Walsh and Lillie Ellis face the perils of the untamed West, they discover that love's uncharted frontier isn't for the weak in spirit or the faint of heart. (978-1-62639-851-1)

Fake It Till You Make It by M. Ullrich. Lies will lead to trouble, but can they lead to love? (978-1-62639-923-5)

Girls Next Door by Sandy Lowe and Stacia Seaman eds. Best-selling romance authors tell it from the heart—sexy, romantic stories of falling for the girls next door. (978-1-62639-916-7)

Pursuit by Jackie D. The pursuit of the most dangerous terrorist in America will crack the lines of friendship and love, and not everyone will make it out under the weight of duty and service. (978-1-62639-903-7)

Shameless by Brit Ryder. Confident Emery Pearson knows exactly what she's looking for in a no-strings-attached hookup, but can a spontaneous interlude open her heart to more? (978-1-63555-006-1)

The Practitioner by Ronica Black. Sometimes love comes calling whether you're ready for it or not. (978-1-62639-948-8)

Unlikely Match by Fiona Riley. When an ambitious PR exec and her super-rich coding geek-girl client fall in love, they learn that giving something up may be the only way to have everything. (978-1-62639-891-7)

Where Love Leads by Erin McKenzie. A high school counselor and the mom of her new student bond in support of the troubled girl, never expecting deeper feelings to emerge, testing the boundaries of their relationship. (978-1-62639-991-4)

Forsaken Trust by Meredith Doench. When four women are murdered, Agent Luce Hansen must regain trust in her most valuable investigative tool—herself—to catch the killer. (978-1-62639-737-8)

Her Best Friend's Sister by Meghan O'Brien. For fifteen years, Claire Barker has nursed a massive crush on her best friend's older sister. What happens when all her wildest fantasies come true? (978-1-62639-861-0)

Letter of the Law by Carsen Taite. Will federal prosecutor Bianca Cruz take a chance at love with horse breeder Jade Vargas, whose dark family ties threaten everything Bianca has worked to protect—including her child? (978-1-62639-750-7)

New Life by Jan Gayle. Trigena and Karrie are having a baby, but the stress of becoming a mother and the impact on their relationship might be too much for Trigena. (978-1-62639-878-8)

Royal Rebel by Jenny Frame. Charity director Lennox King sees through the party girl image Princess Roza has cultivated, but will Lennox's past indiscretions and Roza's responsibilities make their love impossible? (978-1-62639-893-1)

Unbroken by Donna K. Ford. When Kayla and Jackie, two women with every reason to reject Happy Ever After, fall in love, will they have the courage to overcome their pasts and rewrite their stories? (978-1-62639-921-1)

Where the Light Glows by Dena Blake. Mel Thomas doesn't realize just how unhappy she is in her marriage until she meets Izzy Calabrese. Will she have the courage to overcome her insecurities and follow her heart? (978-1-62639-958-7)

Escape in Time by Robyn Nyx. Working in the past is hell on your future. (978-1-62639-855-9)

Forget-Me-Not by Kris Bryant. Is love worth walking away from the only life you've ever dreamed of? (978-1-62639-865-8)

Highland Fling by Anna Larner. On vacation in the Scottish Highlands, Eve Eddison falls for the enigmatic forestry officer Moira Burns, despite Eve's best friend's campaign to convince her that Moira will break her heart. (978-1-62639-853-5)

Phoenix Rising by Rebecca Harwell. As Storm's Quarry faces invasion from a powerful neighbor, a mysterious newcomer with powers equal to Nadya's challenges everything she believes about herself and her future. (978-1-62639-913-6)

Soul Survivor by I. Beacham. Sam and Joey have given up on hope, but when fate brings them together it gives them a chance to change each other's life and make dreams come true. (978-1-62639-882-5)

Strawberry Summer by Melissa Brayden. When Margaret Beringer's first love Courtney Carrington returns to their small town, she must grapple with their troubled past and fight the temptation for a very delicious future. (978-1-62639-867-2)

The Girl on the Edge of Summer by J.M. Redmann. Micky Knight accepts two cases, but neither is the easy investigation it appears. The past is never past—and young girls lead complicated, even dangerous lives. (978-1-62639-687-6)

Unknown Horizons by CJ Birch. The moment Lieutenant Alison Ash steps aboard the Persephone, she knows her life will never be the same. (978-1-62639-938-9)

Divided Nation, United Hearts by Yolanda Wallace. In a nation torn in two by a most uncivil war, can love conquer the divide? (978-1-62639-847-4)

Fury's Bridge by Brey Willows. What if your life depended on someone who didn't believe in your existence? (978-1-62639-841-2)

Lightning Strikes by Cass Sellars. When Parker Duncan and Sydney Hyatt's one-night stand turns to more, both women must fight demons past and present to cling to the relationship neither of them thought she wanted. (978-1-62639-956-3)

Love in Disaster by Charlotte Greene. A professor and a celebrity chef are drawn together by chance, but can their attraction survive a natural disaster? (978-1-62639-885-6)

Secret Hearts by Radclyffe. Can two women from different worlds find common ground while fighting their secret desires? (978-1-62639-932-7)

Sins of Our Fathers by A. Rose Mathieu. Solving gruesome murder cases is only one of Elizabeth Campbell's challenges; another is her growing attraction to the female detective who is hell-bent on keeping her client in prison. (978-1-62639-873-3)

The Sniper's Kiss by Justine Saracen. The power of a kiss: it can swell your heart with splendor, declare abject submission, and sometimes blow your brains out. (978-1-62639-839-9)

Troop 18 by Jessica L. Webb. Charged with uncovering the destructive secret that a troop of RCMP cadets has been hiding, Andy must put aside her worries about Kate and uncover the conspiracy before it's too late. (978-1-62639-934-1)

Worthy of Trust and Confidence by Kara A. McLeod. Agent Ryan O'Connor is about to discover the hard way that when you can only handle one type of answer to a question, it really is better not to ask. (978-1-62639-889-4)

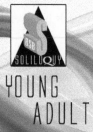